ALSO BY PAULA QUINN

Lord of Desire

LORD of TEMPTATION

Paula Quinn

NEW YORK   BOSTON

Warner Forever is a registered trademark of Time Warner Book Group Inc.

Cover design by Diane Luger
Cover illustration by John Paul
Typography by David Gatti
Book design by Stratford Publishing Services

Warner Books

Time Warner Book Group
1271 Avenue of the Americas
New York, NY 10020
Visit our Web site at www.twbookmark.com.

Printed in the United States of America

First Paperback Printing: February 2006

10 9 8 7 6 5 4 3 2 1

To Samantha, my gentle-hearted girl,
this one is your favorite.

To Danny and Hayley,
my teenage knight in shining armor
and our little weasel . . .
I love the three of you with all my heart.

And for my husband,
the most honorable man I know.

Acknowledgments

VERY SPECIAL THANKS to God for the many blessings He's given me. Thank you, Mom and Dad, for being so wonderful and supportive. I love you both. Thank you, Ryan Roth, for making me such a fantastic Website. Suellen Marita Deeg and Lindsey B. . . . Yours is a love from the beginning of time . . .

LORD of TEMPTATION

Chapter One

ENGLAND, 1071

"REMEMBER, CASEY," GIANELLE SAID while she twisted the heavy rope into one more knot, "an hour after Lord Bryce and his guests retire to their chambers, we will make our escape." She pulled on the knot as tightly as she could and then double-checked the other end, which was tied to one of the four legs on her bed. She tugged, bracing her weight against it. It would hold. She hoped.

"What if he wakes up and looks for us?" Casey watched Gianelle shove the long rope under the bed. She didn't like this idea at all. The thought of flinging herself out the window made her stomach ache. If only there were another way to escape. But Gia was right. They had to leave Devonshire. Their master was bad enough, but it was his brother who truly frightened them both. He rarely laid a finger on them, but it wasn't because he didn't want to. At least in that, their master protected them. But Edgar Dermott found ways to make their lives miserable, especially Gia's. His hooded eyes were ever on her. If she consumed more than her scarce share of food allowed Devonshire's servants, he was there to accuse her. When anything went awry at the castle, he blamed her, taking immense pleasure in her punishment.

"He will not look for us," Gianelle assured her. "Casey, this is the best night to go. With all the guests here for his feast, even if he does wake up, he will not realize we are gone until we are halfway to York."

Casey wished she had the same confidence as her best friend. She wasn't certain which part of the plan frightened her more: descending Devonshire's walls on a rope, or actually making it to the ground, where the true dangers would begin.

"Do you have the coins?"

Casey nodded and lifted her skirt to show Gia the small pouch dangling above her knee.

"How much do we have?"

"Ten pence is as high as I can count," Casey reminded her. "We have a little more than that." She twirled her long chestnut braid in her fingers and chewed her lower lip. "What if the guards see us running away?"

Gianelle crossed the room and took Casey's shoulders in her hands. "You know they fall asleep every night. You must not worry so. Think of our lives after tonight." The determined spark in Gianelle's eyes made them glimmer like polished amber. Her normally sallow cheeks dusted pink with excitement. "We shall be free. There will be no more masters to tell us how to think or how to behave. No more punishment if we raise our eyes to our betters. We shall be able to say what we want, eat when we are hungry, and bathe in clean lakes instead of in a basin behind the kitchen."

The thrill in her friend's voice was contagious. Even though Casey didn't care half as much about freedom as

Gia did, she found herself nodding and smiling with anticipation. They had to go, and Casey would never let her dearest friend leave without her.

"Now come. Let us get above stairs and be the dutiful servants our lord thinks we are." Gianelle clasped Casey's hand and pulled her toward the door.

"Gia." Casey paused just before they slipped into the hall. "Are you certain he won't wake up and catch us? You remember the last time we made him angry . . ."

Gianelle patted Casey's hand to reassure her. "I promise, Casey, Lord Dermott will not wake up."

Gianelle pushed a loose tendril of hair away from her face with the back of her hand and lifted the silver tray, heavy with a fat roasted pig. She ignored the groans of her belly as she stumbled and teetered backward from the weight of the tray. She swore under her breath. For the mercy of God, what had they fed this swine? She didn't think she would make it to the great hall and stopped twice to rest the tray on her knee. Her blasted hair wasn't helping matters, either. Even braided, the unruly waves managed to escape. She blew another golden strand out of her vision before preparing to continue onward.

The corridors of Devonshire Castle bustled with servants, vassals, and an occasional stray guest searching out the garderobe. Today, Lord Bryce Dermott celebrated the summer solstice festival and had spared no expense to please his noble guests. He had hired two extra cooks to help Maeve prepare an array of delicacies fit for the king himself. Minstrels knelt by the hearth fire issuing forth melodies of love and fidelity, while colorfully dressed jugglers tossed balls high over their heads, and midget acrobats somersaulted between the rows of banqueting tables set up for the feast.

From the dais where Bryce Dermott sat with his quieter and even more black-hearted brother, Lord Edgar Dermott, Gianelle's master spotted her struggling with the tray after an acrobat tumbled into her path. "Move your arse, wench!" He snapped his fingers at her. "We are hungry."

Gianelle gritted her teeth, but lowered her head and pressed forward. She finally reached the dais and laid the tray down. She nearly tripped over her own feet when Baron Douglas Landry, one of the guests who sat at a lower table beneath her master, pinched her backside. With a flaming oath battering against her teeth, she turned to glare at him, but he lifted a challenging eyebrow at her.

"Fill my cup," he demanded.

"Of course, my lord." Gianelle dropped her gaze to her feet and curtsied. "There is a freshly opened barrel of wine in the kitchen." She snatched his goblet off the table and headed back to the kitchen with a smile curling her lips.

Since the kitchen was normally the place where gossip ran rampant, Gianelle didn't think it strange to find several of the serving wenches gathered around Maeve, the cook, while she basted an ox turning over the spit.

"I heard tell the earl single-handedly rescued twenty of King William's warriors from the dungeons of Edgar the Aetheling shortly after the conquest. Sarah, old Ingram's daughter, says he is taller even than Lord Edgar, with hair as black as a raven's wing, and eyes the color of fine pewter."

"Aye," said Sylvia while she prepared a tray of poached

eggs. "I caught a glimpse of him when I visited my sister in Dover last spring. Came riding right into the village and stopped to have a word with some of the fishermen as if he were no better than they. Yet he's wealthy as they come with lands in Norwich, and even France. My sister's husband said the people of Dover love their lord well. Especially the women." Sylvia threw a wink at Maeve. "I tell you, girls, Lord Dante Risande is finer than any man sitting in the great hall."

Maeve chuckled. "Makes me wish I was serving tonight." When she saw Gianelle, she waved her ladle at her. "Have you seen him, Gia?"

Gianelle shook her head and walked past the huddled women to where Casey stood setting apple tarts on a long, bronze serving tray. "I told you yesterday when you were all going on about his arrival, Maeve, I've no interest in any man who is eager to order me about."

"Alas, I fear even the face of a god could not turn our Gia's head." Lydia, a swarthy wench, looked up from the swan she was stuffing. She popped her hand out of the fowl's body and pointed a greasy finger at Gia. "You'll die an old maid if you don't find someone to love soon, girl."

"Love is for poets, Lydia." Gianelle pinched a bit of daffodil from one of the many jars lining a shelf above the chopping table, and dropped it into Baron Landry's goblet. "I do not waste my thoughts on such romantic drivel."

"What are you doing with the daffodil?" Casey asked her when Gianelle poured some red wine into the cup next.

"Baron Landry pinched my backside," Gianelle told her with a mischievous grin curling her lips. "Now he will pay the price."

"He'll be expelling my delicious ox before it reaches his guts." Maeve threw her head back and laughed.

"Well, it's better than losing a tooth or two like Lady Millicent last month when she slapped Gia for looking at her dour old husband," Casey reminded them.

"How was I to know that sticking those pebbles in her honey cakes would break her teeth?"

The women laughed when Gianelle held up Baron Landry's cup and offered a quick prayer for his poor intestines. She eyed the apple tarts. She had one more thing to do before she left the kitchen.

She passed Margaret, another of Dermott's serving girls, on the way out and rolled her eyes when the wench announced to the others that she had just seen Lord Dante, and the Almighty should roast her arse if he wasn't the most magnificent beast of a man she'd ever clapped her sorry eyes on.

When she entered the great hall, Gianelle didn't bother to look around for the man causing such a stir in the kitchen, but set her gaze on Douglas Landry and headed straight for him with a satisfied hum rolling off her lips.

"Your wine, my lord," she said quietly and set the goblet on the table before him. When she turned to walk away, she hit a wall of solid rock.

Strong, broad fingers closed around her arms to keep her from bouncing backward and landing in Landry's lap.

"Pardon me, *mademoiselle*."

Before she had time to stop herself, Gianelle looked up. She caught a glimpse of dark hair and pale gray eyes an instant before she dutifully dropped her gaze. God's teeth, the oaf was huge. His frame blocked everyone behind him from her vision. But it was the scent of him that overwhelmed her. A rich blend of leather and salty tang that filled her nostrils and went straight to her head. The moment he loosened his grip on her, she tried to step around him. Something tugged her back.

"A strand of your hair is caught on my button." His voice was deep and smooth, rumbling from someplace within the wall of his chest, a few inches from her nose.

This must be the famed Earl Risande, she thought while she watched his fingers deftly untangle her hair from a small button on his surcoat. None of Dermott's other guests spoke to her with such gentleness in their voices, and not many of them spoke with the sensual inflection of her homeland in Normandy.

"There. You are free."

Normally Gianelle would never risk a second, bold glance at a noble, especially one standing this close to her. She wasn't certain if it was his voice or his words that tempted her to do so now.

When she looked up at him, he captured her gaze with his and held it. Damn the kitchen wenches, they were right. His eyes were fashioned of beaten silver. Thick lashes, as coal black as his hair, made them appear even more piercing, more penetrating. His nose was straight and strong, his jaw rugged, his lips carved for pagan pleasures. He reminded her of a wolf whose magnificence made one forget the danger of getting too close. There was the same feral beauty in his eyes that captivates prey seconds before it is ensnared. Gianelle stood mesmerized for a moment before he smiled at her, flashing a frivolous dimple and tilting her world on its axis.

"Then you will excuse me, my lord." She managed a slight curtsy and hurried away.

Lord Dante Risande watched her departure. His gaze followed the length of her long, golden braid down to the alluring swell of her buttocks.

"*Merde.* Did you see that, Balin?" He turned to another man waiting patiently at his right.

"See what, my lord?"

"That face." Dante turned again to find the serving girl in the crowded hall. "Those glorious eyes. Find out what her name is."

Balin expelled a great sigh. "Someday you're going to find yourself father to a dozen sons you didn't know you had," he grumbled while he went to do his lord's bidding.

Dante smiled, catching a glimpse of her weaving her way out of the hall. "Mayhap if I'm fortunate, thirteen before I leave this castle in the morn."

Chapter Two

DANTE LIFTED THE SILVER GOBLET and inspected its elaborate etchings with eyes that matched the flagon's shining brilliance. The old Saxon workmanship was quite beautiful and crafted to withstand years of wear and tear, much like the people themselves. Looking around the great hall, Dante was pleased to see Norman and Saxon nobles sharing wine and laughter. Enough blood had been shed in England. The time had come for peace between the two different inhabitants of the land. But not everyone wanted peace, and that was why he was here: to find anyone allied with Hereward the Wake, leader of the resistance to the throne.

As a warrior, Dante understood why some Saxons still fought against William. The new king was a foreign invader in their eyes, and while he did try to preserve their laws after the conquest, much of their land was given to the Normans. But William was fair with the natives for the most part. If a Saxon noble, like Bryce Dermott, swore fealty to the king, then most of his land remained in his name. It was the resistance that William sought to end, and Dante hunted the leader of that resistance.

Something warm and soft brushed against his arm, scattering his thoughts of duty and bringing them to his other favored pastime. He turned his head and offered Lady Genevieve LaSalle a languorous half-smile.

"Mademoiselle?"

Ah, his voice . . . the sound of black velvet and steel heated Lady Genevieve's loins. She bent over his chair, her milky cleavage temptingly close to his mouth. "Is that all you have to say to me, *mon cher?*" Her red lips hovered over his. She licked them, causing Dante's smile to harden into something less polite. "After our last"—she paused and bit her lower lip—"encounter, I would think you would at least call me *amoureuse.*"

His eyes moved over her with the arrogance of a man fully aware of his sexual power. She held her breath, suddenly not as in control as she'd thought. Damn him! Why did he have to emit such fire from those smoldering eyes and that full, sensuous mouth? Lady Genevieve fidgeted where she stood, wishing now that she had taken a seat, for her knees felt too weak to hold her up. With a measure of demure charm not lost on her admirer, she lifted a self-conscious hand to her pale, wheat-blond hair. Her pearls were still in place, woven neatly through her plaited tresses.

"I don't think one tryst gives claim to us being lovers, my cherub," he pointed out while his attention turned for a moment to Baron Landry, who had just bolted out of his chair and was running toward the doors clutching his belly.

"How about two, then?" Genevieve offered, nuzzling closer to him, drawn by his deep, husky tone. "We could slip away right now."

His gentle laughter yanked her from her delicious reverie. "Mayhap another time, *mademoiselle*."

Words laced in honey licked her flesh like hot, sultry fire, but Dante was already pulling away from her, dismissing her as though she were a mere serving wench who couldn't keep her pesky hands off him. How dare he! Genevieve boiled. Had he forgotten that she was the daughter of Count LaSalle of Flanders? Any man would count it a blessing from God that she would give him her attentions, much less her body. Oh, but she had given Dante that . . . and he had given her so much more . . . a night she would never forget, kisses that ignited fires so hot she had screamed out, careless if her father heard while he studied in his solar down the hall.

She stared down into his dusky eyes. Her ruby-clad fingers ached to slap that grin off his face—or tunnel through his hair. Her indecision infuriated her until moist beads of perspiration formed and trickled down between her breasts. Thoroughly humiliated, and yet aching to feel his strong arms around her again, Lady Genevieve whirled on her heel and stormed away.

Watching her, Dante laughed in his seat, admiring the gentle sway of her voluptuous hips beneath her saffron gown. Count LaSalle would most certainly demand they wed if he found out about what Dante had called their "tryst," which actually had been more like a battle in a winter storm, leaving Dante aching for something warm when he was done. She was definitely beautiful—with long, elegant legs and full, firm breasts that could tempt a monk to sin. Pity she made him feel as empty as the nets his fishermen pulled out of the straits below his castle in Dover last winter.

With Lady LaSalle forgotten as quickly as she had appeared, Dante shifted in a carved oak chair that felt too small to house his long legs. He scanned the great hall until his gaze settled on Bryce Dermott tearing at a cooked pig in front of him. He sincerely doubted the man was the rebel King William suspected. For while the lord of Devonshire was reputed to be a self-indulgent tyrant, he didn't have the sense to plan his day, let alone a revolt against the king. Dante's careful gaze moved to the man seated at Bryce's right. Here was the man who heightened Dante's suspicions. Edgar Dermott bore no resemblance to his older brother, either in appearance or in temperament. He sipped his wine, watching Dante with the same cool, calculating gaze that a hawk uses to size up its prey.

"Think he knows why we're here?" Balin slid into the chair beside Dante and glanced toward the dais once more.

"He knows who I am. He knows what happened when Hereward brought his Saxon rebels and the Danes against us last winter." Dante tossed Edgar Dermott a challenging smile. "He does not look favorably upon me, does he?"

"Well"—Balin shrugged shoulders that were only a hint narrower than Dante's—"if he is indeed one of Hereward's cohorts, then that murderous glare he just shot you makes perfect sense. After all, it was you who led the king's army in Peterborough and decimated the resistance."

A time I would prefer to forget, Dante thought to himself. It wasn't the bloody battle at Peterborough that weighed so heavily on his heart that at times he thought he might go mad. It was what he'd found when he returned home.

"Her name is Gianelle."

Dante leaned his back against the chair and rubbed his jaw, trying to forget. "Who?"

"The serving wench you admired earlier," Balin reminded him. "Her name is Gianelle Dejiat."

Dante cast Balin a dark frown. "She's Norman?"

"So it would seem."

Sliding his gaze back to Bryce Dermott, Dante wondered how a Saxon came to possess a Norman woman as a servant. His eyes found her again pouring wine into guests' cups around the table. Candlelight flickered over her profile as she bent to her work, seemingly oblivious to the nobles she served. She was frightfully thin beneath a coarse, woolen overdress of drab brown. But while her body lacked the full curves Dante normally found more to his liking, there was something about her that mesmerized him. Mayhap, he allowed as she worked her way closer to him, it was the delicate look of her that made his breath falter in his throat, or how she looked so out of place amid ladies who giggled coyly behind their perfumed handkerchiefs, and who forever lifted their beringed fingers to their hair, making certain no pearl or silvered clip was out of place. Gianelle was real and needed no adornment to punctuate her beauty. Edgar Dermott obviously thought the same, Dante noted. The baron's brother watched her movements with something akin to a starving man's hunger in his eyes.

When she finally reached him, Dante swept his gaze over her features. She glanced at him beneath a veil of long, tawny lashes.

"Is it safe to drink?" he asked her.

She blinked and looked directly at him; a tiny hint of panic made her cheeks flush. For the second time that evening, the extraordinary beauty of her huge, golden eyes arrested Dante.

"Pardon, my lord?"

"I only ask because Baron Landry looked quite ill after he partook."

Gianelle clutched the pitcher of wine to her chest. How was it possible that he suspected what she'd done? "If the Baron is ill, I'm sure it has naught to do with me."

Dante knew she was lying.

He had watched her enter the great hall and set Landry's cup in front of him, already filled. Why hadn't she filled it from the pitcher she used now, dipped from the keg at the front of the hall? His years at King William's table had taught him how easy it was to do away with an enemy with nothing more than tainted wine. He dreaded the idea that this lovely woman might be working in cahoots with someone to poison Bryce Dermott's Norman guests. Pity if she turned on her own countrymen. Even more so if he had to arrest her and bring her before William.

He covered his cup with his hand to prevent her from pouring wine into it and offered her a candid smile when he said, "I prefer to keep my wits about me. And the contents of my stomach where they belong."

He was about to comment on her pale complexion when another serving girl placed a trencher in front of him.

"Some ox, my lord?"

Dante turned to look at the plate, and then at the servant. With a muffled oath he vaulted to his feet, almost knocking Gianelle over behind him. For a moment, he could not find his voice to speak. He could not breathe, nor form a coherent thought save that his sister Katherine had returned to him.

"Balin?" he said without taking his eyes off the girl.

"I see her, lord," Balin confirmed, stunned almost to silence himself by the resemblance.

Dante lifted his hand to touch the maidservant's cheek, but dropped his arm to his side when she recoiled, her clear blue eyes wide with fear. "My God, who are you?" His husky voice faded to a choking whisper.

"My—my name is Casey, my lord."

"Casey." He repeated her name as if he had never heard such a profound sound before. "You look like someone very dear to me."

Gianelle was quite familiar with the tricks men used to seduce women, but the anguish in his voice when he spoke to Casey immobilized her. She stared at him, trying to decide if his sorrow was real.

"Gianelle!"

The warning roar from Bryce Dermott caused her to drop the pitcher. Red wine splattered across the rushes and onto Dante's boots and the hem of Gianelle's skirts. The great hall fell silent, save for the beginnings of a prayer being whispered by Casey.

"My guests thirst. Must they wait all night for their wine while you gape at Lord Risande?" Dermott clenched his teeth and met Dante's gaze from across the hall. "Please accept my apologies. The wench has never learned obedience, and is a constant source of distress in my otherwise content life. See? She stares at me even now."

When he rose to his feet, Gianelle could only watch him as he left the dais. She knew she should lower her gaze, but she couldn't. Gripped by fear and hatred, she stared at him, unblinking, while he stormed around one table and then another in order to reach her.

"I will teach you to respect your betters." He was almost on top of her now. The promise of violence gleamed his eyes to glacier blue.

Gianelle took a step backward and bumped into something inviolably hard. She knew her master was going to strike her. There was naught she could do to prevent it now. Her eyes scanned the faces staring back at her. She met Edgar Dermott's rueful smile, aware that he wished it were his hand about to strike her. Gianelle was sorry she hadn't sneezed on his supper while she carried it in. She raised her chin in defiance of the shame that was to come.

"You will know your place, insolent bitch!" Dermott lifted his hand to strike her. Gianelle finally closed her eyes. But the blow never came. She opened her eyes to see her angry lord's wrist shackled within larger, broader fingers directly in front of her face. The growl she heard above her head was so menacing and deadly she would have fled if her master wasn't blocking her path.

"I give you fair warning, Dermott. Lower your voice and your hand, else you will be the one struck down."

Bryce Dermott looked from Dante to Gianelle. The threat of retribution in his hard gaze made Gianelle look away.

"Touch her," Dante's voice was as lethal as his words, "and I vow I will spill your blood right where you stand."

Dermott nodded and did not even glance at Gianelle when Dante released him. Rubbing his wrist instead, he turned to his brother, who was watching from his seat. Edgar Dermott nodded subtly at him, and then returned Dante's murderous glare. For an instant, his eyes glittered with revenge. But then his face relaxed into a wide grin.

"A toast to King William's royal commander." He lifted his cup to Dante. "Dashing protector of"—he glanced at Gianelle over the rim—"the fairer sex. Let us hope it never gets him killed."

"And that the man who attempts it," Dante added, his cool, gray gaze untouched by the challenging smile he offered Edgar Dermott, "has enough strength and skill to at least cause me to break a sweat before he fails."

The confidence in his voice convinced Gianelle that Dante Risande did not lose many battles. She had no more time to dwell on it, though, because he shifted slightly and she realized with a mortified sigh that her back was plastered against his formidable body. Without sparing a glance to the man who had just saved her, she lurched away from him and crossed the hall to the next table to continue her duties.

For the next hour Gianelle busied herself with every task she could find that would keep her away from Lord Risande's table. He had already proved how sharp his eyes were, how cleverly he had deduced that she had slipped something into Baron Landry's drink. And why hadn't he gone straight to Lord Dermott with that bit of information? He suspected her of a heinous deed, yet he protected her from her master's anger. Why? It was a question she would ponder for a fortnight to come, she was sure. He was a shrewd one, up to something she could not figure out. The few stolen glances she cast his way confirmed the careful surveillance he kept on everyone while sipping wine he had accepted from Sylvia. Would a simple glance at Casey reveal to him their plans to escape? She couldn't take the chance.

She stayed away for another reason as well, one she

found more difficult to admit. He tempted her to look at him. Even now, while she replaced a melted-down candle with a newer one, she wanted to look at him. He was laughing. The sound was rich and throaty, and completely male. He was probably beguiling some purring maiden with his devilish dimple and knee-buckling smile. Foolish twits, Gianelle mumbled to herself. She had better things to think about than Lord Dante Risande, like living out the rest of her days in freedom with Casey. Mayhap they would travel to Scotland and raise sheep. Gianelle wondered if men kept servants in that faraway place. If they did, it wouldn't do. But they would find a place. She would never stop searching, just as her father had never stopped. She hoped Henri Dejiat had found his longed-for freedom.

She looked up while she was still thinking of her father, sensing Dante's compelling gray eyes on her. To her surprise and dismay, he was walking toward her. What did he want? She had a sinking feeling he wanted to question her further about Baron Landry, who had returned twice to the great hall, only to run from it twice again, as green as a summer glade. Her heart beat wildly in her chest, and for a fleeting instant she thought about flinging a candle at the towering earl to stop his advance. But she couldn't move, save for a pitiful blink. She took in every inch of him, and saints, but there was a lot.

He was the epitome of elegant masculinity in a closely tailored, unbuttoned surcoat of cobalt blue that reached just below his knees. Beneath, he wore a white shirt shot through with gold thread. A broadsword sheathed in thick leather dangled from his hip under his surcoat. Black woolen hose and soft leather boots encased his long, muscular legs. His dark hair was pulled away from his face in a neat queue at his nape. Instead of fighting the effect his appearance had on her, Gianelle tapped her foot, impatient to have him question her and be on his way. The problem was, she couldn't stop staring at him. He didn't seem to take offense, though, and stared right back at her until he reached her.

"Forgive me, lady," he said in a low voice, "but I am compelled to find out what it is about replacing an old candle that causes such a wistful look to come over you."

He was a sorcerer who could read her thoughts. Gianelle tried to step around him before he pointed his finger at her and shouted every defiant misdeed she had ever committed. Could she be flogged for replacing the melted soap with tree sap last month? Or mayhap licking all the apple tarts before they were served would be considered a crime more deserving of the whip.

He blocked her path and tilted his head to capture her gaze. "You have nothing to fear from me."

Gianelle almost laughed. Her head barely reached his chest. The man had muscles pulsing right through the sleeves of his surcoat, and eyes the color of lightning. She had plenty to fear.

"What were you thinking about?" he asked her.

"My father," she replied, not daring to tell him that thinking about running free through some Highland field of lavender heather had more likely produced the longing look he claimed to see on her.

"You miss him then," Dante said, understanding.

"*Non,* my lord. I do not."

Struck by the matter-of-fact coolness in her voice, and curious about how she came to serve Bryce Dermott,

Dante pressed her further. "Did he sell you into servitude?"

"I was born a slave, my lord," Gianelle answered him while she looked around the hall. She wished he would get on with his questions about Landry. Do whatever he was going to do instead of causing her to worry this way.

"Where did you come from before you came to be here?"

She finally lifted her gaze to probe his eyes, and the slight quirk of her brow almost made Dante smile.

But Gianelle was just beginning to realize that he was even more clever than she had first accredited him. He wanted the names of her former masters so that he could question them about others to whom she may or may not have caused misfortune. Well, she was just as cunning as he. She would give him all the names he wanted, just not the true ones. "I don't know what that has to do with anything, but if you wish to know, then I cannot refuse to tell you. Let me see, my first master, when I arrived in England, was Lord Harold . . . um . . . Hampton. After that . . ."

Dante narrowed his eyes on her and stopped another smile from creeping along his lips. He had absolutely no idea why she was lying to him again. It should have made him suspicious of her, but she looked so delightful trying to keep up with him, he had to command all his control not to laugh. "I've never heard of this Lord Harold Hampton. What region does he hold in honor for the king?"

"Region?" She drew her lower lip between her teeth and tried to think of some of the regions in England. The problem was that she had only traveled to three of them in the six years she had been here, and didn't know the names of any of the others.

Dante clasped his hands behind his back and allowed his grin to shine full force on her. "Just say whatever wanders into your head, Gianelle. I vow on my sword you could tell me this Harold Hampton holds court at the bottom of the sea and I would only have to look into your eyes to believe you."

Gianelle studied him carefully, but she couldn't decide if he had just given her a compliment or if he was calling her a liar. She guessed it was the latter, since no noble in his right mind would compliment a servant. The conclusion made her angry immediately. How dare he call her a liar? "If you are done interrogating me, I can get on with my duties."

He gave her a reproachful look. "I was trying to converse with you, not interrogate you."

"What in heaven's name for?" She placed her hands on her hips and stared up at him with wide, unbelieving eyes.

"Pardon?" Dante was certain his ears had just betrayed him. "Why converse with you?"

"Oui."

"I . . ." He stopped and scowled at her. "Well, I . . ." *Enfer,* never before had he been asked to explain why he wanted to speak to a lady. He had no idea what to say, so he closed his mouth. To his disappointment, she took his silence to imply their conversation, no matter what she chose to call it, was over.

"Wait." He caught her arm before she walked away. Briefly, he pondered whether she might have slipped something into his food. Why else was he chasing her about like a puppy longing to be scratched? He had never done this before with any woman, and he did not want to begin now. His scowl deepened, but his mouth opened anyway. "Walk with me outside later when your work is done."

Gianelle shook her head and said simply, *"Non."*

"I will remain silent, and you can 'interrogate' me."

"But my lord." She raised her eyes to his. "There is nothing I want to know about you."

Dante stood alone for a few moments watching her walk away from him for the third time that night. Her words should have stung him, never having heard any woman speak this way to him before, but he smiled instead. He was a warrior, always up for the challenge of a worthy opponent. Indeed, the thought of winning her to his bed was quite refreshing.

Chapter Three

GIANELLE HAD NEVER IMAGINED how difficult climbing down a rope could be. Her fingers were raw from the prickly twine after only five knots. Twice her feet slipped as she tried to brace herself on the knot below, leaving her to dangle by her fingernails. Casey wasn't helping matters any by squeaking like a rat and quoting scriptures on how fools despise skillful and godly wisdom. Gianelle would have preferred a psalm or two, since she felt thankful that the servants' quarters were on the lowest level of the castle. Had she been a noble trying to escape, she would have been a hundred feet higher up.

"How many more knots?"

Gianelle looked up and prayed that Casey didn't fall on top of her. "I cannot tell. But we are almost there."

"Look down and count them, Gia."

"*Non,* you look down and count them."

"My cheek is bleeding."

"Well, don't press it so to the rope, Casey."

Soon they would be free. Gianelle repeated it to herself over and over to keep the pain in her hands from overwhelming her. Just the very thought of no longer living under someone else's control had always given her the strength and courage to face even her worst days. And now it pushed her on despite her fear of what lay before them, her aching fingers, and Casey's foot on her head.

"Be careful, will you?" She glared up at the soles of Casey's slippers.

"I think the rope is slipping." Casey squealed so loud Gianelle was certain she woke everyone in the castle. "Did you just feel that?"

The double knot came undone from around the leg of Gianelle's bed, and both of them plummeted the remaining few feet to the ground. Gia landed hard on her rump, legs sprawled out in front of her. Casey landed on top of her, and the rope came next, hitting them both on the head.

Busy cursing the rope and untangling herself from it, Gianelle didn't notice the man standing casually against the castle wall, even though pale beams of moonlight shone directly on him. When he spoke, Casey yelped and Gianelle went deathly still.

"Going somewhere?"

Damnation, what was *he* doing out here? Gianelle pounded her fists into the hard dirt beneath her. Casey vaulted to her feet and took off running.

"Go get her, Balin," Dante commanded the darker figure to Gianelle's left. "Bring her back to her room and assure her that we will tell Dermott nothing of this."

Gianelle still had not moved a muscle. She wondered why this stranger would protect her yet again. He wanted something. But what? She also wondered if she was strong enough to strangle him with her rope. Another look at him and she decided it would be futile to try. She desperately wanted to curse him while he stood there with his arms folded across his chest and a ridiculous grin spread across his face. Why, he'd probably watched her and Casey the entire way down.

"What curse has befallen me that sent you here?" She wanted to weep. She wanted to scream as her hopes of escape crashed to the ground as hard as she had.

Dante stepped away from the wall and squatted beside her. "Do you always say the first thing that is on your mind? Because—" His gaze settled on the silhouette of her leg, and then slowly up to her bare thigh where her skirts had ridden up in her fall. He found it nearly impossible to tear his gaze away and almost sighed out loud when she yanked her hem back down. "I would have you know that your contempt hurts me deeply. To be called a curse . . ." He watched her rise to her feet and blow a stray lock of hair off her nose.

"Why are you not asleep like the others?"

She sounded heart-wrenchingly defeated to Dante's ears, and he had the urge to take her in his arms and comfort her. "I could not sleep," he told her, rising to his feet. He stood directly in front of her and closed his eyes so that he could concentrate on his words rather than on her full, pouting mouth so temptingly tilted toward his. "I was having a walk with Balin, talking about you, as a matter of fact."

Gianelle narrowed her eyes on him. "In the middle of the night?"

"*Oui.*" He had no intention of telling her that he and Balin had also waited for everyone to fall asleep so they could rummage through Bryce Dermott's solar. They hadn't yet found anything connecting him to Hereward the Wake when Dante heard the fervent prayers rising up from somewhere outside the solar window and went out to investigate.

"Why should you have anything to discuss about me with your man Balin?" Gianelle asked him suspiciously. She didn't trust this mysterious stranger with his sharp eyes and roguish smile. The way he looked at her made her feel like a scantily clad wench.

"Shouldn't I be the one asking you the questions?" He stepped around her and bent to gather the bundle of rope on the ground. "For instance, why were you and Casey trying to escape?"

Gianelle turned to face him again, but lowered her gaze to the ground. "You would never understand."

"Tell me anyway."

"We want to be free."

Dante had the feeling that he was the first man to hear her speak those words. Her present lord would certainly punish her if she admitted her desire to him. Still, Dante wanted to ask her why she would want to be away from these thick walls that protected her, from kitchens where cooks prepared warm meals to fill her belly. But Gianelle probably did not weigh more than a silken veil if the look of her told the truth. And living with a man who would strike her had obviously made these thick walls her prison, not her protection. But the world outside Devonshire was so much worse than the tyrant who lived inside. Dante knew this firsthand.

"Where did you and Casey plan on going after this?" He held the rope up and then tossed it over his shoulder.

"Wherever our feet led us," she admitted and raised her chin, reminding Dante of a proud mare.

"Not a very thought-out plan. Have you a dagger hidden somewhere on your body?"

Gianelle stared at him and blinked. *"Non."* Why hadn't she thought of bringing a knife? She admitted to herself that not having one was foolish, but then reminded herself that she didn't know how to use one anyway. "We have a pouch of coin." After she said it, she squeezed her eyes shut since it was too late to do the same to her mouth. Now he would demand to know from whom they had pilfered the coin.

"Well, at least the robbers who killed you would get something for their trouble."

"We would not have been killed," Gianelle argued, and then jumped backward when he came toward her.

"With these scrawny arms"—he pinched her upper arm gently between his thumb and index finger—"you would be lucky to inflict a welt on the face of your attacker."

Gianelle would have liked to test his theory on his cheek, but his fingers caressed her as they slid down to her hand. His gentle touch sent a quiver along her spine. She tried to pull away, but he applied a little more pressure and held her still.

"A woman's hands should not be so bruised. Come, let me take care of this bleeding."

"You take care of *me?"* She would have laughed if she still didn't feel like weeping. Before she could refuse his odd offer, though, he tucked her hand into the crook of his elbow and began leading her back inside.

Gianelle did not fight him. What was the point? He had foiled her plans for freedom, but then again she had been too eager and had not thought out her plans. "Do you truly think Casey and I would have fallen to robbers?"

"*Oui, petite fée.* Maidens should never be alone in the woods."

Something in the way he spoke these words, the way his pitch dipped with sorrow, made Gianelle believe him. Still, she paused and cast a longing look over her shoulder just before they entered the castle.

The kitchen was dark. Dante slammed his shin into the chopping table hard enough to rattle the jars above it. He swore mightily in French just before he nearly sent them both tumbling over a barrel of turnips.

Shaking his arm off her, Gianelle stepped over a stool and lit a good amount of candles before Dante got them both killed. When she finished lighting the last one, she turned and caught the lopsided grin he cast her. She was still angry with him for ruining her escape, but for an instant she felt like laughing.

"Where's the cellar?" he asked her. Gianelle pointed to a doorway down the hall and watched his hulking form disappear into the shadows. "I just want to get rid of this rope. Do not go away."

"You have already seen to that," Gianelle murmured while turning to a large cupboard where Maeve kept some clean cloths. There was still some fresh water in a pot beside the trivet. She dipped the cloth in and pressed it against her bloody fingers with a French curse of her own.

"Here, let me."

God's blood, but his voice behind her shattered the last shred of her nerves. She spun around and looked up into his glittering eyes, then turned her face away from his.

"Do they pain you much?" His velvet voice was a whisper that sent his warm breath across her cheek.

She shook her head while he began to clean her wounds.

She glanced at him once, and then again. He met her gaze and smiled.

"Your eyes are a very odd color, my lord."

"Do they frighten you?"

"Why would eyes frighten me? They are just . . . odd. There are tiny flecks of green in them I hadn't noticed before."

His dimple deepened and made Gianelle mumble an oath beneath her breath. He really was an arrogant rake. "You have a terribly aggravating way about you," she said, hoping to sting his pride. "You are like an itch that comes at the most inopportune time. And no matter how much you scratch it, it will not go away."

Dante stopped wiping her fingers and let his gaze drift over her features. "You have not scratched me yet."

Gianelle was sure it was her imagination, but the man sounded like a big male lion, purring.

"I just might before the morn comes, my lord," she warned, emboldened by the warmth in his eyes.

"Call me Dante. And I like to be scratched right here." He slid his hand, and hers with it, to a place just below his right rib.

Gianelle pulled her hand back and tugged the cloth from him. She would tend to herself. Dante stepped around her and made himself busy by surveying the kitchen.

"Have you ever heard Dermott or his brother talking about Hereward the Wake?"

"Hereward the what?" She looked at his back while he reached for a jar above the chopping table. Maeve and the others would drop dead if they saw the careful way she noted the candlelight playing over his dark hair that fell between the powerful breadth of his shoulders.

"The Wake," Dante repeated. He popped the cork off a small jar and turned to point it at her. "Is this what you used on Baron Landry?"

Gianelle opened her mouth to deny his charge for the last time. But there was something in the casual way he asked her, the certainty in his glance that told her she should not bother lying. And why should she indeed? He had caught her trying to escape but had not dragged her off to be punished. Gianelle knew she should not trust him, but so far he had not given her a reason not to. In fact, he was the first man who had ever asked her questions without bellowing at her answers, even when she was a little rude. He was the first noble who not only allowed her to look him in the eye, but seemed to enjoy it. As mad as that notion was, it gave her a sense of equality.

"Do you want the truth on the matter?"

"It would be a refreshing change," Dante said. His quick eyes caught the shadow of a smile on her lips.

"Very well, then, my lord. I have never heard of this Hereward the Wake. And that is pepper you are holding."

Dante looked into the jar, then brought the rim to his nose and inhaled. Gianelle clamped her hand over her mouth to muffle a giggle when he sneezed and sent a cloud of pepper in her direction.

"*Oui*, it's pepper." He wiped his eyes, corked the lid, and returned the jar to its place. His fingers moved over the next jar.

"Cinnamon," Gianelle told him. "Though Maeve does not use it often. It is very costly. My lord's brother has the bark sent here from another continent, though I am unfamiliar with its name."

"India." Dante eyed the spice. "Odd that the younger

brother of a Saxon baron can afford such a luxury." Unless he found a way to acquire coin for services unknown to the king.

"And this?" Dante pointed to another jar. "Another rare spice?"

"That is sage." Gianelle gave him a confounded look. "May I speak freely, my lord?"

A half-smile played around his beautifully chiseled lips. "It would give me great pleasure if you would."

That response stunned her and deepened her confused expression. He certainly had a way of scattering one's thoughts, and she wondered if there was a purpose behind it. "How is it you know where cinnamon comes from, yet you do not know what a jar of pepper looks like?"

"I like cinnamon in my mead," Dante explained. "But I don't prepare my own food."

"Of course." She felt foolish for allowing herself to forget he probably didn't even know what his kitchen looked like.

"You look quite irresistible when I befuddle you, by the way."

"You don't befuddle me," Gianelle hastily retorted. "And the next jar is daffodil; quite tasteless when dried and powered, and added to a lecherous noble's wine."

Dante grinned at the way she looked at him when she spoke those last three words. "And what effect does it have on the lecherous noble?"

"Vomiting." Gianelle waited for his reaction now that his charges were validated.

He shrugged his shoulders. "Uncomfortable, but harmless. Was Baron Landry deserving of such a malady?"

"He was." Relief relaxed the tight knots behind her neck. She suddenly felt very sleepy.

Dante watched her yawn and thought about offering to carry her to her bed.

"May I ask you a question, my lord?"

"Of course," he replied on an uneven breath, and let his visions of her sprawled out beneath him vanish.

"If he was undeserving, would you have struck me?"

For a moment, Dante simply stared at her. He knew why she asked him that heartbreaking question, and it angered him to think of a hand coming down on such a fragile thing as she. *"Non,"* he answered gently, drawing a step nearer to her. "I would never strike you, Gianelle."

His eyes were smoky and warm when she looked into them; his rugged features were softly defined in the candlelight.

"You're very unusual, Lord Risande."

He caught her hand and covered it with his own. "I've been thinking the same thing about you all night." *Merde,* he had to kiss her before he went mad.

A piercing scream shattered his thoughts. "What the hell . . . ?"

Footsteps pounded in every direction. The castle came awake as a woman screamed over and over again.

Lord Bryce Dermott was dead. He was dead; poisoned in his own bed.

Without taking his eyes off hers, Dante released Gianelle's hand and stepped away from her. Her heart nearly stopped when he looked over his shoulder at the jars above the chopping table.

Chapter Four

A CORNER OF THE GREAT HALL pulsated with flickering light and the frantic whispers of Devonshire's servants. They had all been herded into the hall by Edgar Dermott, but had been given no more information than what they already knew. Their lord had been poisoned and died while he slept. Lady Genevieve LaSalle apparently had been sharing his bed at the time, since she was the first to discover him upon awakening.

"How do they know he was poisoned?" Margaret asked the small assembly. "Mayhap his heart gave out after rutting the noble harlot. I overheard Lady LaSalle offering herself, *for the second time,* to Lord Risande earlier this eve. I'd wager my arse that any woman who could go two rounds with that stallion would likely kill a bloated toad like our master."

"Gia?" Casey tugged on her friend's sleeve. "Think you it is possible for a woman to kill a man by rutting him?"

"I don't know," Gianelle answered vaguely and continued staring at the doors, waiting for Dante to enter and declare her guilty. She had seen the suspicion narrowing his eyes after he looked at those jars. She'd admitted to poisoning Baron Landry, and now he suspected her of poisoning her master as well.

"Gia?" Casey tugged her sleeve again. "Edgar Dermott will be our master now, and you know how cruel he can be."

Gianelle patted her hand to offer her friend some comfort from that terrifying thought. Not that she would suffer under his hand. *Non,* she would be hanging in the courtyard before nightfall, if she was fortunate. She cursed Dante Risande to Hades. If he had been sleeping like everyone else, she and Casey might be halfway to Scotland by now.

The doors opened, and the hush that spread over the great hall stilled Gianelle's heart. Edgar Dermott entered first. He took long, deliberate strides to the center of the hall. His dark hair was still flattened from his pillow, his nightdress tucked haphazardly into his trousers. Dante entered next with Balin, followed by seven of Devonshire's guards. Their footsteps pounded in Gianelle's ears. Her gaze met Dante's, but his expression didn't help calm her nerves. He offered her neither an accusing glare nor a reassuring nod.

"My brother has been murdered." Edgar Dermott's voice shattered the dooming silence. "A cup of wine was found in his chambers. When fed to one of our hogs in his gruel, the beast keeled over and died shortly thereafter."

Someone gasped to Gia's right.

"I suspect one of you, and I will . . ."

"I told you, Dermott," Dante's powerful voice overrode his. "Everyone is a suspect in this castle, including the lords and ladies who have not yet been questioned."

Dermott didn't look at Dante when he spoke but closed his eyes and ground his teeth together with impatience.

"Earl Risande, you of all people should know that a noble would not commit such an offensive deed."

"I know no such thing," Dante replied coolly. "Men, regardless of their title, are capable of many things, even treason against their king."

Dermott chuckled with mocking insincerity. "Forgive me. I forgot that I was speaking to the servant's champion."

"You are speaking to the king's emissary, and the royal commander of his army." Dante corrected him with such authority and command, two of the servants curtsied in their places.

Servant's champion indeed, Dermott thought, his smile fading. The Norman swine shamed the Dermott name this evening when he rebuked Bryce in front of everyone in the great hall, and over a servant no less. They would both pay for that. If Bryce had let him discipline the wench in the past, Gianelle would be cowering at his feet, fat with his third bastard instead of standing there tempting Risande to defend her yet again. Well, tonight was the last time she would be protected by anyone. Of course, Bryce had denied him the pleasure of beating her and taking her to his bed only because Bryce so enjoyed doing it himself. His brother was dead, and Gianelle was finally his, but now he had Risande to deal with. How far would the royal commander go to defend her when the king's own law was put to him? It was an ingenious plan of his, really. If he accused Gianelle of the crime, no one could stop him from doing whatever he wanted to her, not even her new champion. Edgar's only regret was that Risande wouldn't be there to watch.

"Then as the king's emissary," he said with a wry smile,

"you are aware of the law. Since I am the victim's brother, it is my right to exact punishment on the murderer. I formally request that you not stand in the way of justice. One of these servants has taken the life of my brother." He turned to settle his gaze on Gianelle. "I saw the hatred in her eyes tonight. She enjoyed what you did to my brother. She has been heard twice before wishing death on her lord after being punished for her insolence. I myself have fallen ill after merely scolding her. Alas, my brother wouldn't heed my warnings of her treachery. Now he is dead. Surely you will not continue to defend her."

"You have proof of what you say?" Dante asked him.

"I know her. You do not."

Dante flicked his gaze to Gianelle and smiled. He had plans for remedying that soon enough. He turned his attention back to Dermott. "That is not good enough, and since your accusations are based on nothing more than wounded pride, I will protect her."

Dante knew by now that he had gone completely and undeniably daft for continuing to protect Gianelle. Everything pointed to her as the offender. He knew nothing about her, save that to the untrained eye she appeared perfectly obedient. But Christ, she took her revenge on Landry like a trained assassin. She had half-climbed, half-dangled her way down a considerable length of poorly tied rope to escape a man she obviously hated, perhaps ensuring he would never catch her by killing him. Every instinct in Dante cautioned him to be wary of her. Logic told him she was probably guilty, but he didn't care. He intended to have her, and he wasn't about to let Edgar Dermott or a murder stop him. The little worm knew the law and would probably insist on an inquiry, which could take months to conclude. If Dermott had time to request it of the king, Gianelle could be ordered to remain here until she was proved innocent. Dante couldn't allow that. Guilty or not, he wanted her. *Oui*, even now the slightly belligerent curl of her mouth tempted his body to harden with thoughts of where he might compel those lips to taste him. He had to get her out of Devonshire, and quickly.

"Your deep concern for justice does not go unheeded, Dermott," he said, hoping his plan would work. "I will personally conduct an inquiry into the murder. The captain of my guard, Sir Balin DeGarge, shall ride back to Graycliff immediately and gather twelve of my most astute men to aid us. When they return we shall proceed, questioning the nobles first, as I think they will be eager to leave Devonshire by then."

"The . . ." Edgar Dermott formed the word around his lips, but produced no sound. Stunned disbelief soon turned into anger. "You expect me to hold barons, earls, and dukes prisoner in my brother's castle while your man travels to Dover and back?"

"Don't think of them as prisoners." Dante flashed him an infuriating grin. "Request that they remain here. If they refuse, *then* we can consider them prisoners." Dante knew that what he proposed was risky, even so far as testing his friendship with William. Every noble in the castle would go to the king the moment they were released and make formal charges against him for refusing to let them leave. He said a silent prayer that Bryce Dermott's brother understood that keeping so many people here for a long period of time would drain what was left of Devonshire's coffers. And if losing his funds didn't worry him, Dante hoped spoiling the Dermott name would.

"I'm certain that after a pair of years your peers will forgive you the blemish of suspecting them of murder."

"My lord, you cannot be serious. I will send a missive to the king and . . ."

"Wait for his reply." Dante concluded for him. "That will probably take a little more time, perhaps a se'nnight or two." He leaned his backside against a table, folded his arms across his chest, and sighed. "If I must remain here an extra fortnight while your missive is answered, what choice do I have? It is my duty."

Panic rushed across Dermott's cheeks, painting them crimson. "We can question the servants now while allowing the others to leave. When your men return, they can take up the inquiry in the lords' own castles."

Dante thought about it for a moment, then shook his head. "*Non,* it would take months in travel, probably a year before we find the murderer. Certainly, you wouldn't want to wait that long to bring the scoundrel to justice."

"I don't care how long it takes. You would do all this to protect a murderess?" Dermott's jaw tightened so that he spoke between clenched teeth. "I will not have my name soiled, nor will I go broke because you insist on—"

"There is no murderess. But the inquiry could end quickly." Dante cut him off, his voice no longer blasé, but deadly. "We merely need to determine who would profit from your brother's death. You will make your request to King William to be made Lord of Devonshire, will you not?"

Dermott visibly blanched as Dante's unspoken threat

became clear. "This is a crime of vengeance, not profit," he argued.

"That is yet to be determined," Dante countered. He turned and searched the faces of the servants. "I will see that you are all treated fairly. No matter how long it takes. I suggest you each retire to your beds, and I will do the same. There will be trying days ahead."

He crossed the great hall in a few strides and was about to leave when Dermott's voice stopped him. Before he turned to face him, Dante exhaled deeply.

"Lord Risande, I appreciate your desire to bring"—he tightened his lips over his teeth, hating having to admit defeat—"my brother's killer to justice. But there must be another way."

Dante brought his index finger to his lips and thought about it. "Now that you mention it, King William will be returning to England in a few weeks or so. When he holds court, all his great vassals must attend. They can give their account of this night to him. The innocent will not take offense to this since they must travel to Winchester anyway, and will be happy to aid you in capturing the murderer."

Dermott narrowed his eyes at Dante. The ploy had not been carefully thought out, but it ceased to matter the moment the king's royal commander insisted on keeping everyone here. Of course, Dermott could have agreed to hold more than seventy nobles in Devonshire just to watch what Risande would have done next. But he had no idea how far the Norman would take this farce, so he conceded. What infuriated Dermott the most was that Risande didn't care if his plan was discovered or not. The arrogant bastard stood there smiling, daring him not to do things his way. Dermott had no choice, but there was one consolation: Risande would be gone by morning, and with Bryce dead, there would be no one to stop him from taking Gianelle to his bed.

"You have my thanks for solving this problem without catastrophe, Lord Risande. But you left out one final detail. Who will question the servants?"

Turning to face them all, Dante allowed his victorious smile to widen into a cheerful grin. "Their champion will, of course. I will do so in the morn before I leave."

"But 'tis almost morning now, my lord," Maeve pointed out.

"So it is. We will do it now then, and be swift about it."

Dante returned his attention to the man glowering at him. "One more thing, Dermott. I am taking Gianelle and Casey back to Dover with me."

"Nay! You cannot. Their innocence has not been . . ."

"If you refuse to let them go, I will have no choice but to take offense and bring you to the lists, where I can assure you, you will surrender them to me. Do you refuse?" Dante almost hoped he would.

"You and I shall have our day," Dermott snarled. "I vow it."

"I look forward to it." Dante's diamond-hard gaze lingered on Dermott while he shoved his fingers into a pocket inside his tunic. "A thief I am not." He handed Edgar Dermott two silver coins, one for each woman he was taking, and left the great hall.

Gianelle wanted to weep and never stop. In fact, she felt misty eyed, which infuriated her further. Wanting to cry and actually doing it were two entirely different things.

She hadn't cried since the day her father had abandoned her, and she vowed after that unabashed bawling never to do so again. But tonight she almost lost her control twice, and Dante Risande was to blame. She admitted that having her freedom snatched away was a good enough reason to wail until her lungs ached. But watching him so brilliantly take command over Edgar Dermott, knowing that he did everything he could to protect her, even when he believed her guilty, could have given her years of tender songs to sing had she been a bard. She felt relieved and filled with hope again when he told Dermott that he was taking her and Casey with him. Surely, she had told herself, he would free them the moment they left Devonshire. She even imagined the "servant's champion" might escort them to wherever they wanted to go, ensuring their safe journey to liberation. But then he had bought her and Casey. Oh, if that wasn't reason to cry, she didn't know what was. The songs went flat. Gianelle gritted her teeth as she left the great hall. She hated bards anyway.

Dante studied Gianelle's face while she sat in absolute silence across from him in Dermott's solar. The downward brush of his gaze took in the worn folds of her skirts, her raw fingers clenched tightly in her lap.

"Did you do it?"

"Do what, my lord?" She stared at her hands.

"Did you poison Bryce Dermott, Gianelle?"

"I was with you, my lord."

Dante ran his hands down his face and tried to remain patient. She was being deliberately evasive. "Do you think it hasn't occurred to me that you could have done it before your attempted escape?"

"I fully admit that I've no idea what goes on in your head."

"Gianelle, I'm tired. You're the last person to be questioned. Answer me so we can get the hell out of here."

"*Oui,* I am tired as well, and I fear I've forgotten the question."

That did it. He slammed his palms down on his thighs and swore an oath fit only for the company of men. "Look at me," he demanded. She did, but only for a moment before she dutifully lowered her eyes again. "What has come over you? Do you avoid looking into my eyes because of your guilt?"

"There would be no guilt in me for killing a man like Bryce Dermott, my lord," she said benignly. "Do you shout at me because I am your servant now?"

Dante tried to keep the frustration she was causing him out of his voice. He found it very difficult. "You are not my servant."

"You paid for me," she insisted. "You are planning on freeing me then? And Casey as well?"

There it was. Now he understood why she worked so hard at driving him mad. She wanted him to let her go. For a moment, he was tempted to do it. To bid her farewell and cease thinking about kissing that sulky mouth of hers. He thought about places he could send her where she would be safe. The nunnery came to mind, but he quickly dismissed the idea of her covered from foot to crown in black robes. He would much rather see her lying in his bed wearing a robe of a much sheerer nature. He frowned when visions of her smashing him over the head with a bowl invaded his original thoughts.

"I told you already. You and Casey would not survive a day without protection. I cannot give you what you want."

"I understand, my lord." The quaver in her voice said otherwise.

"You have my word that you will be free to do as you wish in Graycliff Castle."

"I will wish to leave it. I will not be free to do that."

Enfer! Dante wanted to go find a guard with a strong nose he could beat to a bloody pulp. He had no idea how to handle this wisp of a woman. And it frustrated the hell out of him. All she wanted to do since she met him was get away from him. It clipped at his ego and compelled him to prove to her that he was a better man than the ones who made her want to run away.

"We have a full day's ride before we sleep. Do you want to stay here a few more hours and . . ."

"Non," she answered hastily. "I wish to leave now. If the choice were mine to make, I mean," she added quietly.

"It was. That's why I asked you." The clip of annoyance in his voice tempted Gianelle to smile, but only after he rose to his feet and turned to leave the solar. And only because what he said, and how he said it, made her forget how angry she was with him. She had never been given a choice before.

"Are you coming?" he asked, waiting for her at the door.

God help her. If he didn't start acting like a master, she might even forget how badly she wanted to dislike him.

An hour later, Dante's patience was tested again while he waited upon his stallion for Gianelle and Casey to gather what little belongings they possessed and then bid farewell to every servant in the castle. Just when his patience had reached its limit, Gianelle stepped up to him and looked around the courtyard.

"Which horse will I be riding?"

"This one." Dante leaned down, snaked his arm around her waist and lifted her off her feet.

Wincing when her backside landed hard in his saddle, she yanked her skirts down over her knees that dangled over the mount's right haunches, and clamped onto Dante's shoulders when he flicked the reins. Casey rode in the same fashion with Balin a few paces behind.

"Are you comfortable?" Dante asked her as they trotted out of Devonshire.

Gianelle wanted to tell him that her spine felt like dry timber ready to snap with every step his horse took. Her buttocks were slipping and her sore fingers were already aching from digging into his granite shoulders.

"*Oui*, I am fi . . ." Her rump went first, her fingers followed, and she landed facedown in the dirt.

"*Merde!*" Dante swore and leaped out of the saddle. "Are you injured?" He slipped his hands under her arms and brought her back to her feet.

"*Non*." She spit a twig out of her mouth and dusted off her skirts.

Dante took her by the shoulders and tilted his head to meet her gaze. "Have you ever ridden a horse before?" he asked gently.

"Of course, many times. All right," she admitted when he lifted a doubtful eyebrow at her, "only once. And I was tied to it so I managed to stay on."

Balin and Casey passed them at a slow canter. The captain shook his head at Dante, but said nothing.

"Come on then. You will have to sit in the front." Dante leaped back up and then bent to her and lifted her onto his lap.

She winced again, for his thighs were as hard as his saddle. She wiggled into a more comfortable position, but frowned at the way her backside fit so neatly between his legs. "This is unholy!" she protested, though she could not deny the safety of his arms encasing her when he reached for the reins.

"Only if you move upon me like that again." His voice rumbled low like a seductive battle drum.

Gianelle went stiff. "How long will it take to reach Dover?"

"Three days." Dante smiled above her and plucked a piece of hay out of her hair. "You will like it there, *fée*. The cliffs still steal the breath from me . . . as you do."

He heard a sound from her like a mocking grumble and leaned forward, putting his lips to her ear. "You may speak freely with me." He knew his next request was a mistake, for framed by wisps of hair the color of beaten gold, her delicate profile intoxicated him. "And I would prefer it if you looked at me when you speak."

"If you insist," she said, and angled her face toward his. "You have a deceptively smooth tongue."

He gave her a smile that sent her pulse racing. "I wish that was a compliment."

"I'm sure you get enough to coat your ego quite nicely." Out of habit, and a desire to protect herself against the shimmering potency of his gaze, she averted her eyes and smiled at Casey riding beside her with her cheek pressed against Balin's back. Her friend smiled back and closed her eyes.

"You think I'm a rake then." It was more of a statement than a question.

"I don't think about you one way or the other. I only speak from what I have observed."

"And what is that?" Dante was surprised to find himself brooding over her indifference.

"I heard you bidding Lady LaSalle your charming farewell. And for a woman who woke up with a corpse, she recovered quickly enough. Lady Humphrey and the Duke of Stamford's daughter both giggled uncontrollably when you addressed them. Do you have the same effect on all women?"

"All but one."

Gianelle nodded and turned again to face the forest that loomed ahead. "One with good sense still left in her head."

Dante scowled at the back of her head and then glanced at Balin when he heard his captain chuckle.

"Pay attention to Casey," he growled. "She's asleep and about to tumble out of the saddle."

Balin slowed his mount and reached behind him, and Dante put his heels to his horse.

At first, Gianelle clung to Dante for dear life as they sped away. But the wind in her face and the landscape blurring by her made her feel like she was flying. Pressed against his chest and cradled snugly within the muscular circle of his arms, she began to relax, and finally closed her eyes when they reached the woods.

"This time," she said, letting her body drift off to sleep, "I have come prepared." Her hand slipped to her thigh and her head sank into the crook of Dante's arm.

Chapter Five

❧

Dante hated himself for doing it, but when she began to snore, he lifted her hand and felt her thigh. He whispered a blasphemous oath as his fingers molded to the hard shape of a dagger beneath her skirts.

"While she's asleep, you scoundrel?" Balin cast him an admonishing frown.

"She has a dagger, Balin," Dante whispered back at him. "Think you I would grope her while she sleeps?"

Balin ignored his lord's incredulous glare. "I honestly don't know what you would do anymore."

"What is that supposed to mean? And turn away for a moment while I retrieve her weapon."

"She's getting under your skin," Balin told him, fixing his eyes on the trees.

"I assure you she is not." Dante carefully lifted the hem over her knee.

"You believed she murdered Lord Dermott and instead of arresting her, you're bringing her back to Graycliff."

"After questioning her and the other servants, I no longer think she killed him." His breath stalled in his chest as he gazed at the shapely contours of her thigh.

"Did she deny the charge?"

Dante shifted his gaze to her face and knit his brows together. "*Non*, she managed to distract me quite nicely." Damn him, but he hadn't even realized it until this moment. He plucked the dagger, which turned out to be a small kitchen knife, from the leather strip tied to her leg and pulled her skirt back down.

"Dante, you don't get distracted. You don't care if she killed Dermott, do you?"

"Not particularly."

Balin turned back to him. "Why bring her home?"

"Because Dermott would have strung her to a high branch without posing a single question to her. Why do you think he only called the servants to the hall? He wanted this unpleasant matter dealt with swiftly. He had no intentions of questioning his brother's stately guests. Gianelle was an easy victim. He planned on accusing her because she brought shame to his brother through me. I couldn't leave her there not knowing for certain if she was guilty or innocent."

He didn't tell Balin that he couldn't leave her there because something in her drew him like a siren song. Even now his gaze was drifting back to her, to revel in the temptation of her softly parted lips that had hurled more insults at him in one night than he had heard in the last five years. He longed to touch the alluring curve of her slender jaw and bask in the guileless beauty of her eyes for two lifetimes.

"You took this one because of Katherine."

Dante heard Balin's voice and blinked his gaze away from Gianelle. "*Oui*, I did." He didn't look at Casey's sleeping face right away. He found that he needed to prepare himself over and over each time he did look at her. It was becoming easier, though. "She looks so much like my Katherine, yet her eyes lack the spark of living my sister possessed."

Balin nodded and sighed deeply. "I fear these two have led a harder life than any of the vassals at Graycliff. I don't wish to spend my years worrying about them."

"You are soft, *mon frère*." Dante's voice was low and lacking condescension.

"*Oui*, but I can live with only you knowing it."

They rode until nightfall and finally made camp in a small clearing on the outskirts of Hertfordshire. Gianelle and Casey slept the entire day, which worried Dante. If he fell asleep and Gianelle awoke, she would surely run. The empty strap on her thigh attested to her future plans. He could tie her to him, he reasoned while he laid her down gently on his pallet. But that would only make her feel more like a captive. He rubbed his tired eyes, knowing he would have to stay awake. He had gone without sleep before, but there was no reason Balin should be denied the luxury.

Balin offered to build the fire first. When it was done, he sat down a few feet away from Casey and poked a stick into the flames. "Simone will be madder than a hellcat when she sees how you look at Gianelle."

"Simone is no longer my lover. You know as well as I that it's been over a year since she's been in my bed."

"That doesn't mean she doesn't want you still."

"I grew tired of her manipulations."

"*Oui*, you tired of her, just as you tire of them all. As you will tire of her." Balin ran his hand over his stubbled jaw and slanted his dark eyes toward Gianelle. "What if you break her heart? You've done it before."

Dante was about to refute the comment, but then realized Balin was probably right. "Go to sleep," he ordered his captain instead.

A few minutes later, Balin's breathing evened out to a quiet snore and Dante sat staring into the flames. He thought about Balin's question. He certainly didn't want to break Gianelle's heart. He hadn't wanted to hurt any of the women he was with, and most of them, like Simone, had other lovers besides him. They did not fall to pieces when he ended their affairs. He couldn't imagine Gianelle falling apart over him, either. She didn't even like him, and it was beginning to vex him mightily. What had he done to her that was so terrible? Was he such a devil for wanting to hold her instead of releasing her to a world she didn't know? *Enfer,* she couldn't even ride a horse. He looked down at her. Her eyes snapped shut.

Unable to help himself, he smiled. "I know you're awake. I saw you staring at me, *ma fée.*"

Damn his quick eyes. Gianelle released an exasperated sigh, but kept her eyes closed. "It was more like glaring at you."

He laughed softly. "What have I done now to kindle your fury while you slept? Did you dream of me, perchance?"

"I did not," she retorted, angry with herself for getting caught. She had heard his conversation with Balin, and the last thing Dante Risande's male ego needed was to think she had been studying his features. "It's simply your face that angers me."

"If you insist on insulting me, I would like you to look me in the eye when you do it."

"No, thank you." She crossed her arms in front of her chest.

"What are you afraid of?"

Her eyes shot open and she glared at him with a spark that set her eyes aflame with defiance. "Nothing!"

Dante met her challenging gaze with a warm one of his own. "Did you ever speak your mind to Bryce or Edgar Dermott?"

"If I didn't, it was to protect Casey, not myself." When Dante knit his brows, she explained, "They sometimes punished me by punishing her."

Dante's eyes flashed like smelted steel when he looked into the flames. "Then I understand why you may have wanted him dead."

"*Non,* you don't." When Dante said nothing more, she sat up and hugged her knees to her chin. "Why do you call me *fée?*"

He slid his gaze back to her. "Because I imagine you are what a faerie would look like, all golden and petite, enchanting, and mischievous."

And you are what a wolf would look like before he eats me alive, Gianelle thought to herself.

"Have you slept?"

"Not yet."

"Hmm." Gianelle sighed and touched her hand to her thigh. Her eyes opened wide at her discovery. "You took my knife, you . . ."

"What?" He merely smiled, a maddeningly handsome crooked smirk that exposed his intoxicating dimple.

"Lout!"

"Is that it?" he coaxed.

"Knave!" Her voice rose another octave. Dante yawned, and Gianelle erupted. "You son of a grunting sow!"

"That's much better." Dante winced.

"You are the one who's afraid." Gianelle let loose on him, and by God, it felt exhilarating. "You're afraid I will escape. You will not close your blasted eyes because you know you cannot hold command over me."

Casey woke up at the sound of her friend's shouts and nearly fainted when she discovered whom Gia was yelling at. "Gianelle, hush, I beg you."

But Gianelle hardly heard her plea. This was something she had wanted to do for years, and now that she had begun, she couldn't stop. "I *licked* your apple tart! *Oui,* I licked them all. What do you think of that?"

Dante shrugged his massive shoulders. "I did not eat one. Now I wish I had."

"Do not strike her, my lord," Casey begged him.

"I've no intentions of striking either of you. Ever," Dante promised Casey. "I'm simply waiting for her to finish her tirade."

"I'm finished!" Gianelle screamed at him and then threw herself down onto his pallet.

"Do you feel better now?" Dante asked gently, knowing she needed to trust his temper and hoping he had just proved that she could.

"*Oui,* I do."

"Are you crying?" He listened carefully to the sounds muffled into his pallet and was about to reach for her when Casey interrupted him.

"Gia never cries, my lord."

"Thank God for that," Dante declared. He could stand

her shouting at him, but tears were a whole different matter.

A twig cracked somewhere beyond the shadowy trees and Dante vaulted his feet.

"What was that?" Gianelle sat up and wiped her eyes with the backs of her hands.

Dante held his index finger to his lips to quiet her, his eyes unblinking on the stand of trees to their left.

"Casey," he whispered. "Wake Balin quietly, please."

Casey moved carefully to the sleeping captain and shoved him until his eyes opened. She kept silent, but pointed to Dante.

"Hide them," Dante ordered Balin when he appeared at Dante's side an instant later. "Go now. Don't leave their sides."

Balin grabbed Gianelle's arm and then Casey's, just as a small swarm of men rushed out from within the trees. Gianelle stopped, almost breaking free of Balin's hold. Terrified, she stared at Dante standing his ground while he slowly, almost artfully slipped his sword from its sheath. When Balin tried to draw her away she resisted and turned to him.

"He's alone. Will you not fight with him?"

Balin shook his head and pulled her again, dragging her away. He pushed her and Casey behind a huge rock and knelt at its edge to watch. After cursing the guard for hiding with her, Gianelle peeked her head around the boulder and watched as well.

She had seen a man die by the sword before, a sword driven through his back by Edgar Dermott. It was a cowardly deed, to be sure. What she witnessed now was nothing like that. Two of the seven men who attacked Dante were killed before she set her eyes on the scene. The other five circled him, swords poised and ready to swing. But the fear Gianelle felt for him facing an ambush alone vanished. For bathed in the soft, amber hue of the firelight, the hilt of his great broadsword gripped in both hands, Dante stood perfectly still, save for the warning throb of his muscles. An unmistakable air of self-confidence exuded from every pore. Each subtle nuance of movement, even the slight curling of his fingers on his hilt, spoke of a man at ease with his deadly skill, confident of his devastating power. A man to his left shifted nervously. Dante angled his head a fraction, and then looped his blade to the right, killing a third man where he stood. He moved in a blur of speed after that, striking with the deadly precision of a supreme killer.

Gianelle wanted to look away. But she stared, captivated by Dante's skill, his terrifying beauty. He lunged and parried with effortless elegance, killing two more. His sword flashed beneath the moonlight as it danced in his powerful hands. Blood from his sixth victim sprayed across his cheek, creating for Gianelle the illusion of a predator bloody from a kill. An upward thrust of his lethal blade ended the last man's life quickly.

The clearing was silent save for the frantic thudding of Gianelle's heartbeat in her ears. Balin helped Casey to her feet first. When he took Gianelle's arm, she looked up at him, her eyes as wide as saucers. "He didn't need any help at all," she whispered.

"*Non*, he didn't," Balin quietly agreed. "Come on, both of you. He will want to see that no harm came to you."

"But we were hiding," Casey pointed out.

"Still, the forest is dangerous. Come."

Gianelle looked over her shoulder into the darkness and shivered. Dante had told her the same thing last night. If these two men meant to frighten her, they were succeeding thoroughly. She and Casey would not have survived the space of two breaths had they been alone. Mayhap, God had answered Casey's prayers and sent Dante to stop them when they climbed out the window of Devonshire Castle.

A thought occurred to her, and she looked up at Balin. "Why does he travel with only one guard if it is so perilous?"

Balin only shrugged his shoulders. "He doesn't need an army at his back."

That was for certain, Gianelle realized. The man was a force to be reckoned with.

She met Dante's gaze over the floating embers of the bonfire, and this time he was the one who looked away. He walked off alone and stopped when he reached his horse, tied to a tree. The stallion greeted him with a shake of his head. Dante ran his hand down the beast's long black mane, then searched his saddlebag for a cloth to clean his face.

~

"Dante!"

He swung around at Balin's shout and found his captain waving him back to the clearing.

"The ladies say they know this man." Balin tapped his boot into one of the fallen when Dante reached them. "Who is he?"

"I've seen him at the castle," Gianelle told him.

"Aye, his name is . . . was Trevor the Black." Casey glanced at the body briefly, then looked away.

"He's in Dermott's guard?" Dante asked them, not surprised by the discovery.

"*Non.*" Gianelle shook her head. "He visited on occasion, but his brother is Sir Conrad Lowell, my deceased lord's emissary."

"Edgar Dermott sent them, Dante," Balin fumed. "Let's go back and kill him."

"*Non,* we wait to speak with William. I believe Dermott is one of the rebels we seek. I want him to lead us to Hereward before I kill him."

"Who is this Hereward?" Gianelle asked. "You spoke of him last night."

"He is a Saxon who was exiled by the late King Edward," Dante told her while he began wiping the blood from his sword. "He returned after William became king. The Normans seized his father's estates and killed his brother, for what reason I do not know. He went on a rampage and murdered many Norman warriors because of it, becoming the leader of the Saxon rebels. Last winter he plundered the abbey of Peterborough, but when we arrived he was gone. He is called 'the Wake' because he is watchful and wary of the king's movements. He has spies throughout England who report William's plans for him before the king has time to carry them out. He's intelligent and a skilled warrior. He eludes the king at every turn and William wants him stopped."

"Do you hate all Saxons then, my lord?" It was Casey who asked, staring down at her hands as if dreading his answer.

"Only those who follow the Wake."

"Because they hate the king?" She ventured to look up at him, and he shook his head at her.

"*Non,* because they killed my sister."

~

They left the dead scattered around the ashes of the extinguished bonfire and headed out of the clearing. Gianelle knew Dante had to be exhausted. She worried that he might ride them straight into a tree in the dark. He hadn't said a word since telling her about his sister, remaining instead pensive while they traveled. In the absence of his rakish charm, there was something more vulnerable about him: sorrow that Gianelle felt she could identify with, almost touch.

She didn't want to have anything in common with him. She wanted to believe that he was as coldhearted as Bryce and Edgar Dermott, but everything about Dante was different from any other man she knew. It was that notion that prompted her to speak.

"How did she die?" The question was asked on a whispered breath filled with trepidation that this might be the topic to push him over the edge of his patience. But she wanted to know, and his kindness so far gave her the confidence to ask. He didn't answer her right away, and Gianelle closed her eyes, awaiting chastisement when she heard Balin expel a withering sigh.

"She was out for a ride with two of my men when a band of Hereward's followers came upon her. It was an act of revenge toward me while I was away fighting at William's side in Peterborough."

"Did they kill her in the woods?" She knew they had, even before Dante confirmed it. It explained why his warnings to her about the dangers of the forest were spoken with such conviction. "You weren't there." She turned her head to look up at him and saw the deep regret that made his eyes glisten. "How do you know it was Hereward's men who did it?"

"I was able to find six of them shortly after I returned to Graycliff. They confessed before they died. I don't wish to speak of it anymore," Dante said, his words tinged with pain, not anger.

Gianelle nodded and leaned her back against his chest. She felt his muscles stiffen, and then relax again.

He whispered her name, stirring a strand of her hair across her cheek. His voice sounded husky with weariness.

"My lord?"

"You're too skinny. You should have taken bites out of the tarts instead of just licking them."

He made her smile. *Oui,* Lord Dante Risande was a different kind of man.

Chapter Six

HE WAS A ROGUE! Even passed out behind her, he sought to beguile her.

When the even rhythm of Dante's warm breath fell against Gianelle's neck, and his body relaxed around hers, painfully reminding her of his awesome size, she realized he had fallen asleep. Her first instinct was to push him away. He didn't budge. She whispered to Balin, casting him a panicked, helpless look, but the captain merely reached for the reins and assured her that Dante wouldn't fall out of the saddle. It was too dangerous to stop now, he told her. Who knew if there were more of Dermott's men following them?

Gianelle didn't care about Dermott's men at that point. Her backside was slipping slowly, torturously toward the earth, and Dante's weight was bringing her there faster.

"Balin, I'm slipping!"

"Swing your leg over the other side. It will give you more balance." He slowed the horses to a near stop, brought his mount closer to hers, and anchored her while she struggled to do as he instructed. "You will need to pull your skirts over your knees."

Gianelle tossed him a wary scowl that he answered with an impatient nudge. When her legs were finally spread apart, she shifted her weight to the center and tried to brace her shoulders against Dante.

"Saints, he's heavy." Her mouth snapped shut and her eyes grew large as Dante's arm snaked around her waist and pulled her bottom half closer to his. As if she were his favored pillow, he hugged her to his frame and groaned with pleasure.

She strove to free herself, but the more she moved, the more erotic his hold on her became. His palm flattened against her belly, broad fingers splayed and grazed over her with such sensual leisure there may as well have been no woolen barricade between them, the touch was so intimate. She squiggled forward, feeling light-headed from his caress, but he bent forward with her, wedging her between his hard thighs and crushing her spine beneath his chest. He angled his head to a more comfortable position, one that pressed his mouth to the pulse beat along her throat.

"I think he's dreaming of you," Casey reasoned, watching Dante position his body.

Balin gave his lord a hard shove, and then another until Dante lifted his heavy lids.

"You're crushing Gianelle, and are doing it indecently," the captain informed him.

Dante blinked slowly and sat straight up, dragging Gianelle with him. "Christ, you're bony."

Her mouth fell open in indignation. She was about to jab him hard in the ribs when his head dipped over her shoulder, brushing his rough cheek along hers.

"I'm sorry if I hurt you."

Gianelle tried to turn the astounded look his apology brought to her face on him. But he settled into her again and began to snore, so she didn't dare move a muscle.

Morning came quickly, and Gianelle offered worshipful thanks to God that it had, for with the rising of the sun Dante also rose off her shoulders.

He stretched behind her, offered Balin and Casey a large grin, and leaned forward over the hunchbacked woman in front of him. "Are you awake yet, *fée*?"

"*Non*," she groaned. The pain radiating from her bones and sore muscles made her feel nauseous. "I think I died during the night." She arched her back and sighed with relief at the soft cracking sounds the movement produced.

"Some food will make you feel better."

Dante's cheerful demeanor almost earned him the jab in the ribs he'd missed getting a few hours before.

"There's a stream past that meadow." Balin motioned with his chin. "Let's stop there so the horses can quench their thirst."

They rode for a few more moments and stopped just in time to avoid Gianelle being sick all over her new lord. He dismounted first, then spanned his fingers around Gianelle's waist and lifted her out of the saddle. When he set her on her feet her legs collapsed beneath her. With lightning-quick reflexes, Dante caught her before she hit the ground.

"Are you sore?" he asked her with traces of concern and regret etched on his face. "What in blazes possessed you to straddle my horse? When you're new at riding it pains you more to sit that way."

"I hate you." Gianelle glared at him and held on to his stallion, rather than him, for support.

"Oh, we're back to that, are we?"

"Leave me alone and let me die in peace." She buried her face in his steed's mane, and then moaned right in Dante's face when he snatched her off the ground and cradled her in his arms.

"Put me down!" she demanded somewhat weakly, while he strode toward a grassy opening nestled beside a running stream.

"Stop being so stubborn. You can barely walk."

She had to admit he was right. Her body ached so badly even the thick muscles in Dante's arms pained her flesh. He set her rump down beside Casey, then bent over her and smoothed her hair over her forehead. "There. That wasn't so bad, was it?"

He was close enough to kiss, or claw out his eyes. His sexy dimple made Gianelle want to do both.

"Thanks to Maeve," he said, straightening to his full height, "we have enough food to last us a journey back to Normandy."

Gianelle shut her eyes, sickened by the very thought of being on a horse that long. She felt someone tug on her sleeve and opened her eyes to find Casey staring back at her. Her friend leaned in close and whispered in her ear.

"What is it, Casey?" Dante folded his long legs and sat down in the grass near Gianelle. He untied one of the sacks Balin had carried over from the horses and shoved his hand inside. "You're free to eat whatever you like."

Casey cut a quick surprised look at Gianelle, then shifted nervously before she spoke to him. "You're very kind, my lord. But I . . . I fear I need to . . ."

Dante stopped rummaging through the bag and looked at her. Her eyelids began to droop and she twisted her mink braid around her fingers in her lap. He sighed, wishing he had removed some of Bryce Dermott's teeth, before someone else got to him, for commanding such timid submission from his servants. It might be too late for revenge, Dante thought, but it wasn't too late to give these women back some of their dignity. He broke off a small piece of black bread from the loaf Maeve had provided and threw it at Casey.

The morsel hit her on her forehead. She looked up and giggled, seeing the playful spark in his gray eyes. Her anxiety melted and she smiled at him, then blushed a warm shade of claret. "I have to relieve myself."

Dante pointed to a huge oak a few feet behind her. "You too?" He glanced at Gianelle and she nodded. "Do you need help getting there?"

"I think I can manage," she replied succinctly. But Casey helped her to her feet anyway.

Casey slipped behind the tree while Gianelle waited beside the thick trunk and gazed at the sun-dappled stream. She wondered where it led.

"I think Lord Risande fancies you, Gia."

"It would seem he fancies anything in skirts," Gianelle retorted. *And then he tires of them and breaks their hearts,* she reminded herself. Not that she would ever give him the chance to do either.

"He's quite handsome, and kind spirited as well," Casey went on.

"Hmm. He's not difficult to look at." Gianelle put her hands behind her back and leaned against the trunk. Her eyes drifted over the dew-drenched meadow to where Dante sat with his arm extended over his bent knee and his other long leg stretched out before him. He brought an apple to his mouth and laughed at something Balin said. He looked so carefree Gianelle almost sighed, envying him.

"What think you of Balin?" Casey appeared around the trunk, straightening her skirts.

Gianelle recalled the concern for her in the captain's voice the night before when he'd admonished Dante on her behalf. "It's best if we don't think anything of them, Casey."

"Why not?"

"Because," Gianelle said as she disappeared behind the tree, "we will be gone from here long before you form any attachments."

"But what if I like it at Graycliff, Gia?"

Gianelle stepped around the tree after another moment. "We are still servants. He paid for us like chattel, Casey. Don't you want to be unconstrained and unrestricted, free to make your own choices?"

Casey shook her head and stared into her best friend's eyes. "Gia, where do you get these ideas? We are born either noble or peasant. Neither are truly ever free. Do you forget my father was the Baron of Colchester before he died? My mother did not make her own choices, but obeyed him. I do not want to be independent. It frightens me. And it frightens me further to think that someday your unconventional ways of thinking will get you killed."

Casey's eyes shimmered with unshed tears. Gianelle knew there was no point in arguing right now. Casey would come to her senses after a few weeks of suppression and control from their new master. Gianelle could wait until then.

"Come, Casey." She smiled and pulled her friend forward. "Before those two eat everything."

An hour later, Gianelle rubbed her belly and moaned. She hadn't been this stuffed with food since the Dermotts were away last summer and Margaret snuck into her room with half a lamb and four loaves of honeyed bread. It was one of the rare times either of them had eaten so much. Bryce Dermott had been a gluttonous pig who hated sharing his food almost as much as he hated sharing his women. But today she ate to her fill while Dante watched her, coaxing her to eat more and fill her skin with something more than just bones.

She released a burp that could have belonged to a drunken pirate. Luckily no one heard it. Balin and Casey had gone for a walk, and Dante was crouched at the edge of the stream washing his face. He had removed his surcoat and untied his mane of black hair. She watched him for a few moments before she realized how much she enjoyed it. With a muttered curse at herself, she decided to completely and permanently ignore him. She lay down so that she was not tempted to look at him again.

She hadn't planned on falling asleep. She dreamed she was flying over a sun-soaked field, looking down at a great black wolf that leaped into the sky and landed on her back. Oddly, the beast didn't weigh her down, but filled her lungs with a scent that was unfamiliar and alluring.

Gianelle smiled in her sleep and buried her nose deeper into Dante's shirt. She curled her hands under her chin. The wolf's warm breath above her head erupted into a loud snore.

Her eyes shot open. A great expanse of white linen and gold filled her vision and squished her nose. It was

Dante's chest, she realized as the effects of sleep wore off. Mortified that she had nestled herself into the curve of his body, she tried to sit up, but her long braid was pinned under him. She was able to move a scant few inches away and hoped he didn't wake up before she put more distance between them. She raised herself up on her elbow and followed the trail of her thick plaited hair to where it disappeared behind his shoulder. God's blood, how did her braid get under him? She tried pulling on it. He rolled from his side to his back. His arm came up and almost banged into her face before it fell again, over his head. Where the hell were Casey and Balin to help her? Lord, but Dante was huge all sprawled out beside her. And how did the man manage to still smell so good after fighting seven men?

Against her will, her gaze strayed over the length of him. A rush of warmth trickled down her spine at the thought of sleeping so close to this strong body. She wondered if he had fallen asleep looking at her, as his position suggested when she'd first awakened.

Enough! Gianelle chastised herself. *He's your master. He's a rake who uses women to satisfy his needs and then disregards them. Get your damned hair out and get away from him.*

She moved up a little to give herself more leverage to move. Frowning, she noticed that his arm now covered her braid as well. She would have to move it. She reached up and closed her fingers around his corded bicep. Moving very slowly, she chanted a prayer that he didn't wake up while she maneuvered her way closer over his body to free herself. She looked down directly into his face and felt her heart pumping madly against his chest. With no other choice, she squeezed her eyes shut and gently pulled on his arm.

"What are you doing?"

His whispered voice washing over her startled her so much, she was certain her heart had just ceased beating. She opened her eyes, already forming an excuse in her mind for why her face was so close to his. So close that if she had ever learned how, she could have counted every one of the sable lashes ringing his extraordinary eyes.

A slow, sensual grin tugged at his lips. "You needn't have waited until I was asleep to throw yourself all over me, *fée*. I would like to participate if you don't mind."

She wrenched on her hair, more eager to be away from him than ever before. "Strange. I thought you woke up, but I see now that you are still dreaming." She yanked again when Dante's rich laughter filled the meadow. "Would you mind moving yourself off my hair so that I can get up?"

"*Oui*, I would mind." He traced her features with his bemused gaze. His eyes grew warm when they settled on her mouth. "But I will do it to save you the temptation of kissing me."

Gianelle glared at him with mute fury and he laughed again before he rolled his shoulder off her hair. She sprang to her feet, before he said something else that would make her want to kick him, and stormed away.

Dante's gaze followed her lithe figure for a moment and then he took off after her. "Where are you going?"

"To find Casey."

"Balin took her to a castle belonging to a friend of mine not far from here. We will meet up with them."

"Fine." Gianelle stopped walking, turned to him, and

crossed her arms over her breasts. "Point me in the right direction, and I will walk there."

She was just beginning to fully enjoy her newfound belligerence when Dante reached for her, his eyes darkening to a smoky charcoal. His hand clamped the back of her neck and, without touching her anywhere else, he hauled her mouth to his. Tasting her fully, he swept his tongue into her, molded her soft lips to his own, and kissed her until he felt her knees buckle. Then he lifted her into his arms, surprised that he felt as dazed as she looked, and carried her to his horse.

Perched upon his lap, Gianelle clutched Dante's wrist with both hands while they rode out of the meadow. She didn't realize she was doing it; she needed an anchor to keep her from falling, or floating away. His wrist was the most solid thing within her reach.

He'd kissed her! Dear God, he'd kissed her, and it was nothing like when Edgar Dermott did it. Dante's kiss was like wine, and she felt drunk from it still. But it wasn't just his kiss that turned her bones to tree sap. It was the way he looked at her just before, like he held within him the power to bend her to his will with ease, and he fought it with all his being. But he did have his way, she told herself. She intended to walk, and he made her too weak to stand. Still, he could have ordered her to move her arse or he would drag her off by the hair for her cheek. He would have the right as her lord.

She lifted her gaze to his rugged jaw, the decadent fullness of his lips. What was he thinking right now? He was probably severely disappointed. Well, it served him right. She hoped he hated kissing her. She looked down at her fingers, firmly secured to his wrist. His hand holding the reins was as beautiful as the rest of him. She let him go. It did no good to hold on to something that wasn't real. Her father had taught her that.

Behind her, Dante closed his eyes when Gianelle released her death grip on him. Silly, but he liked the idea of her wanting to touch him, even needing to.

"Gianelle, I—"

"Please," she interrupted him. "You must never kiss me again."

Dante stared at her profile, her downcast eyes, and then he looked away, muttering a tight oath that sounded pained to Gianelle's ears.

They rode in silence until they came to a small keep of stone and timber. Old planks that made up the drawbridge creaked and groaned beneath the heavy hooves of Dante's stallion. The small inner bailey was overrun with squealing pigs and honking geese. A tanner sat behind a large stone, hammering a thick swatch of leather that was spread out across the stone's flattened top. He waved at Dante when they passed him. A serving girl carrying a bucket under her arm called out to Dante next, much to Gianelle's astonishment, and then blew him a kiss across the bailey.

"Who is lord of this castle that allows his servants to take such liberties with his guests?" Gianelle turned a curious eyebrow on Dante and saw him smiling at the wench.

"His daughter Brynna is my brother's wife." Dante turned his smile on her. "His name is Lord Richard Dumont, Earl of Salisbury. And his servants are quite free to do as they like, while respecting him, of course."

Free to fling themselves into your bed, it seems, she thought. Gianelle didn't look at the wench again, and secretly wished the girl would trip over a chicken. "Are we in Salisbury now?"

"*Non, fée.* Salisbury is at least four days' ride away. The king gave Lord Dumont this land a few years ago, and Richard left it as it was when his Saxon brothers ruled it."

Gianelle was only half listening. She had spotted Casey and Balin with an older man whom she guessed to be Lord Dumont, judging by the richly embroidered, quilted tunic he wore. The three of them stood in front of a wooden fence, their eyes fastened to what was on the other side.

A breathtaking white mare kicked and bucked, tossing her mane of long, snowy waves wildly about. The man atop her did his best to hold on, but she arched her fluid back and bucked again, sending him flying ten feet away.

"My God, she's beautiful," Dante breathed as he dismounted. Without taking his eyes off the now strutting mare, he helped Gianelle to her feet.

"Dante, you rogue!" the older man turned and called out cheerfully. Gianelle could only agree with such a fitting description. "I was expecting you a month ago." He gave Dante a gentle pat on the back and his voice grew more serious. "How do you fare since last we spoke?"

"I am well." Dante answered him truthfully, since the time Lord Dumont referred to was only a few months after Katherine's murder.

"Ah, that is good news for my ears," Lord Dumont said. "You and your guests will stay the night."

"*Non,* Richard, I want . . ."

"I insist, and I'll hear no more about it. Besides, I want to hear the latest news on Hereward." Richard clapped him on the arm when Dante agreed.

"And who is this?" Richard turned his attention to Gianelle, and she noticed that he had kind, chestnut-colored eyes and dark hair peppered with gray streaks, before she dipped her gaze to her feet.

"Lord Richard Dumont, may I present Gianelle Dejiat."

Richard lifted her hand to his lips and placed a polite kiss there. "A pleasure."

"Don't be fooled." Dante looked at her and winked. "She's a hellcat."

Gianelle shot him a murderous look and stomped off toward Casey. Let him explain *that* to his friend.

Watching her, Dante laughed softly. As he walked with Richard toward the others, he turned his gaze to the mare. "Where did you get her?"

"A gift from my Turkish friends. She is called Ayla. The name means 'moonlight' in their tongue. She's untamable. None of my men have been able to break her in. Still, she's difficult to part with."

"You may have to." Dante's eyes glimmered with excitement when he reached the fence and the mare charged toward him, as if warning him to come no closer.

"You think you can ride her?" Richard challenged him.

"*Oui,* I do."

The mare whinnied and rose up on her back legs, her glorious mane flying, then ran off kicking her legs behind her.

Arrogant fool. Gianelle sighed at the confidence in Dante's voice. She didn't want to see him injured, but he almost deserved the thrashing he was going to get if he tried to best *that* female. "What makes you think you can ride her when no one else can?"

Dante tore his gaze away from the mare and probed Gianelle's eyes, and, it seemed, her thoughts. "Because, *fée*, I will not try to break her."

"If you can ride her with no bucking," Richard said, "she's yours."

Dante slipped through the fence, eager to get to her. "I'll pay you handsomely," he called over his shoulder.

"Don't think she's yours yet, whelp," Richard replied, grinning from ear to ear. "You have to ride her first." He chuckled and said in a lower voice, "He's about to bruise his arse, ladies. You might not want to watch."

Casey covered her eyes, but Gianelle smiled and looked on.

Dante approached the mare cautiously. She stopped and eyed him, her muscles twitching with coiled energy. She lowered her head and pawed the ground with her front hoof. Gianelle watched Dante lift his hand to her mane, not to touch her, but to calm her. He spoke, but his voice was too low for Gianelle to hear. The mare trotted sideways, avoiding him, but Dante's hand shot forward. He grabbed hold of her mane and swung himself onto her bare back even while she rose up, clawing the air with her deadly hooves. He held on, though not for long. The mare threw him twice before she even took a step, bucking so hard Gianelle feared the horse might toss Dante clear to Normandy.

But he rose to his feet and mounted her again. This time she took off, kicking both back legs high into the air. Dante clamped his strong legs around her middle and let go of her mane. He almost fell, but he bent his body low and wrapped his arms around her neck. The mare charged the fence and the onlookers scattered in terror. She arched her spine to throw her rider but he held on, eyes closed with his cheek pressed to her elegant neck.

Gianelle saw his lips moving and imagined that he was gently coaxing the mare to rant and rave all she wanted; he would never take the whip to her.

Suddenly the horse stopped. She swung her massive head around and opened her mouth to chomp at Dante's face. Everyone gasped, and Casey cried out, covering her eyes again. But Dante lifted his hand to the mare's huge nose, and held her back. She kicked one last time while he scratched her muscled jowl.

"Now, ride her," Richard Dumont whispered on a breath of exhilaration.

Sitting up, Dante clutched a handful of her wintry mane and dug his heels into her flanks. The mare thundered forward, foam coating her sleek fur and mouth. She ran around the perimeter of the enclosure, once, twice, biting at the air.

Dante rode her toward the fence and when he reached Richard, the mare snorted and pawed the ground again.

"I'll be damned." Lord Richard looked up in awe.

Dante's breath came as hard and as fast as the mare's. He stroked her and spoke quietly to her, and when he smiled down at Gianelle, she knew the magic this magnificent sorcerer possessed. It was more dangerous than any weapon. It was tenderness.

Chapter Seven

THEY ATE SUPPER IN THE GREAT HALL, which was about half the size of the hall at Devonshire. Fire from the central hearth warmed the bones while casting the hall in a cozy, golden hue. Because this keep was not one of Lord Dumont's permanent dwellings, there were only a handful of servants in attendance. Gianelle and Casey both headed for the kitchen, but Dante stopped them and seated them at the table with Balin, Richard, and three of Richard's knights who had escorted him from Salisbury.

When the food was served, Gianelle stared at her roasted quail for a long time while the men's voices filled her ears. She had never dined with nobles or knights before, and doing so now made her uncomfortable.

She glanced at Casey several times. Her friend had been the daughter of a Saxon lord before the invading Normans burned her castle and her parents perished. Casey was familiar with this setting and merely picked up where she'd left off five years ago, before Bryce Dermott had found her in the rubble and made her his servant.

"My dear, the food doesn't please you?" Lord Dumont

stopped talking to Dante and directed his attention to Gianelle.

"It smells delicious, my lord," she said into her chest.

"Perhaps you should eat it then, *fée*." Dante winked at her effortlessly when she looked up. "Your belly is rumbling," he added with a smile.

"During my visit to Warwick Castle," said a dark-haired knight to Gianelle's left, "several of the ladies at court preferred to be fed by the men." He stared at Gianelle boldly with his dark blue eyes. "Perhaps this lady would like someone to feed her."

"Or perhaps not, Frederick." The savage curl of Dante's lips made it clear to the knight that he would think nothing of cutting Frederick's fingers off his hand if they went anywhere near Gianelle's mouth.

Gianelle ate on her own after that, avoiding anyone else's attention.

Dante told Richard about Bryce Dermott's untimely death with as much interest as he would show a slow-growing plant. He didn't tell his host about Baron Landry, though, or Gianelle's knowledge of herbs.

"I'm leaving the questioning of Dermott's guests to William."

Richard chuckled and took another bite off the drumstick of his quail. "He will appreciate that."

They didn't discuss the ambush and Edgar Dermott's role in it, since one of the knights at the table had come into Richard's service only recently, and Hereward had a reputation for planting spies.

After supper a plump, elderly serving woman showed Gianelle and Casey to their chambers. Frederick left the table; the conversation turned more personal soon after that.

Dante learned that since Brand's last missive, his brother had become a father for the third time.

"A boy," Richard proclaimed. "His name is Richard, and he came out with a louder voice than his brother before him."

"A fact I'm certain will irritate the hell out of William when you tell him." Dante laughed and then looked up and saw Gianelle coming back toward the hall with Frederick.

"Of course," the proud grandfather confirmed. "Brand and Brynna's second child may be named after the king, but their third will be a more fearsome warrior."

"Brand is blessed to have a wife who gives him . . ." Dante's voice trailed off when Gianelle smiled at something the knight said to her.

Lord Dumont followed Dante's lethal stare across the hall. "Have you given any thought to a wife yet?"

Dante ground his jaw. "*Non.* Searching for Hereward keeps me busy enough. I don't need a . . . excuse me."

Gianelle looked up from the knight's hand on her arm in time to see Dante stalking toward her. He looked angry, somehow larger and less manageable. When he reached her, he seized her hand and pulled her away from the knight's grasp.

"I thought you were going to bed." He stormed toward the stairs, towing Gianelle behind him.

"Please, let go of me!" She dug her heels into the rushes and tried to pry his fingers off her hand.

Dante stopped and pivoted around to face her, his brows a dark slash against the brilliance of his eyes. He opened his fingers, releasing her as she asked, and walked away without a word.

What in hell had come over him? Dante raked his fingers through his hair and shook his head at himself as he climbed the stairs. *Merde!* He was jealous! He almost laughed, but he felt too sick to his stomach for even feigned mirth. She never smiled at him that way, and did he hear her screeching to Frederick to let her go the way she did to him? Damn him, was he losing his mind? Since when did he care about such trivial matters with a woman? Simone took other men to her bed even when she was his lover, and he never lost a night's sleep over it. Every woman he knew had perfected the coy smile and flirtatious giggle. He never cared who they practiced on. But Gianelle wasn't the kind to practice. *Non,* what she did was real. In those luminous eyes of hers, he could read almost every thought that crossed her mind. Christ, he loved to watch her face; it was so expressive. He frowned to stop himself from smiling at the thought of her, and fought the urge to go back to the great hall to see if she returned to the knight, mayhap to make plans to run off with him. He didn't care if she escaped. Perhaps Balin had been right: Gianelle was getting under his skin. He would stop it before she defied her way even more deeply. He could never be happy with just one woman, he told himself as he entered the chambers he would be using for the night, and slammed the door shut hard enough to rattle the timber walls.

Gianelle fumed. What had come over Dante? He couldn't possibly be so angry because she met Sir Frederick on the way back down the stairs. Unless, she mused, her expression darkening, she wasn't permitted to exchange a few pleasantries with anyone. So that was how it was to be then, she thought miserably.

"Rotten lout," she mumbled. "He deserves hot coals in his boots."

"Pardon, my lady?"

"Oh, there you are!" Gianelle smiled at the woman who showed her and Casey to their room. "You left in such a hurry before. I think you gave my friend and me the wrong room."

The woman looked at her as if she had just sprouted another head. "The wrong room?"

"*Oui*. You brought us above stairs."

"Aye."

"Well, we're not ladies."

"You're not?"

"*Non*, we are Lord Risande's ser—"

"Oh, forgive me!" the woman cut her off and gave the cloth around her head a pat. "He is in the chambers directly across from you."

Gianelle dipped her brows in confusion, and then the woman's meaning slowly dawned on her and heat radiated across her cheeks. "Oh, *non*, I didn't mean . . ."

"Fergie!" Lord Richard called from inside the great hall. "What have you done with my cup of ale?"

Fergie rolled her eyes, lifted her skirts above her pudgy ankles, and stomped toward the hall. "It's right where you left it, on the table!"

Gianelle watched her leave, then eyed the stairs. Imagine the woman thinking that she wanted to share Dante's room. She guessed, as she made her way back to her room, that Fergie had heard that particular request many times in the past when Dante was their guest. She couldn't blame the woman for making such a ridiculous assumption.

When she reached her door, she paused and looked at the one opposite it. She really didn't appreciate the way Dante released her hand, as if it were a disease-ridden rag. Was it her fault that he hadn't been clear about whom she could speak to? And wasn't he the one who insisted she look up when she spoke? Did he mean she could only look at him? If he did, she would just have to wash his bed linens in the hog trough. That was, of course, if they had pigs at Graycliff Castle.

She didn't know why his anger nagged at her so. She suspected it was the same thing that had bothered her when he paid for her. He could be quite nice when he wanted to be, and at times he felt more like a friend than a master; that was, when he wasn't looking at her like he wanted to take her for a tumble across the first flat surface he came across. She needed to know if he planned on being a tyrant like the Dermotts, so she could hate him and plan her escape sooner.

With her heart pounding furiously in her chest, she tucked a few loose tendrils of her hair behind her ears and gathered her mettle to go ask him her questions.

She lifted her knuckles to his door and almost changed her mind. Finally, she took a deep breath and knocked.

"Oui?"

Gianelle opened the door just as Dante finished tugging his shirt over his head.

"This is a surprise," he drawled, standing there wearing nothing but his woolen hose and boots.

Gianelle's eyes opened wide. She blinked and took a step back out of the room. His mocking chuckle drew her back. He thought his appearance affected her. She tried to laugh but swallowed a huge gulp of air instead.

"I . . . I . . ." Gianelle's mouth grew so dry she feared her lips might stick together. She hated herself for stammering, and even more for staring at the soft play of muscle along his corded arms. The dark, crisp hair on his sculpted chest glistened in the soft glow of the candles that lit the chambers. He ran his hand over a stomach taut and ribbed from years of battle. Gianelle couldn't help but look there. She had never seen a man in such perfect physical condition.

"Well?" Dante asked, arching a black brow. He tossed his shirt to the floor and stared at her. "I'm tired and I'd like to get out of these hose sometime this eve."

Jolted by the very thought, Gianelle blinked and quickly regained her composure. "I would like to know why you're so angry with me."

"You would?"

"Oui."

His steady gaze on her was unsettling. Gianelle turned to look at the door, rethinking her determination to stay. She tried desperately to look anywhere but at the sensual contours of his face, or his flat belly, or his long, powerful legs.

"Sir Frederick was being most polite to me, and . . ." Her voice wilted at the scowl he aimed at her. He looked positively primitive, the embodiment of pure male power. He was so dark, yet his eyes gave off a light that compelled her to move closer, or turn and flee for her life. The tallow candles burning around him only served to accentuate the shadows and carved curves of his splendid physique.

"Am I not permitted to speak to others?" she asked him after a few seconds passed and he still hadn't said anything.

"You can speak to whomever you wish." He sat down on a chair by the hearth and yanked off a boot.

"Then why are you so angry?"

He wanted to shake her—better that than truthfully answer her query. "I'm not angry," he practically growled at her. "Go to bed." He snorted with disgust at himself. There was no more doubt in his mind of his lunacy. She had come to his room, there was a bed not two feet away, and he was demanding that she leave! He ripped off the other boot and flung it at the wall.

Gianelle was torn between running out the door or storming out of it and giving it a good slam behind her. She stood her ground instead. Her eyes darkened to a burnished gold when she looked at him. "I don't understand you. You don't lose your temper when I insult you, but then you lose it over nothing. And it really doesn't matter to me if you're angry or not. I would simply like to know your desires so that I don't have a raving madman as my lord again."

His gaze brushed her face, a titillating caress she felt all the way through her body. "My desire," he told her with a darkly sensual smile upon his lips, "is to get up out of this chair and kiss you senseless. I'm trying very hard not to do that because you asked it of me when last I kissed you. But I warn you, Gianelle, if you don't leave immediately, my control will shatter."

"Very well." Gianelle's breath sounded ragged to her ears. "Thank you for telling . . ."

She was gone. And Dante threw himself back into his chair, not knowing whether to laugh or curse.

⌒

Dante helped Gianelle into his stallion's saddle the next morning, then lifted himself to the mare's back with a single leap. He exchanged a few words with Lord Dumont, reminding him of what they'd spoken about earlier. Richard assured him that he would keep his ears alert to Edgar Dermott's name.

Gianelle was about to ask Dante what to do if she began to slip in the saddle again when he nudged his restless mare and took off. Gianelle swore silently at his back and inched her leg over the saddle to straddle the stallion. When she felt a bit more balanced, she flicked the reins and almost toppled over backward when the sinewy steed galloped forward. She held on, determined not to fall again, and clenched her jaw to keep her teeth from rattling while she bounced. Thankfully, Balin took her reins and slowed her horse to a pace in time with his own.

⌒

They reached Dover by midday.

The forest had long since fallen away, its absence settling upon Gianelle a new sense of hopelessness. The woods had comforted her with their deep shadows and towering pillars, where one could get lost and never be found. She looked around and surveyed the low, rocky hills, void of any color but slate gray dotted with patches of green. She inhaled the familiar fragrance that laced the moist air and made her hair curl. The scent was his, her dark new lord's. She shifted in the saddle, trying to decide what it was about the strange salty scent that pleased her so.

An enormous wall of solid rock cast its great ominous shadow on the road, blocking out the sun and warning Gianelle that her new prison would extend far beyond mere castle walls. The precipice rose up toward the cloudless swath of blue sky, where hundreds of large, strange-looking birds soared on great white wings tipped with black, screeching as though their flight was painful.

Gianelle gazed at the birds wistfully, envying their freedom, wondering why they chose to remain in this grim-looking place with its harsh planes and colorless hues when the forests were so much more beautiful. A moment later when they turned around a steep incline, she found the answer to her question.

The precipice fell away like an enormous curtain to reveal a hidden, glorious world soaked in dazzling rays of sunshine. The light glittered like tiny diamonds upon a surging, tumultuous blanket of water that stretched farther than Gianelle's imagination could take her. Swollen waves came rushing out of the ocean to hurl themselves against sheer, jagged cliffs of pale gray, and erupted into sea spray that laced the air with icy mist.

Gianelle gasped so sharply at the sight before her that Dante pulled in on Ayla's reins and stopped to see if she had injured herself. She sat perfectly still, her eyes wide with wonder as she gazed across the ocean while the crisp breeze blew silken strands of her hair across her flushed cheeks. Dante's chest tightened looking at her. He tried to deny the effect she had on him, but she continued to appear more beautiful, more desirable, though he didn't know how that was possible.

"Gianelle?"

She swung her gaze to him, breath still held in her throat. "You live here?"

He pointed to the silhouette of a castle high upon the cliffs cloaked in silvery fog. Ayla pranced impatiently beneath him. With a rumbling snort she tossed her head and bucked slightly. Dante moved with her. Horse and man seemed to become one, for both appeared as wild and inviolable as the land.

"Come," Dante beckoned. Balin tugged her reins, and she had no choice but to leave this glorious place.

Castle Graycliff seemed to be carved out of the massive cliffs that encompassed it. Its spires punctured the thick clouds that hovered low in the sky, drifting west from the sea and casting the castle in an ever-present fog.

As they climbed the steep pass, the waves crashed against the rocky crags below. Gianelle looked out over the jagged bluff at the roaring sea and had the urge to weep at the brutal grandeur surrounding her. They climbed, and gulls met them in the air before diving into the salty waves for herring that were smashed against the cliffs. When the party reached the gatehouse, Gia was still reveling in the briny sea smells that reminded her of being pressed against Dante's shirt while she slept. He was Graycliff.

They stopped when a squeaky voice echoed from high atop the battlements along the great stone walls of the castle and surrounding cliffs.

"Who goes there?" A figure peered precariously over the edge of the sun-bleached ramparts.

"I, you bloody fool! Open the gate," Dante shouted up to him and cast Balin an irritated glance.

His captain shook his head, but the corners of his lips were already lifting into a sardonic grin. "I told you long ago to put the old fool out of his misery." Balin chuckled as he passed Dante and waited patiently until the portcullis was finally lifted.

Her new home loomed before her. Gianelle shivered at the sight of it. Shadows from two towers swallowed up the small bailey where a few scrawny chickens squawked around a pig the size of a small pony. Unlike the land around it, the castle's appearance was gloomy, and Gianelle realized that her new home, with its magnificent rising towers and wrought-iron gates, was as confining as it was impenetrable. There would be no climbing out windows here.

Inside the castle, strewn sunlight from dozens of arched windows fell across a rush and mint-sprinkled floor and illuminated the long corridors where colorful tapestries and gilded candle stands lined the walls. More than a dozen knights and squires greeted Dante when they stepped inside, but none of them, it seemed to Gianelle, were as happy to see him as the women in the castle. It didn't matter if they were dressed in fine gowns or peasant skirts; they all giggled and fussed over him before running back to whatever they were doing, making Gianelle turn to Casey and roll her eyes.

A man as ancient as a rowan scurried down the long, curved stone stairway, his eyes squinting into the entryway until he spotted his lord. Or at least the one he thought was his lord.

"James, what were you doing keeping watch?" Dante tugged at his gloves and eyed the withered little man who was blindly searching the hall.

The sound of his lord's voice directed the old man toward him. "Milord, I just could not stay in the kitchens another day. Ingred batters on like a clucking hen day and night till me just cannot take it anymore."

Dante stared at him with amusement sparking his eyes like fiery crystals. "But you cannot see, man."

"But I can hear!" James countered with a measure of pride that straightened his scrawny shoulders. "I can hear better than anyone in this castle. I heard Balin tell ye that ye should put me out of me misery."

Dante turned to his captain and lifted an amused brow, then pivoted slowly back to his determined watchman. "Despite that quite amazing feat, you must leave the battlements to Roland."

"Oh, all right," the old man grumbled, turning away. "But Roland cannot see worth a squirt at night, whilst I can hear the rabbits multiplying in the next village."

"Fine if we're going to be attacked by mating rabbits," Balin mumbled under his breath as he left the hall.

"I heard that!" James called out, turning the long corridor.

Dante beckoned to a fair-haired, stocky man who stood waiting in the shadows. "Talard, these two ladies will be living here with us. See to their chambers and have baths prepared." He barely looked at Gianelle, but turned to a steward who was waiting for him, impatiently clicking his heel against the floor and drumming his fingers along a bundle of parchments clutched to his chest.

"Any news from the king, Douglan?"

Talard touched Casey's elbow. His ruddy complexion paled when she smiled at him. He whispered Katherine's name and Casey whispered her own name back to him.

He nodded but still looked like he'd seen a ghost. He set his eyes on Gianelle, relieved that she didn't resemble anyone, alive or otherwise, and urged them forward. He shook his head and pulled her to the right. An instant later, he looked up the stairs just as a woman appeared at the top of them.

"Welcome home, my lord." Her voice was laced with the foreign tones of one who came from the East. Her hair was as black as obsidian and as straight as a taut harp string, her skin the color of Dante's fine leather scabbard. Gold powder lined her eyelids, which opened and closed as lazily as a cat's lounging in the sun when she gazed at Dante. She didn't walk down the stairs, but rather swayed down them, her voluptuous figure barely concealed beneath layers of colorful gauze. Her full red lips curled at the corners when she strode right up to Gianelle and lifted a honey-colored strand of hair in the air to inspect it. "Where did you find her?"

Douglan sighed exhaustively and tapped his heel even louder.

"Simone, Gianelle and Casey." Dante flipped his fingers and pointed in the opposite order, making the full introductions. Douglan pinched his lord's shirtsleeve and began to usher him away. "Talard," Dante said, walking backward toward another doorway, "why are you still here?"

"I don't understand what these two women will be doing here." The burly vassal waited for his lord to explain, but Dante cast him a look of annoyance.

"Sewing new gowns, I imagine. Or planting . . . hawking." He thought of some of the things his sister used to do. Other than her, he had never bothered himself with knowing how women filled their days. "How am I supposed to know, Talard?"

"They're not servants, then?" Simone called out to him. *"Non."*

Simone tossed Talard a knowing smirk. "Concubines."

Gianelle and Casey both opened their mouths to protest, but Dante cut them off.

"They're not my concubines. They are . . ." He threw his hands up and finally turned to leave with Douglan. "Whatever they want to be."

Chapter Eight

WHATEVER WE WANT TO BE? Gianelle tried to determine what Dante meant while Talard led her and Casey up the stairs. The fact that they were to have a chamber above stairs stunned Gianelle. Servants' quarters were always on the main floor. Lord Dumont's serving woman, Fergie, hadn't known any better and mistakenly put her and Casey above stairs for the night, but this was different. Dante actually said they were not servants! If they weren't serfs here, then what were they? Talard was obviously as baffled by his lord as she was, so no help would come from that quarter, and Casey was too busy absorbing the rich beauty of her new home to even care. Gianelle glanced over her shoulder at the woman following them up the stairway.

So this was Simone. She didn't look madder than a hellcat, as Balin had suggested she would be. In fact, she appeared to be as serene as a lake on a windless day. What exactly was the exotic beauty's position here if it was true that she was no longer Dante's lover? She certainly wasn't dressed like a servant. Gianelle had no more time to dwell on this when they reached the landing. They followed

Talard down a long corridor lit by candled sconces, caked in dripping wax. Dozens of thick walnut doors bracketed with wrought iron lined the hall. Talard stopped in front of one of those doors at the easternmost end.

Simone stepped in front of Talard and turned to face him. "That will be all." She reached up and swiped her thumb across his bottom lip. The smile she bestowed on him was so seductive he nearly crumbled under his weakened knees. "Have their baths prepared and leave us." She led Gianelle and Casey into their new chambers like the perfect chatelaine, delighted with Casey's gaping approval.

The bed is enormous! That was the first thought in Gianelle's mind when she stepped inside. Fine cream muslin draped a canopied bed large enough to fit a harem of women, which was probably just what Lord Dante Risande had. A burgundy brocade chair sat in front of a cold hearth whose mantel boasted twin swords fired from the finest metal. A rich walnut table was set against a wall dressed with tapestries of rich gold and ruby reds. She almost tripped over the gold-fringed edge of a knotted, deep cobalt blue carpet.

"I fear someone has erred giving these chambers to us," Gianelle told Simone.

"You would prefer separate chambers?"

"Oh, *non*," Gianelle hastily explained. "I only meant that this room is too fine."

Simone's voice was like music, lilting and erotic when she laughed. "Too fine for what?" When Gianelle lowered her gaze, Simone understood. "Ah, you are servants."

"Were," Casey politely corrected her.

Simone turned and studied Casey's face with eyes as

dark as coal. "He must have killed for you. You look very much like his sister. Who did he take you from?"

"Lord Risande didn't kill Bryce Dermott!" Casey argued, then lowered her pale blue gaze when Simone narrowed her eyes and took a step closer to her.

"We are servants," Gianelle said quickly to distract Simone's attention from Casey. "Dante has been kind to us, but I must admit, this room is . . ."

"Dante?" Simone echoed. She tilted her head slightly and sized Gianelle up in a whole new way. "I see. Well, you are not the first serving girl he took his pleasure in, and I'm certain you will not be the last."

"But, I'm not . . ."

The door opened and Talard returned with a single line of male servants hefting a tub and a dozen buckets of hot water. Simone slipped her bare arm through Talard's and whispered something into his ear, then left the chamber.

Gianelle watched her go and stomped her foot. She didn't want Simone thinking she was Dante's lover, but then she couldn't bring herself to care when she met Casey's gaze over the steaming water filling the bath. They almost couldn't contain the wonder and sheer thrill of it all.

"Please give Lord Risande our most heartfelt thanks for such a lovely room," Casey implored.

Talard nodded, then held the door open and waited for each servant to leave before closing the door behind him.

When they were alone, Gianelle and Casey looked at each other, grabbed each other's hands, and leaped onto the lush feathered mattress, screaming with delight.

A knock at the door vaulted them back to their feet. They waited for the door to open, but when the knock came again, Casey turned to Gia. "They're waiting for us to allow them entry."

"Oh." Gianelle giggled. Here was something else that would take getting used to. "Come in," she called out.

The door opened and a woman who was definitely not a serving wench stepped inside. *Probably another one of Dante's lemans,* Gianelle thought with a sinking feeling. The woman was very beautiful, not much older than she and Casey, with pale flaxen hair, and eyes of cornflower blue. She wore a gown of indigo wool that looked as soft as her creamy complexion. She carried a small bundle of gowns over her arm and held them out in front of her.

"I met Dante on his way to the solar with Douglan, and he told me you were both here and in need of these."

Casey stepped forward and accepted the offering with great enthusiasm. She spun around to Gia, her eyes wide with delight.

"I'm Lady Dara, Sir Malen's wife."

"Oh," Gianelle said, surprised by the relief settling over her. And why should she feel relieved anyway? she thought angrily to herself. What did she care who Dante took to his bed?

She stopped thinking about it and introduced herself and Casey, then asked Lady Dara if the gowns were hers.

"Aye. I think they'll fit you both." She moved across the room and when she reached the window, pulled open the shutters. She turned to Gianelle as the sound of the roaring sea below filled the room. "Yours may need a little taking in, and yours . . ." She smiled at Casey again and when she blinked, a dewy haze made her eyes shimmer. "Yours will need to be shortened about two inches."

She touched the back of her hand to her cheek, feeling flushed.

"Would you like to sit down?" Casey offered her the chair by the hearth. "You look a bit ill."

"It's just that you remind me of someone."

"Katherine," Casey confirmed.

"Aye." Dara nodded, staring at her more openly now. "She was younger than you, and very dear to me. Katherine's death has been difficult for everyone at Graycliff. It devastated Dante."

"He doesn't look at me often," Casey admitted to her.

"He wasn't here to save her," Dara told them. "He is very hard on himself about it."

Gianelle remembered the night she had tried to speak to him about his sister. He seemed so vulnerable to her then. She knew he still grieved for Katherine. It was obvious when he spoke of her. But knowing that such a mighty, capable warrior, not to mention a powerful lord over a castle like this, was defenseless against guilt and sorrow made him more substantial, more genuine.

"How terribly sad." Casey let out a mournful sigh and then, not wanting to bring those tears back to Lady Dara's eyes, tried to change the topic.

"He likes to look at Gia all the time." She laughed softly when her friend glared at her. "She's very stubborn, though."

Dara looked up at the blushing, golden-haired beauty who mumbled under her breath. "Well, a woman who doesn't fall over him may be just what he needs."

Gianelle met Lady Dara's warm gaze and knew they would be good friends.

"Your bathwater is getting cold while I stand here

keeping you both." Dara made her way toward the door. "I'll have Talard send up more water for whichever of you is taking her bath next."

"Thank you, Lady Dara."

"Just Dara, sweeting," she told Gianelle. "I will send my handmaiden Nora up to tend to you."

"Can she arrange my hair in those pretty knots like yours?" Casey asked her.

"Of course." Dara waved her fingers at them and left the room.

"Oh, Gia." Casey nearly squealed the moment the door closed. "Isn't she wonderful?"

Gianelle pushed her backside up onto the bed. "*Oui,* she is." She looked around at the lavish surroundings. How easy it would be to get used to all of this. It was a pity that she wouldn't be here long enough to do so.

~

The great hall bristled with people, most of whom were Dante's garrison, which numbered over one hundred men. The fragrance of mint rushes on the floor blended with the aromas of ale, sweet wine, roasted pheasant, freshly baked bread, and fish sautéed in mushrooms. The delicious aromas assaulted Gianelle's senses and made her stomach groan the moment she stepped inside with Casey and Talard. Laughter echoed along the walls, where the men sat at six long trestle tables set in a large rectangle, each table overflowing with various delicacies. Pheasant was ripped from bones and tossed to large hounds gathered in the center of the hall, where they ate with the rest of the residents of Graycliff Castle. Dozens of tall gilded candle stands lit the hall while an enormous hearth warmed the flesh. There were ladies in attendance as well, some serving while others, dressed in a bit more finery, sat among the men. Simone was there, tossing her lusty head back as she laughed between two feverish-looking knights. Casey spotted Dara dining with a handsome auburn-haired man and took off to greet her.

Gianelle's eyes found Dante a moment before Talard ushered her to her seat. He stood by the enormous hearth, a cup clutched in one hand and his head slightly bent toward a red-haired serving girl. Against her will, Gianelle noted the width of her lord's shoulders and the way his lustrous black hair fell slightly over them as he bent forward. He wore it loose tonight, tied only at the temples, giving him a more roguish appearance. He said something to the wench and she threw her head back and laughed. He looked up just as Gianelle took her seat and his slow smile made his eyes sparkle like polished steel. He shared a few more words with the purring redhead and then left her and made his way toward Gianelle.

If Gianelle thought him handsome before, the sight of him now stole her breath away, from his dusty black boots that hugged his muscular calves to his thighs of steel, encased quite snugly in black woolen hose, up past the giant broadsword dangling from his lean hips. He wore a loose-fitting shirt of undyed linen, and its wide, pleated cuffs fell over his long, powerful fingers as he strode closer.

"Ruby suits you well, *fée*," he said, referring to the color of the gown she'd chosen to wear. He wanted to stand her up and feast his eyes on all of her again. He thought her beautiful even when she was dressed in drab, oversized peasant's garb, but tonight his petite faerie looked especially ravishing. Her hair was gathered up at the sides by combs hidden beneath thick, glossy waves. A few loose tendrils fell around her temples and he ached to touch them. Her gown fit her body perfectly, accentuating curves Dante hadn't noticed in her servant's skirts. The ruby garment was made of either the softest wool, or fine linen. In the firelight, he couldn't tell unless he touched it, which he planned to do. The fabric clung to her hips and breasts, sending fire through Dante's veins.

"Do your chambers please you?" His deep, mesmerizing voice caressed her.

"It's so big, Casey and I almost lost each other in it." She looked up at him to find him smiling. She folded her hands in her lap and looked at them instead. "I should be serving."

"*Non.*" He shook his head and pulled out a chair to sit beside her. "You should be served. Besides, it's my duty to keep everyone at Graycliff safe, and if I allow you in the kitchen, who knows what might fall into the drinks?" He lifted one corner of his mouth in a rakish grin when she opened her mouth in her defense.

His presence consumed her as he leaned closer, filling her senses with his scent and blanketing her in the feral warmth that emanated from him.

"You look like a queen, Gianelle."

She felt like one, but none of this was real: the room, the gowns, his attention. How long before he turned somewhere else? And what did she care about his attention anyway? The sooner she and Casey escaped him, the better off she would be. *They,* she corrected herself. But what if Casey didn't want to leave all this? How could her friend deny this temptation after sleeping on a straw bed behind the kitchen for so many years?

"What are you thinking about that creases your brow with worry?" Dante lifted his fingers to her hair.

Startled, she pulled away. Dante's expression hardened, and instead of touching her, he lifted his hand and motioned to another serving maid to come fill his cup.

Within the space of a breath, a dark-haired beauty appeared, poured his wine, and then threw herself in his lap. "What else can I get you, lord?" she practically cooed at him. "Something hot, mayhap?"

"Bring Gianelle some food, Beth," Dante said blandly, and gave her a little shove to get her on her feet.

"Who's Gianelle?" Beth asked. Dante pointed across his chest.

When Beth was gone, an uncomfortable silence passed between them. Finally Gianelle turned to face him. When she spoke there was no contempt in her voice. "My lord, I've had but one duty my whole life: to serve others. I don't know many things, but I know people. People like you."

"Like me," Dante intoned with a noticeable sting in his voice.

"Don't sound so insulted. You know as well as I that you're a rogue." She was prepared for his anger, but he leaned back in his chair with his arms folded casually over his chest. He clenched his jaw and waited for her to continue with that anger seething beneath the surface. But it was there, making his eyes burn. "You are used to getting your way," she continued, albeit a bit more gently, afraid to push him too far. "I don't believe you truly care about one woman you have seduced, and I would like to know why . . ." She closed her mouth when Dante's glare impaled her. "Forgive me, it's not my place to speak so."

"Why stop now, Gianelle?" he drawled out in a deceptively calm voice. "You've been telling me my faults since we met."

"Well, you have many, my lord," she reasoned.

He stared at her for a full minute, his lips twitching with a mix of wounded pride and amusement. Finally he tossed her a soft chuckle, then lifted his cup from the table and downed its warm liquid.

"Are you going to get drunk and brood all night now?" Gianelle asked him quietly.

"Enfer." Dante leaned over the table and dropped his head into his hands. "I think I liked you better when you were afraid to speak to me."

"Of course you did." Gianelle spoke in a soft, mocking voice. "You would rather have an eyelash-batting mindless twit in your lap than a woman who might challenge your precious ego."

"You're quite wrong about me, Gianelle." Dante stood up and offered her a dimpled smile that had stopped many hearts, including Gianelle's. "And if you happen to come across a woman who can challenge my *precious ego,* bring her to me and I shall prove it to you."

Gianelle bit her lip as he walked off. She wanted to curse him, but Beth had returned with a trencher of steaming food and the swearing would have to wait. Sinking her teeth into a tasty piece of herring, Gianelle couldn't decide if it felt better to eat such delicious food or tell Dante exactly what she thought of him. Well, she thought, trying the pheasant next, she didn't tell him *exactly* what she thought of him. It was better that she'd left out how kind she thought he was, and how that certain half-smile of his made her heart palpitate. She realized, while she shoved a hunk of black bread slathered with butter into her mouth next and washed it down with heavenly wine, that she didn't really want to curse Dante. No matter what he said, he still allowed her to speak her mind. For that, she could never thank him enough.

When her stomach was finally full, she let her gaze scan the enormous hall. The stone walls were carved with bare-breasted nymphs astride giant dolphins. They stared down at her with cold eyes from the four corners of the hall, jutting outward as if they were about to dive onto her. Gianelle shifted uncomfortably in her chair and looked for something else that wouldn't make her cheeks burn.

Casey sat at the far end of the hall, laughing with Lady Dara. Her dancing eyes found Gianelle and she waved her over. But Gianelle's gaze involuntarily drifted back to Dante.

He sat with Balin and a few other men at a table across the room. Gianelle watched him dip his fingers in his trencher and bring some food to his mouth. He listened to something Balin said and nodded. The men around him laughed and tossed scraps of food to the hounds. Astonished, Gianelle noticed Talard among them. She looked around the rest of the hall and saw some of the male servants who had carried water to her chambers sitting with Dante's knights. The wenches laughed as they carried jugs of ale high over their heads, away from hands that reached for them. This scene was so different from Bryce Dermott's great hall. Everyone seemed so comfortable here, so at home. Even Casey looked like she belonged here amid the laughter and warm acceptance of people who didn't care whether they were servants or nobles.

Suddenly Gianelle felt more alone than ever before. What was her place here? She might have felt more comfortable serving; at least then she would understand the longing that plagued her heart. She ran her fingers across the delicate fabric of her gown and closed her eyes. She felt like a play actor in someone else's bizarre dream. She didn't belong here, and yet she didn't want to wake up.

"Gianelle, why are you sitting here alone?"

She looked up into Dara's tender smile and answered with a slight shrug. "It's where Talard sat me."

"Oh, sweeting." Dara folded herself into the chair Dante had occupied earlier. "You can sit wherever you wish. Come, meet my husband and the others. Casey's there," she added, to coax Gianelle to go with her.

"*Non,* I think I will go to my room. I must confess I'm dying to sleep in that bed."

Dara looked as if she might erupt into tears. "Balin told my husband that you and Casey were servants, and that you were treated unkindly."

"That is all past now." Gianelle waved away Dara's concern. "Da . . . Lord Risande has been more than kind to us."

"And to me and my husband as well. Malen has been in his service for over two years." While Dara spoke she noticed Gianelle glancing at the door as if she wanted to make a run for it.

"Stay and share a cup of wine with me." She covered Gianelle's hand with her own and smiled when Gianelle nodded.

~

By their second cup of wine, Gianelle was feeling much better and found herself laughing more than she had in years.

"Goodness, Casey was right." Dara giggled, looking across the crowded hall. "Dante does look at you often."

"He's a rogue," Gianelle muttered.

"Aren't they all," Dara agreed with a sigh. "He's just better looking than the rest."

They laughed again, and Dara called for more wine.

~

Chuckling softly, James passed Dante's chair and patted his lord's shoulder sympathetically. "What can ye do when fair lasses have such fun at yer expense?"

"Pardon?" Dante turned in his chair and stopped James's slow shuffle.

"The new lass and Sir Malen's fair maid." James lifted his eyes to the women and then chuckled as if he were in on the joke. "They find ye quite handsome, but wicked. Actually, 'tis the new one who finds ye wicked."

Dante followed his gaze. "Is that so? You can hear her?" When James nodded, his lord pulled an empty chair close and motioned for him to sit. "Tell me what she says."

"Are ye sure ye want to know?"

"Tell me." Dante's lips lifted into a darkly curious smile.

Slipping into the offered seat beside Dante, James leaned into him conspiratorially. "According to the new one, yer an arrogant, conceited swine with beautiful thighs." James frowned and shook his head. "That would be *eyes*."

"Go on."

"Now Lady Dara is telling the other about yer woman, Bridget." James slapped his thigh. "I remember her, milord! She was the one with them mammoth-sized . . ."

"James." Dante pressed his index finger to his lips and then pointed at the ladies again.

"Sorry, milord," James repented sheepishly and inclined his ear back to the ladies. "The new one suspects that ye don't meet yer lovers' expectations and that be why none of them stay with ye." James tilted his head and aimed a sympathetic frown at Dante. "That be a cutting blow to yer manhood, eh?"

"Oui," Dante agreed, staring at her. "She has a tongue sharper than an executioner's blade."

"And a devious nature to her, as well. She says when next ye bring a woman to yer bed, there'll be ants in it. The biting kind!"

Dante's mouth hooked into a satisfied smile. "Ants in my bed, eh?" Could it be that she was a tad jealous? Well, she had nothing to worry about; she was the only woman he planned on taking to his bed.

"I'd be careful of that one, milord. She doesn't seem to like ye very well. Milord?" James felt Dante's chair, but his lord was no longer in it.

Gianelle's gaze roved boldly over Dante's muscular body, from his boots to his sexy dark hair falling over his shoulders. She could hardly catch her breath as he strode toward her.

When he reached them Dante flicked his gaze at Dara in acknowledgment and then let it return to Gianelle. "May I have a word with you?"

"Why, of course." She offered him a sweet smile.

Dante didn't intend to talk to her here in front of hundreds of eyes, so he asked Dara to excuse them and turned on his heel to head for a quiet corner. He completely missed Gianelle stumbling into the table, then turning to laugh with Dara. By the time he reached the secluded corner and turned around, Gianelle had managed to steady her steps. She was still smiling at him. That was a good sign, he thought. When she seemed to pretend to trip over her own foot and landed in his arms, he wanted to toss his head back and shout in victory.

"You're not going to kiss me, are you?"

Her voice was a husky, drawn-out purr that drove him mad. His broad hands flexed on her back and drew her in closer. "I want to do far more intimate things to you than just kiss you, *fée.*"

Her head rolled back. Dante felt himself go hard as he dipped his mouth to the tender throat she exposed to him. It took him a moment to realize her entire body had gone limp. Lifting his head from her neck, he looked at her.

"Gianelle?"

She was out cold.

Dante swore violently in French and swooped down to lift her in his arms. He met Malen on the way out of the great hall with an unconscious Dara hauled over his shoulder.

"They enjoyed a pleasurable night, my lord," Malen called out over his wife's rump as he climbed the stairs in front of Dante. "But they'll pay for it tomorrow."

"Oui." Dante looked down into Gianelle's beautiful face. He should be upset that his plans were overthrown by cheap wine, but she had had a pleasurable night. He was glad for that.

When he reached her room, he laid her down on her bed and leaned over her. "Ah, woman, you test my control to the limit." He traced the sensual dip of her lower lip with his thumb, then bent his face closer and kissed her good night.

Chapter Nine

❧

GIANELLE HEARD CASEY CALL HER NAME, distantly at first. But then the voice she had come to think of over the years as sweet grew louder, until it sounded like a peal of thunder. The lightning came next—a white-hot bolt that pierced her skull and sealed her eyes shut a moment after she opened them.

"Gia, wake up. It's nearly noon."

"Don't shout at me, Casey," Gianelle pleaded and winced at the pitch of her own voice. "Dear God, did I fall down the stairs and land on my head?" Cautiously she lifted her fingers to her head and felt around for lumps, or even blood.

"It's from the wine."

"What?" Gianelle tried to lift her eyelids, but they hurt.

When she groaned, Casey scooted farther up on the bed to reach for her. "You poor dear," she lamented. "Lord Risande told me that your head would pain you so I should wake you gently."

"Then pray, do as he commanded and quit yelling."

"I'm not. You drank too much wine with Dara last eve, and now the demon comes to claim you. You remember what the chaplain told us at Devonshire when our master drank too much wine. He said it was debauchery, and . . ."

"Casey, please." Gianelle turned her head into the pillow, but the motion made her sick to her stomach. She had to admit she did feel like a demon had come for her. "I don't remember drinking more than two cups."

"You passed out as if dead."

"I did?" Gianelle opened her eyes and focused on her friend's nodding head.

"Lord Risande had to carry you to bed."

Ignoring the blinding pain shooting across her eyes, Gianelle looked down at herself. When she saw that she wore nothing but her chemise, her face paled to a sickly shade of white. "He undressed me, that . . ."

"Nay, I did," Casey advised her. She clutched her hands in front of her and went to the window. "Gia." She had to tell her, but she couldn't bear to see the disappointment in Gia's eyes. "I like Lord Risande. I like it here."

Gianelle had known this was coming. She feared Casey would be drawn into this fantasy of feathery beds and fine gowns, of having her belly full without having to lift a finger to prepare the food, or sneak off to the kitchen in the middle of the night to pilfer some. Gianelle understood, for she, too, could get used to sleeping with luxurious drapes around her bed instead of nosey mice. But she wouldn't let herself succumb to the temptation. As painful as it was going to be for Casey to hear, it was time she knew the truth of it.

"Casey, why do you think our new lord has given us such a lavish chamber when we are nothing more than servants?"

"But we're not servants," Casey argued. "You heard him tell Talard."

"He paid for us," Gianelle insisted. "Why would he purchase us, then ask nothing from us?"

Casey turned to her, wringing her new powder blue gown in her fingers. "I look like his sister, and he . . ."

"What about me, Casey?" Gianelle asked her quietly. Slowly, she pushed herself up on the bed to a sitting position. Casey saw Gia biting her lower lip and rushed to help her, propping her up on the fluffy pillows.

"He believed me guilty of poisoning our master, and still he purchased me."

"He never believed that!" Casey raised her voice, then lowered it again when Gianelle cried out. "Gia, you would never hurt anyone. He took you from Devonshire because he fancies you."

"*Oui*, he fancies me, and he gave us all this to win my favor."

"And what is so wrong with that?" Casey asked. "I think it's terribly sweet."

"Sweet?" Gianelle laughed, and then clutched her head. "Is it sweet of him to want to get me in his bed?" Her friend tried to answer, but Gianelle cut her off. "He's a man used to winning. You saw how cleverly he dealt with Edgar Dermott. And how he fought those men in the forest. Even Lord Dumont's spirited mare could not deny the spell of his tender touch and kind voice. But I have resisted his enchantment from the very first moment he spoke to me, and *that* is why we are here in this beautiful room instead of scrubbing floors. He is determined to win me."

Casey took her hand and sat beside her on the bed.

"Then let him win you, Gia. Mayhap God has sent him to you to teach you the love you deny so vigorously."

"Love has nothing to do with this." Gianelle shook her head and her voice went flat. "Once Dante succeeds in his quest, he will find another woman to conquer. He shared Simone's bed, and I'm quite certain that the serving wench Beth is familiar with his beguiling smile and wooing words, yet last eve he barely paid her any attention. He tires of them all. I heard it from Balin's own mouth."

"You're afraid he will tire of you then?" Casey cast her a knowing look.

"*Non,* I'm afraid this will all be taken away when he does."

Casey let Gianelle's words sink in. Her eyes grew large and misty, and she laid her head on Gianelle's lap. "I couldn't bear it if he changed toward us. I don't want to be a servant again."

"I know," Gianelle soothed her, stroking Casey's hair over her head. "That is why we cannot remain here. We will find happiness that is ours and that no one can take away."

"Aye." Casey nodded and closed her eyes, letting Gianelle's strength comfort her. It always did. From the time they first met, when Bryce Dermott had dumped her at the other servants' feet, it had been Gianelle who cared for her, changing Casey's grief to hope.

Casey didn't think Gia was right about Lord Risande, but that didn't matter. If Gia left Graycliff, she would go with her. "We will find our own happiness. And we will never leave each other," she said, repeating the very first promise she ever made to her dearest friend. They would leave it all, but Gianelle was wrong about their new lord, of that Casey was certain.

⁓

"My lord?"

Dante turned from the window in his solar, where the memory of Gianelle's hooded eyes and lusty smile from the night before invaded his thoughts. He had to have her; on a table, in his bed, against a wall, it mattered not. He ached to taste her on his lips, feel her softness beneath the hard, hungry heat of his body. He shook his head and sighed again, willing her to cease haunting him.

"Forgive me, Douglan," he said, returning his thoughts to the matters at hand. He shuffled some parchments on his cherrywood table and sat down in a heavy, high-backed chair. "Where were we?"

Douglan glanced down at the parchment in his hands and read. "Bryce Dermott died with no sons, so the one to profit most from his death is his brother, Edgar."

"*Oui.*" Dante closed his eyes and brought his hand to his forehead. "I found no evidence at Devonshire to feed my suspicions that Lord Dermott was one of Hereward's men, but we were ambushed in Briarwood Forest by several of his men. There were no survivors to question, but I believe the order came from Edgar. I have dispatched Sir Thomas the Swift and ten of my other men to ride back to Devonshire and keep me abreast of Dermott's movements."

Douglan's quill bobbed back and forth as he wrote. When he was done, he looked up from the table. "Is that all?"

Dante opened his eyes, erasing Gianelle's image from

his mind. "Inform him that the uprising in Kent last month has been ended, with less bloodshed than he had anticipated. Before he died, Lord Evansey informed us that Hereward was hiding in Colchester, but we searched for over a fortnight with no sign of him. The English aren't fond of us, and most offered no help. Those who did I have rewarded with coin and promised to mention their names to you, sire." He read off a list of names to his steward. When he was done, he fingered the stack of parchments on the table and frowned. A moment passed and he rubbed both hands down his face and groaned. Was there something he was forgetting? *Enfer,* but he couldn't seem to think straight. He couldn't get her image out of his mind.

"Is there something troubling you, my lord?" Douglan asked quietly, seeing his lord's silent frustration. Having been in the Earl of Graycliff's service for four years, Douglan knew this man was not one who was ruled by his emotions. Dante Risande was a decorated warrior, almost unfazed by the horrors he had witnessed during the Conquest. Only once, when he had found his sister's body, did Dante's emotions rage, and that day would remain in Douglan's mind forever, like a black, rancid hole in an exquisite tapestry.

"Is it the lady, sir?"

"Non—oui," Dante admitted, rising to his feet as if his chair were a cage and he had to escape. He paced the room, washing his hands over his face again. "She is a mystery to me, Douglan. One moment she smiles at me and she looks like an angel dropped from the golden clouds strewn across the sky, but before her next breath is drawn she snubs me, rebuking every attempt I make to please

her. She frustrates me, and at the same time . . ." Dante ground his jaw, remembering their kiss and how she clung to him afterward.

From his chair, Douglan cast his lord a stunned stare. "Do you care for her?"

Dante stopped in mid-stride and laughed. "Don't be absurd."

Douglan sighed and tossed his quill on the table. "Of course. Forgive me. I grew eager thinking you might actually settle down someday and save me from the tedium of writing your regrets to ladies who probably cannot even read."

Dante cast his steward a brooding scowl. "I hope you appreciate my good nature, Douglan. You've no idea how cruel some lords can be when their stewards speak so freely to them."

Douglan flashed him a cheerful grin. "It's why everyone at Graycliff loves you, my lord."

Dante grunted something indistinguishable, then headed for the door. "I'm going riding."

"What of the castle affairs?" Douglan asked. "We must discuss the problems with the village, not to mention all the chickens that are falling dead, and we cannot eat a one. And what about—"

Dante held up his hand to silence him and gave him a look full of meaning. "Later, please. I need to go."

Douglan nodded quietly and offered Dante a gentle smile. Everything would get done, it always did.

~

Gianelle made her way down the stairs at Casey's insistence that she join Casey for supper. Gianelle mumbled on her way toward the great hall. She doubted she could keep a bite of anything down. Fine thing too; she finally had all the food she wanted just waiting to be consumed, and she couldn't eat it. She promised herself she would never drink wine again.

Her thoughts turned, as they had from the moment she woke up, to her lord. She hadn't seen him all day. Casey said he'd visited her room early that morning to check on her condition, but Gianelle was sleeping. A ghost of a smile traced her lips thinking about it. Sleeping most of the day away was a luxury she had never been afforded. Never in her life had she lived amid such finery, nor had she ever been able to exhaust her temper on a man only to have him grin at her. She liked standing up to Dante. It was very . . . liberating. And she liked Dante as well, as much as she hated to admit it. He made her smile, when he wasn't infuriating her with his cocky arrogance. He didn't order her about, but used an unending store of forbearance, smiles graced by a disarming dimple, and an alluring glint that sparked his eyes when she entered a room, to lure her. She didn't feel trapped by his gossamer snare. She felt more alive than ever before, and that worried her. If she let him, he would have her. She had to be careful. She couldn't let herself think about any kind of permanency here in Graycliff. Everything would change after Dante grew bored with her.

Reaching the great hall, Gianelle turned her thoughts to the cliffs outside the castle and the sea beyond. Odd that such a savage landscape made her feel so peaceful, so content. She looked around her. She appreciated the warm atmosphere of Dante's castle, but she just couldn't sit here another night pondering her tenuous position, not while the rolling, roaring waves called her.

Retracing the steps she had used to enter the castle the day before, Gianelle found the front doors. She slipped out of Graycliff and into a world of mist and fading sunlight. The first thing she did was inhale a deep, cleansing breath, then she looked around. The bailey was deserted save for a lone pig and a few of those odd-looking birds picking at the ground. She ran toward them, dissolving the fine mist that clung to her ankles, and laughed when the birds spread their long wings and hovered over her, their screeches piercing the damp air. But her mirth vanished a moment later when she reached the lowered portcullis.

Clenching her fingers through the cool iron, she peered out at the clouds curling over the cliffs. Heedlessly, she yanked on the giant gate, tried to shake it in her frustration, and finally rested her forehead against the cold metal.

"Are you going to run away, Gianelle?"

She whirled around and pressed her back against the barricade when she saw Dante. He stood propped against the castle wall, watching her like some dangerous beast, his arms folded over his chest, his boots crossed at the ankles. His gaze was brooding, incredibly sexy.

"I wanted to take a walk," she told him. She glanced out of the corner of her eye and saw a stable hand leading the beautiful white mare into the stable.

"Alone?"

"I'm not afraid."

"You should be."

His eyes smoldered beneath his rakish black hair. Gianelle could feel that shimmering silver cutting through her like forged steel; penetrating her skin and making it tingle with a sensation that thrilled the breath right out of her.

"You could easily get lost, or slip on the cliffs and fall to your death." He pushed himself off the wall and walked toward her slowly. "You're very naive, *ma fée.*"

"Not as naive as you would hope, my lord," she threw back at him. She pressed her back farther into the metal gate when he came closer.

"I think my hopes would shock you." He stood over her, dark and compelling. The scent of the powerful ocean clung to his clothes, his hair. Gianelle could almost see him and his magnificent steed charging across the shoreline while the wind fed them its power and saturated Dante's spirit with wildness.

She thought of Simone, and Beth, and even Lady LaSalle. Each one falling under Dante's spell of pure seduction. Determined not to be his next victim, Gianelle lifted her chin in defiance of the undeniable effect he had on her. "You are the naive one to think I will ever surrender myself to you."

Dante's eyes darkened with something primitive as he dragged his gaze over her face—her eyes, her mouth, her sweet, rebellious chin—and then lower to her soft, heaving bosom. When he spoke, his voice was harsh and low, revealing the fire she ignited in him. "I don't want you to surrender, though your eyes tell me you could. I want you to come to me of your own free will."

"You must be drunk." Gianelle tried to step around him to go back inside, but he shackled her wrist with his strong fingers and then looked up to the tower guard.

"Roland! Raise the portcullis."

Dante watched her as the grinding metal of two enormous chains lifted the gate. He let go of her wrist and swung his arm across his waist, offering her an unhindered exit.

Glancing at him warily, Gianelle stepped forward. Dante followed her.

"What do you want to see?" he asked.

She knew Lord Dante Risande was the only true danger to her, though that danger had nothing to do with her physical being. She shouldn't go anywhere with him. She already thought about him too much. The very sight of him weakened her. If she had any sense at all, she would make a run for it now. But the crashing waves in the distance beckoned her, so she looked into his eyes and said, "Everything."

He wasn't drunk after all, Gianelle decided while he led her over a jagged crag, his steps as sure and agile as any cat's. He held her hand to keep her from slipping, which only muddled her concentration and made her slip more. When they came to a steep slope blanketed in moss, he fitted his hands around her waist and lifted her to a narrow path carved into the rock. She came to the top ledge of the hundred-foot precipice before him and sucked in an awe-filled breath when she cast her eyes over the sea below.

Dante reached her side and gazed with her at the spectacular view. "Beautiful, *oui*?"

"Oh, God . . ." Gianelle wanted to say more, but her heart felt like it was lodged in her throat, stopping her breath. She wanted to see everything, and Dante showed it to her.

Magnificent white-and-gray cliffs jutted out over an

immeasurable surface of pulsing waves, set afire with a path of orange light from an enormous half sun dipping below the horizon. A hundred feet below her, the swelling tide thrust frothy whitecaps against the wall of rock and then upward in the air like a geyser. Like nature's music, the roar of the battering surf filled Gianelle's ears, her soul.

"I never knew such a place existed."

Dante turned to her and felt his heart accelerate when a salty breeze lifted her hair away from her profile. "You traveled across the channel when you left Normandy."

"But I never saw it," she told him. "My father and I left Normandy on the darkest of nights. We hid behind some barrels on one of William's boats headed for Hastings. And when we landed. . . ." Her voice drifted off. Mayhap it was because Dante didn't press her for the rest of the tale that she told him. After bringing her here to this magical place, it felt right somehow to tell him. "My father longed for freedom as I do. He said we could find it here in England. He said I would have a better life here now that William is the king." She paused and a wistful smile lifted her lips. "I had no idea he wanted to be free of me as well. When we landed, he left me behind those barrels and said he was going to check if it was safe to leave the boat. I waited for him for a very long time. I was so frightened to even move. When I finally realized he wasn't coming back, I gathered my courage and left. It was night, of which day I don't know. The boat had been dragged ashore and there were men all around, shouting and hammering. I was able to slip past them and ran away, unseen."

Beside her, Dante clenched his jaw around a dozen words that were unfit to utter. He wanted to take her in his arms and simply hold her, but she would run away. She had never stopped running away.

He sat down and rested his arms on his bent knees. When Gianelle sat beside him a moment later, he kept his gaze on the darkening water.

"I like it here," she said, following his gaze.

"Gianelle?"

Imitating his position, she rested her cheek on her folded arms and looked at him when he spoke her name.

"What can I do to make you want to stay here?"

She wasn't sure if it was the warmth in his eyes when he set them on her, or his question that made her go all soft. *Careful, Gia,* she warned herself, *he is more clever than you think.*

"If I said there was nothing you could do, would you let me go?"

Dante had ridden all day, asking himself that same question. He was stunned to find that the thought of her leaving Graycliff made him willing to do anything to keep her here. But he had no right to hold her captive, and the more time he spent with her, the more he wanted to watch her fly. He only wished she would not fly away from him.

"*Oui, fée,* I would let you go. You belong to no one, and no one has the right to keep you."

Her eyes widened into glistening topaz spheres. Her lips parted in surprise, and the need to kiss her nearly doubled Dante over.

"Do you truly mean what you say, my lord?" Her voice was barely a whisper, her breath uneven. Was he willing to give her what she had dreamed of her whole life in order to win her? She was tempted to throw her arms around his neck and declare him victorious. But another thought occurred to her. What would he have won when she left? He hadn't asked her to climb into his bed before she went on her way. He was giving up! He was bored with her already.

"If that is what you want, my men will escort you . . ."

"And Casey as well?"

He clenched his jaw. "If she wishes to go. My men will escort you out of Graycliff. You may go to my castle in Norwich. I rarely visit there, but you would be safe. Or you can travel with Lord Dumont when next he visits Avarloch. My brother is a fair lord, and living in his village will be most pleasing to you and Casey. But you just cannot go out on your own, Gianelle."

She looked out over the waves now dappled by moonlight. She would never see this place again. The fact that Dante did not offer her a place in his village told her all she needed to know. He had no intentions of ever laying eyes on her again. Why, he wouldn't even escort her, but would have his men do it. She had absolutely no idea why his rebuff felt like a hammer to her heart. He was giving her what she wanted and she was happy, delighted, elated!

"We can leave in the morn then?"

Dante vaulted to his feet, then bent down, clasped her hand and pulled her up to face him. "*Oui,* right now if you want to."

"It's better this way." She glared into his eyes.

"What way is that?" he asked roughly.

"Being forgotten before I started to like you."

"Forgotten? What the hell . . . ?" Dante stopped as the full impact of her words hit him. "That's what he did to you, isn't it?"

"Who? What on earth are you talking about?" She tried

to pull out of his grasp when Dante held her by the tops of her arms.

"Your father. He left and forgot you."

"My father has nothing to do with this," she flung at him, struggling harder now to break free. "Let me go!"

Dante loosened his hold and angled his head so that he could look at her before she ran from him. And now he understood why she would. "I'm sorry," he whispered. And he was. She had shared something very personal with him, and he had no right to use it to judge her. "Forgive me, *fée*."

Gianelle nodded. "We should get back." Without looking at him, for she was certain he would see her whole heart in her eyes, she stepped around him and walked away.

A moment later she returned. "I don't know my way back."

Dante went to her and covered her hand in his. Before they disappeared over the ledge, she turned and cast her longing gaze back on the moonlit water one last time.

Chapter Ten

DANTE STARED INTO HIS CUP and then guzzled its entire contents. He clenched his jaw and stretched his legs out in front of him. "So she's leaving in the morning. Casey will probably go with her."

"And why did you allow this?" Balin stood by the window staring into the darkness. "I planned on taking Casey to the village tomorrow." He didn't need to turn around to know Dante was as miserable as he. He only had to listen to his voice.

"What was I to do, Balin?"

"Why didn't you simply ask her not to go? You don't want her to leave, that much is obvious."

"It doesn't matter what I want."

Now the captain pivoted around, his dark eyes surprised. "I knew she was under your skin, *frère*."

Dante shook his head. "She just deserves to be happy." He rose from his seat and poured himself more wine from the small table by the hearth.

"She can be happy here."

"*Non,* she can't." Dante took a swig from his cup and returned to his chair. "Not with me. She needs someone in her life who will love her, and never leave her." Dante's eyes gleamed when he examined his goblet. "She was abandoned, and she's afraid of that happening again. I could break down the defenses she's built around herself, but what will become of her"—he looked at Balin—"when I forsake her?"

Balin didn't ask how Dante knew these things about Gianelle. His lord had a gift for sensing people's true feelings, for getting much information out of little, which was why the king trusted him to find Hereward. Balin did ask him, though, why he didn't ask Gianelle and Casey to remain in the village of Dover.

"Because"—Dante glanced at him from under dark, brooding brows—"someone will eventually promise her those things she needs, and I'd rather not watch it happen."

Dante left the solar then and strode down the long corridor that led to his chambers. On his way, he thought about a young girl hiding in the darkness waiting for her father, her protector, who was never coming back. He had left his daughter on the shores of a foreign island, at the beginning of a bloody war. Dante hoped Gianelle's father found his freedom at the end of a sword.

He entered his chambers and looked at his empty bed. Lush velvet drapes were pulled back elegantly from the posters to reveal a plump, inviting haven of fine goose feathers with sleek furs strewn across it.

His throne.

How many women had he bedded there? How many of them had he taken the time to get to know? How many had he forgotten?

He pulled his boots off and unlaced his shirt, then poked at the embers crackling in the hearth. He remembered when his brother had lived at Graycliff and Collette deMarson almost destroyed him. Brand often complained about being cold. Dante felt that same chilled loneliness now. He closed his eyes and saw Gianelle the way she looked standing at the lowered portcullis earlier today: her windblown tresses, the pink blush of her cheeks, her eyes the color of a summer sunset. He liked to watch her dainty brow dip when he made her angry, and the way her eyes smiled at him when she wouldn't allow her lips to do so. He . . .

He heard her voice outside his chambers, just a whisper urging someone to follow her. Moving toward the door, Dante listened until their footsteps faded. Then he stepped into the dark corridor.

She was still there, a few feet away from Dante's door. He could see her because all the candles on the walls were lit behind her. At her side, old James tilted his head in Dante's direction, then demanded to know what Gianelle was doing, and why she had asked him to direct her path throughout the castle.

"I'm simply getting to know my way around, James," she told him and plucked a candle from its holder. Dante watched the small flame illuminate her face for a moment before she puckered her lips and blew it out. She swore. James advised her that his eyesight might be poor, but he could smell, and he knew she was blowing out the candles.

"Don't tell Dante what I did, and I won't tell him that you fed strychnine to the chickens."

"Now, now, miss. There's no reason for that. Let's hurry and be on our way."

After the last three candles were extinguished, Gianelle and James tiptoed down the darkened stairs. Dante went to the wall and picked up a candle. Why the hell did she blow all the candles out? He carried it back to his room, set it on a small table beside his bed, and tried to figure out what possessed her to shroud the castle in darkness.

His gaze settled on the candle, and a smile crept over his lips. "Son of a . . ."

~

The next morning, Dante met Balin as he left his chambers. The captain looked a bit pale and a little out of breath. "They're in the bailey waiting to be escorted to Norwich."

"Who is?" Dante finished tying off the laces on his sleeve.

"Who? Why, Casey and Gianelle. Casey is crying. I think you should go out there."

Talard raced down the corridor toward Dante next. He stopped to yank a candle from the wall. When he looked at it, he muttered an oath and shook the wax cylinder at Dante. "The wicks have been pulled out of every blasted candle on this landing! By the saints, you could have fallen down the stairs and broken your neck had you come out of your room last eve."

Dante stopped and offered the candle a concerned look and then continued toward the stairs. "A devious thing to do," he called out over his shoulder. "I shall find the culprit and punish them severely."

"Aye, and bring the bastard to me when you're done," Talard called back.

Keeping pace with Dante's long strides, Balin looked back and scratched his beard. "Why would someone pull out the wicks?"

"The same reason she would lick the tarts, or put daffodil in someone's wine. She is angry. And she's not angry because I gave her the freedom she wants." Dante grinned at Balin when his captain finally made sense of what he was hearing and smiled. "She is angry that I'm sending her away."

Dante wiped the grin from his face when he stepped into the bailey. He looked to where Balin pointed at the two women standing by the stable. Casey wiped her eyes with a small cloth clutched in her fingers. Gianelle, as stoic as a freshly carved saint, stared unblinking at the cliffs surrounding the castle.

Dante strolled up to them, hands clasped behind his back. "You're taking nothing with you?"

"Nothing here is ours," Gianelle answered flatly, without looking at him.

A quick glance revealed that they wore the same servant's gowns they had arrived in.

"Casey, why are you crying?"

Gianelle shot a warning glance at her friend, but Casey ignored it and sniffed. "I like it here, my lord."

"I like having you here." Dante almost smiled when Gianelle snorted and mumbled something under her breath.

"Pardon? What was that?" He moved closer to her and inclined his ear.

"Nothing." She tapped her foot and pretended great interest in the screaming birds overhead. "What are those?" she asked, her voice deliberately blasé.

"Gulls."

She thanked Dante and stared at the cliffs again.

She wouldn't look at him. Dante glanced at Balin and

shrugged his shoulders. "Well." He offered them a polite smile. "Farewell then, ladies. Godspeed to you." He turned and began walking back toward the castle. "Pity, though, I really don't want either of you to leave."

He waited a moment, feeling as devious as his little faerie.

"And why not?"

Replacing his triumphant grin with a rueful sigh, he swung back around at Gianelle's question. "Balin wanted to take Casey to the village. He's a loyal friend to me and I hate to see him disappointed." With carefully shielded satisfaction he noted the way Gianelle bit her bottom lip and slanted her gaze toward Casey. "And I had hoped to take you to the sea today and teach you how to swim."

The women exchanged looks, and then Gianelle dug the point of her slipper into the dirt. "I, too, hate to disappoint my friend. I suppose one more day here won't be too unpleasant."

Casey nearly leaped into Gianelle's arms. She kissed her friend's cheek and then ran off, chatting happily with Balin.

"I tell you, he was as cranky as a flea-bitten cellar rat before she came here," Dante said, watching his captain throw back his head and laugh at something Casey said.

"And what were you before I came here?" Gianelle asked him.

He smiled at her and held out his hand. She hesitated for only a moment before she fit her hand into his palm.

"Alas, I was charming."

He still was, damn him, she thought, watching that careless dimple flash when he spoke. She told herself nothing had changed. She would still leave tomorrow without caring if she ever saw his face again. He wouldn't stop her, and that was what she wanted, wasn't it?

⁓

It took over an hour for Gianelle to prepare for her excursion to the sea. She planned on fully enjoying her day, which meant that she would have to be properly clothed for it. Having no idea what to wear in the water, she went to Lady Dara for advice.

"You are going with Lord Dante?" Sir Malen's wife asked her, not bothering to conceal the mischievous grin that curled her lips.

"*Oui*. And you needn't look at me like that, Dara. I'm quite immune to him," Gianelle clarified with stern rebuttal charging her voice.

"Oh, of course," Dara repented, but her smile grew when she turned away from Gianelle and headed toward her wardrobe. "I'm just thankful that he talked you into staying." She riffled through a few garments before she found just the right thing for Gianelle to wear. Nodding her approval, she held the cream-colored chemise up to her chest and spun around. "This is perfect!"

Gianelle stepped forward and examined it more closely, making sure there was no chance of seeing through the heavy linen when it was wet. "It's a bit short, and there are no sleeves," she complained with one hand on her slim hip, noticing that the hem only reached Dara's thighs.

"Just what one needs to move one's arms and legs freely through the water. Otherwise, one would get all tangled up and might need Lord Dante to save her."

Gianelle lifted her scrutinizing gaze from the chemise

and scowled at Dara. "I will take it," she decided and snapped the garment away from Dara's body with an exasperated click of her tongue. "But you can wipe that devious smirk off your face. I will need no saving today."

"Of course you won't."

"I'm not a child and will not venture into the deep waves." Gianelle held the fabric up to her face and peered through.

"I'm sure you won't."

Narrowing her eyes at Dara from behind the linen, Gianelle lowered the chemise and sighed exhaustively, then marched out of the room only to have her hackles raised again by Dara's muffled giggles.

Once in her room, Gianelle slipped into the chemise and brushed her hair until it shone. She clipped it into a thick rope of soft waves over her shoulder, then looked down at her bare legs and frowned. There was more flesh exposed than hidden. Hoping Dante didn't think her indecent, she slipped her gown over her head and tied the laces of her kirtle.

She left her chambers and raced down the stairs, eager, now that she was ready, to get to the sea. She ran straight into Dante's arms. He gave her a smile that made her heart flutter in her chest. Then he took her hand and led her out of Graycliff.

Chapter Eleven

PERCHED BEHIND DANTE ON HIS STALLION, they rode along a boulder-strewn coastline until they came to a sandy shore of glistening gold with flecks of silver. The moment Dante helped her dismount, Gianelle removed her slippers and dug her toes into the warm sand. She waited, simply staring at the rushing waves while Dante untied a sack of provisions from the saddle. She inhaled a deep breath of fresh, salty air and let it cleanse her.

Beside her, Dante paused, watching her. He saw the wonder widening her eyes and the gooseflesh covering her arms and knew that she would come to love this land as much as he did if she stayed here. The idea of it made him happy. Most women didn't like the bleak loneliness of the cliffs, the raw force of the coast. She was utterly feminine, and yet she possessed a wild spirit waiting to be set free. "It's mighty powerful here, *oui*?" he said, his voice low and deep with feeling.

Gianelle turned and looked up at him with awe still lighting her eyes. That awe didn't fade when her gaze drifted over his face. She would have opened her mouth to agree with him, but she realized that everything of beauty lost its appeal when compared to him. Even the ocean's rugged magnificence couldn't halt her heart the way he did. She swallowed and looked down at her trembling hands, knowing that soon Dante would shed his clothes. What was happening to her? She was becoming as wanton as the maids at Devonshire when they saw him. Of course it wasn't her fault; the man was temptation itself with his lusty smiles and gentle fingers.

Much to her relief, he rummaged through his leather sack and pulled out a blanket, then snapped it in the warm breeze and laid it out neatly on the sand. Gianelle hoped he would remain fully clothed and fall asleep on his blanket. But when he began to peel away his riding pants, she watched him in quiet fascination. It seemed right that he was lord of this place, for it was as mighty and powerful as he. Like the waves that stretched toward their feet, Dante was delightfully inviting, yet powerful and dangerous. He was warm and malleable like the sand, dark and as finely chiseled as the cliffs that surrounded them on both sides. But like the sea, he could swallow her up, suck the life out of her body and leave her limp and dead.

Or she could learn to swim.

With timid apprehension at first, Gianelle began untying the laces of her kirtle. She turned toward the crashing waves and set her chin in defiance of their mighty roar. But when she heard the snap of Dante's tunic before he folded it and tossed it onto the blanket, her resolve faded like the sun-bleached wood that scattered the shoreline. She wouldn't look at him. But even as the command became a thought in her mind, her eyes were already turning back toward him. Her fingers shook at her laces and then halted altogether when her sun-soft gaze settled on his expansive shoulders. His bare arms practically trembled with tight, corded muscle, and when he turned, as if sensing her eyes on him, a grin spread over his face, and she felt herself being swept away on the tumultuous sea that was this man. Before she could shift her attention away, he continued to strip until all that remained were tight black hose that reached just below his knees.

He began to walk toward the waves, then stopped and turned back to her. "Are you coming?" His deep, satiny voice reached her ears, but she couldn't move. He was beyond beautiful standing before her with the raging ocean behind him. And she could do nothing but stare at the power in his legs and the way his hose clung to his firm derriere. He didn't wait for her but headed toward the rushing waves like a sea god returning home. Chewing her lower lip, Gianelle ached to look away from him. Dante frightened her more than ever before, not because he sought to command any control over her, but because she was losing control over her own emotions. Even her flesh had begun to react to him. Unbidden thoughts of being ravished under his strong body sparked a flame in her so hot it made her breathless.

Dante stepped into the waves and turned to her with his arms outstretched at his sides. The wind riffled through his lustrous black hair, blowing it across his face and over his stark, molten eyes, making him look like a painted warrior beckoning her.

"Come, Gianelle. Fear not, I will save you if the terrible waves snatch you up," he called out, stepping backward into the water. He knew the challenge would goad her, and he was right. He smiled when her mouth tightened into a determined line and she took up untying her laces. His smile faded an instant later, and then his breath faltered altogether when her gown fell away. He had not been expecting to see so much of her and felt captivated by the sultry beauty coming toward him. Silently appraising her shapely legs and maddening curves, Dante contemplated sitting at the shoreline and simply gazing at her all day. She filled his vision like a feast. Never had a woman brought him to the heights of such frustrated passion, made his body ache like a fresh-faced squire coming into his manhood. He cursed himself, gripping his lower lip between his teeth, then held his hands out to her.

When she reached him, he pulled her close against his hard chest. His voice was silk against her ear. "Are you afraid?"

Wanting to say no, but barraged with the sizzling sparks that rushed through her body when he fit her hands into his and then hauled her into his arms, Gianelle stifled a sharp gasp and nodded.

Dante's dark brows dipped into a crestfallen frown, but his grin was wicked and vibrantly warm. "You, afraid? I don't believe it."

Frothy waves rushed toward them and sprayed Gianelle with icy water. "Ohieeeeee!" Her entire body quivered from the chill, but Dante's arms gathered her in, molding her closer to his sculpted angles. She looked up, completely breathless, and met his heated gaze.

"What's the matter, *ma fée*?" he whispered, holding her in a tight, warm embrace. "Is the water cold?" But before she could answer he broke away and scooped up a handful of water to fling at her.

Gianelle opened her mouth to gasp at the frigid cold and the sudden playful glint in Dante's eyes. She was still trying to recover from the warmth of his gaze one moment and his careless treatment of her the next, when he did it again! He grinned with a dark challenge that prompted Gianelle's revenge. She bent her body to gather as much water as she could into her palms, ready to soak him, but he doused her a third time, straight in the face. He laughed, inclining his head, goading her further until she took off after him. She would have gotten him, too, if she knew how to run in the water. Instead, she tumbled face-first into the waves. Dante was still laughing, harder now, in fact, when she rose to her knees and swiped the salty water out of her eyes. She didn't chase him but remained where she was and covered her eyes with her hands until he rushed to her side with concern filling his voice.

"Are you injured?" While he bent to capture her face in his hands, Gianelle carefully concealed her victorious smile. She slipped both arms around his calves and yanked, hard. Dante went down and Gianelle leaped on him. She tried to dunk his head, but he was too strong. Laughing, he flipped her over and then he was on top of her, holding her head up in the palm of his hand.

"Don't worry, I'm not ready to make you surrender just yet." He grinned down at her, and then for a heart-stopping moment he searched her gaze with something so potent tightening his jaw, Gianelle nearly lifted her fingers to his face. What was it he wanted to say? She didn't find out. His expression changed again. His perfect mouth hooked up at one edge, his dimple charming Gianelle senseless, and then he splashed water into her face and was gone again. This time, he stalked into the deeper water and disappeared beneath the surface. Gianelle followed him but stopped when he went under. She turned full circle, looking for where he would come up again. She never heard him rise out of the water directly behind her, and when he tapped her shoulder, she spun around.

He kissed her.

It was not a long kiss, just a peck square on the mouth, and just enough to set her head reeling. He backed away, smiling, sculpted arms outstretched again. "Come now, you are not going to let me get away with that, are you?"

She took a step toward him.

His mischievous smile grew as he led her into deeper water, too deep for her to follow. He turned and dived into the waves, disappearing from her sight.

After bending to gather a handful of gooey sand, Gianelle waited, and just when alarm gripped her, worrying that he had been under too long, he burst through the shimmering surface like some fabled deity directly in front of her, so close that he nearly knocked her over. Crystal droplets sprayed outward, soaking her all over again. Water cascaded off his glistening shoulders down to his taut belly as he towered over her. "Did you miss me?" He leaned down and whispered close to her lips, ready to kiss her again.

"Oh, were you gone?" Gianelle asked and tossed her fistful of wet sand in his face. She threw her hands to her mouth and giggled at his surprise. Then she spun around and fled.

Confident that he was not chasing her, but rather cleaning the sand from his mouth, Gianelle grinned victoriously when she saw the shoreline inches away. That would teach him to tease her so ruthlessly, she thought, just before she felt his hands around her ankles and opened her mouth into a huge O.

She went down face-first, and before she could gather more sand into her hands to fling at him, Dante flipped her over on her back and slid his body over hers, pinning her under him. Wearing a darkly roguish grin, he held up a much larger handful of sand over her face.

"Surrender to me, and I will show you mercy."

"Never!" She laughed.

"You refuse?"

"I said never, brute. Are you hard of hearing?"

Dante shrugged his massive shoulders as if he had no other choice now. Pinning one of her arms between his belly and hers and holding the other high over her head, he proceeded to smear her cheeks slowly and thoroughly with sand. She thrashed and squealed with laughter beneath him. When he was done, he regarded her with sheer amusement lighting his eyes. And then his gaze changed, darkening with the hunger that raked his body.

"Kiss me, or I'll hurl myself into the waves and end my miserable life."

Gianelle stopped laughing and looked up at him. Her heart began to pump wildly. Dante felt it against his chest like the furious beating heart of a tiny bird.

Her resistance deserted her. She closed her eyes and pursed her lips, ready to receive him. Above her, Dante smiled at the chaste kiss she offered.

He moved his mouth over hers, devouring its softness, tasting her, teasing her while his own breath stalled against the fervent pounding of his heart. His tongue parted her lips, marauding the deepest corners of her mouth, spreading, stroking, and making her writhe beneath him.

His body ached to take her right there while the tide washed over them. Her reaction to him, so sweetly wanton, set every drop of blood in his body ablaze, hardening him until the agony of it ripped a groan from his throat. He broke the kiss, his breath heavy and his eyes burning into hers like sizzling mercury.

"Oh, my," Gianelle whispered with languid wonder. She dragged her lower lip between her teeth, making Dante want to do the same to those coral-colored lips.

"I should warn you," he murmured, a slow grin, heart-wrenchingly sensual, curling his full mouth, "I find your wicked seduction of me completely irresistible."

Gianelle laughed. "I'm not seducing you. You're to blame for this."

He lifted his fingers to her face and wiped the sand off her cheeks with excruciating tenderness. "*Non, ma petite fée,* the very thought of you seduces me." When she rolled her eyes, Dante laughed and pushed himself up on his elbows. "You doubt my words?"

"*Oui.*" Her eyes danced with amusement. "I think you've said them to a score of other women. Why are you frowning so? I am simply smarter than all the others."

He stood up and walked toward the blanket, stopping to dip to the sand and pick something up in his hand. Gianelle giggled watching him, then called out, "Going off to brood?"

"*Oui,* I am highly offended." He turned and walked backward while he spoke. "Come kiss me again, and I might forgive you."

"I'd rather drown." She offered him a radiant smile before she turned away from him and looked out over the water.

"I could arrange that, you little . . ."

Gianelle covered her mouth to stifle her laughter. But a moment later she was up on her feet and following him. "I enjoy insulting you. I don't know why," she teased as she sauntered past him.

She folded her legs under her and sat down on the blanket. Unclipping her hair, she spread the deep bronze tresses over her shoulders to dry, and lifted her face to the sun to let the radiant warmth cover her.

Dante's eyes were on her. She could feel them, hooded, burning, wolf-colored eyes. She looked at him just as he squatted before her.

He said nothing for an eternal moment and then lifted his hand and presented her with a large curled shell. Gianelle accepted the offering, turning it over in her hands with curiosity knitting her brow. With Dante's gentle silence covering her, he took her hand in his and brought the shell to her ear. Gianelle listened. Her eyes opened wide, and she smiled so radiantly the man before her almost groaned, exhaling.

"It's the sea, Gianelle, and now it belongs to you." His gaze drifted slowly over every inch of her face, drawing her in closer until she thought he would kiss her again. To her dismay, he didn't, but instead lifted his fingertips to her cheek and then down to her chin. Her skin tingled everywhere his fingers touched her, and when he slid them over her throat, she gasped at the tight wrenching beneath her navel. Torturously, he continued his fiery path across her shoulder, then down the length of her bare arm until gooseflesh rose from her toes to her head. God's teeth, what was he doing to her? The ache that began somewhere in the pit of her belly ended between her legs.

She met his heartrending gaze, silently begging him to stop, but needing him to continue. His fingers finally reached hers and he closed them, clutching her small hand in his. She whispered his name, and he closed his eyes and brought her hand to his lips, kissing it with such intimacy her breath faltered and she could say nothing more but simply stared at his sun-kissed head.

She didn't want to care about battles, but she had to for her own sake because she couldn't lose this one. Oh, she just couldn't. This was not a man moved by any one woman. She couldn't let herself get close to him, no matter how sweet his words sounded, no matter how torrid his kisses were. But how was she supposed to resist him when he gave her the sea?

"It's so beautiful." She held the shell to her chest and looked out at the roaring waves rather than at him. "This place is so beautiful, I could stay here forever in this very spot."

"*Oui*, this is my love, my sanctuary." Dante sat beside her, his gaze softened with deep emotion as he looked around him.

"You carry its scent upon you."

"After the conquest, I took my sister to Normandy for a year, and every day I yearned to come home. I was born in Normandy, but this is where I want to die."

Gianelle watched him while he spoke, understanding why he loved this place the way he did. The first time she'd seen it, she never wanted to leave. "Are your parents alive?"

He shook his head. "But I barely knew them. My brother Brand and I were sent to William to serve as his squires when we were very young."

"Your brother who is wed to Lord Dumont's daughter?"

"*Oui.*"

"Is he like you?"

Dante laughed and turned his gaze on her. "*Non,* Brand's not a rogue. He fell in love with Brynna and makes her very happy."

Gianelle sighed and turned her attention back to the sea. "Love is a fool's emotion."

"It's strange to hear a woman say that."

She slanted a glance at him and smiled out of the corner of her mouth. "I'm certain in your case it is." She laughed softly when he groaned and shook his head toward the heavens. "Don't dare disagree with me, Dante. How many women have you truly loved?"

"Only one," he admitted. "My sister."

Gianelle grew serious. "Forgive me," she whispered and lifted her hand to his arm. "I didn't mean to . . ."

"It's been a long time since I spoke of her." The intimacy of his smile coaxed a flip from her heart. "She was very much like Brand. She laughed at everything, and cried just as passionately. Everything stirred her, even simple things like a rainstorm, or a feisty horse . . . or trees. She loved to listen to leaves when the wind riffled through them. There aren't many trees here, so she used to beg me to take her to the woods a few leagues away. Madly enough, it sometimes comforts me to know she died listening to that sound. When I found her, though it was winter, there were still leaves on some of the trees."

Gianelle turned her face away and didn't look at him again, even when Dante smoothed her hair off her shoulder.

"*Fée,* don't cry."

"I'm not crying," she argued and swiped her hand

across her nose. When she looked up her amber eyes glistened. "How do you heal from that kind of loss, Dante?"

"I don't know if you ever do," he replied, fastening his powerful gaze on hers. He stared into her eyes, knowing she understood the depth of pain that came from losing a loved one. "I have arisen from my sleep every morn since Katherine died with one purpose, Gianelle."

"What is it?"

"Revenge. It plagues me."

He ground his jaw around words he wanted to say, but they were unfamiliar to him. He didn't know how to utter them. "And then . . ." He laughed softly at his own inability. But when she smiled at him, not understanding, he found the words came out smoothly. "And then I woke up and looked into your eyes, and I haven't thought of anything but you since."

Chapter Twelve

THE SMALL COASTAL VILLAGE OF DOVER lay nestled between a spectacular backdrop of sky painted in streaks of magenta and deep blue, and high, jagged crags encrusted with centuries of shells spewed from the sea.

Gianelle clung to Dante's waist with one arm, and with the other waved to the small children who had come to greet their lord as he rode his horse into the village. They had left the shore, changing back into their clothes, and came here hoping to meet up with Balin and Casey. But Gianelle suspected the true reason was that Dante wanted to show her how resourceful his people were. He pointed to every cottage they passed, telling her who lived in each and what trade they were known for. Young Cameron, who was busy hanging herring and cod to dry, was proving to be as good a fisherman as his father. While Ennis and Kevin the Shark, known for the ten-foot-long blue shark he'd caught three summers past, were the best net makers on the entire eastern coastline. Old Lizzy Somers could string seashells into ornaments fit for Queen Matilda, and Teresa, the daughter of Graycliff's own cook, made clam soup so delicious that Dante was certain Colin, the man herding the sheep across their path, married her so he could be assured of having a bowl each night.

Gianelle smiled at the people Dante spoke of when they called out greetings to him. Everywhere she looked, villagers were stepping out their front doors to smile and wave. Geese and chickens scurried to and fro, while dogs chased gulls away from baskets of eels and oysters.

It was perfect here because these people had a lord they loved, and who loved them in return. Every face was friendly, every child well fed.

Dante dismounted first, then lifted Gianelle out of the saddle. Two men hefting rolled nets over their shoulders patted him on the back as they passed him.

"Does no one bow to you, or wait until you speak before they do?" Gianelle asked him, surprised at how easily Dante fit in here among the commoners.

"*Non,* and if they ever do they'll be hurled off the cliffs." He tossed her a carefree wink and bent his body to pluck a little girl from the ground.

"Greetings, Hilary."

"Greetings, Lord Risande." The child looked to be about five years old. Her flaxen curls bounced around pudgy pink cheeks and a ruby red, bow-shaped mouth.

Watching them, Gianelle felt something tug at her heart. Dante looked bigger and more magnificent holding a child than ever before. For one heart-stopping moment, she allowed herself to think of what her children might look like with him as their father. She fought to chase those images away. Such permanency was impossible with Dante, and it made her want to weep, blast him.

"Do you want to ride my horse?"

Hilary nodded emphatically and kicked her feet when

Dante sat her in the saddle. The stallion swung his huge head around and snorted as if she were as bothersome as a gnat.

"Hilary," Dante said as he picked up the reins, "this is Gianelle." He leaned closer and lowered his voice, pretending Gianelle couldn't hear him. "Does she not look like a faerie to you?"

Hilary's eyes opened wide, and when she nodded her curls bobbed up and down. "Do you have wings?"

"*Non.*" Gianelle laughed and turned around to show Hilary her wingless shoulder blades.

"Are you Lord Risande's wife?"

"*Non.*" Dante answered with a long-suffering sigh and gave the reins a gentle pull. "She said I remind her of a warty toad."

Gianelle nodded and Hilary squealed with laughter.

A woman with wide green eyes and hair as yellow as Hilary's rushed to Dante's side and blushed two full shades of pink when she looked up at him.

"I'm sorry, my lord. Is Hilary pestering you again?"

Gianelle eyed the woman and didn't think she looked sorry at all.

"Of course not, Becky. But you might not want to ask my horse that question." Dante looked up at Hilary, still kicking and now bouncing up and down as well, trying to make the horse go faster.

Looking past her daughter, Becky glanced at Gianelle and smiled. Dante introduced them, then balled up his cheeks and made toad-like faces at Hilary, which must have reminded her why Gianelle wasn't his wife.

"My mama said she would marry you if papa ever went away."

"Hilary!" Becky paled. Her eyes shot first to Dante, who suddenly found his stallion's kneecaps intensely interesting, and then to Gianelle. "I don't know what she's talking about," Becky denied. She lifted her arms and commanded her daughter into them.

"But mama, I heard you telling Caitlin that you . . ."

Becky pressed her hand over Hilary's mouth and hurried off with her before she said another word.

When they were gone, Gianelle cast Dante a terse smirk. "No wonder your ego is the size of France. You don't even have to try, you are *that* charming."

He grinned. "I am?"

Exhaling an exhausted sigh, Gianelle slipped around him. He followed her, toting his horse. "What good does it do me when the one woman I want to charm is immune?"

"I wasn't immune until I kissed those toad lips," Gianelle replied without turning. She spotted Casey and Balin sitting with a group of people beside a fire set within a carved-out niche in the ground.

Dante came up close behind her and bent to her ear. "You melted in my arms."

"I was this close to falling ill," she corrected, holding up her hand and bringing her thumb and index fingers close together. His throaty laughter filled her ears and she smiled in front of him.

Casey looked up and tugged on Balin's arm when she saw them. "Gia, come look at what Balin bought me!" She held up a beautiful shell necklace strung with coral and pearl.

"I didn't expect to see you here," Balin greeted Dante while Gianelle sat down near Casey and the two of them began talking nonstop.

After handing the reins over to a boy who led his mount to a nearby mound of fresh hay, Dante looked around at the faces he knew as well as his own. "I haven't been here in over a se'nnight. All is well with you?"

Dozens of nods and "ayes" answered his query. "Join us, my lord," someone called out. "The crabs are cooking and there's plenty to go around."

The sun dipped low in the sky and the crabs and ale kept coming, along with the people, until the whole village sat together.

Teresa, Colin the sheepherder's wife, sang a haunting song about a man dying at sea and his wife, who waited by the cliffs for ten years for her beloved to return.

While Teresa's soft voice filled the night air, Dante reached for Gianelle's hand and weaved his fingers through hers. The touch was so intimate, she nearly wept. She looked at him and knew she was losing fast. He was too kind and tender with her to resist. He gave her everything she ever wanted, almost everything she needed.

How would she ever forgive him?

How could she ever forget him?

Gianelle lay in her bed many hours later, unable to sleep. Every time she closed her eyes she saw his face, heard his voice. She should have known Dante Risande would have his way. But he had disarmed her with the same speed he used to vanquish the men who attacked them in the forest. From the first night they'd met, he had treated her differently than any other man, any other noble, ever had. Had his insistence that she ignore the rules of servitude and look at him been a ploy to make her notice the broad sweep of his shoulders, the sensual caress of his trousers against his thighs? Did he want her to look into his eyes so that she could see the heated longing he felt for her, and watch him conquer it over and over? Oh, but she didn't have to see it. She tasted his desire on his breath when he kissed her, hot, untamed beneath his iron control. What if she let him have his way with her? When he tired of her she would be free to come and go as she pleased, just as Simone was. Why did she even care if he no longer gave her his attention? Why was she so angry that he was willing to send her away? Wasn't that what she wanted?

She flipped herself over on her bed and cursed the nagging, unfamiliar ache in her heart that kept her awake. He could never love her. When he told her on the beach that he thought of nothing but her, she wanted to believe it. But Dante Risande didn't love the women he courted. And what was love anyway? She certainly didn't know. Her father hadn't loved her. None of her masters ever had. All she knew of love was what she'd heard from the castle bards, and it always sounded painful. She didn't want any part of it. She wanted her freedom, and Dante gave it to her. He gave her the freedom to be who she was without fear, but in doing so, he made her want something more.

She pounded the mattress, unable to find a comfortable position.

"Gia, for heaven's sake, stop moving so much."

She should leave in the morn, but she knew she wouldn't. She loved the cliffs, the ocean, the people. For the first time in her life, she felt like she belonged somewhere, and she didn't want to leave. Casey was happy here, too, finally happy. Casey, she thought as her eyes drifted closed. She would stay for Casey.

~

Dante padded down the stairs the following morning, eager to get to his bed. He had spent the night in the turrets, looking out over the cliffs as he had on so many nights after Katherine died. But last night his thoughts were filled only with Gianelle. He had to find a way to keep her here. At first, he'd wanted time to play the game of cat and mouse. Her rejection was exciting as well as frustrating. And any warrior would rather face a challenging opponent than one who throws down the sword before the battle even begins. When he understood that she needed more than he could ever give her, he let her go, relinquishing his victory. But she ignited a fire in him as no woman before her ever had, and at the same time she gave him peace from the terrible hatred that clawed at him daily. He didn't want to lose that.

He was still deciding the best way to go about asking her to remain at Graycliff when he spotted Talard crossing the corridor.

"Good morn, Talard. All the candles are intact, I presume?"

"Aye, my lord." The vassal eyed his weary appearance and shook his head. His lord had been to the turrets again. He'd gone there almost every night after Katherine died, and many mornings Talard found him asleep within the large alcove facing the cliffs. "I'll have some breakfast sent to your room."

"Thank you, Talard. And have a bath prepared also. I still have sand embedded in my skin."

Talard nodded and retreated to the stairs, but Dante called him back. "Gianelle is still here, is she not?"

"Aye, she dines with Balin and the others in the great hall." The relief that settled over Dante was obvious enough to cause Talard to eye him narrowly. He said nothing, though. His lord's affairs were not his concern.

When Talard left, Dante entered his chambers. He sat on his bed and thought about Gianelle until his bath and food finally arrived. Her mood had changed so suddenly last night at the village, but he hadn't pressed her for an explanation. Although he found it easier to talk to her than even to Balin, he knew her grim expression had to do with him, and he dreaded hearing her tell him she was leaving in the morning. So he simply held her on the way home and let the howling wind rushing across the steep ledges soothe both their anxious thoughts.

When his bath was ready, he dismissed Talard and the other vassals who hefted his water from the well. He pulled off his shirt and boots and picked at his food but found his appetite had deserted him. He looked at his bed and frowned, wishing Gianelle was in it. He had to get her out of his thoughts. Tossing his hose onto the bed, he tried to concentrate on Hereward. Where was the bastard hiding? Did he know about the men who killed Katherine, or had they acted on their own? He had to find out. And how did he leave Edgar Dermott when his suspicions of him were so high? He knew how. He'd done it for her. God's fury, he was growing as soft as a rose petal. What more would he do for her, and why the hell couldn't he stop thinking about her?

He kicked his boot across the floor and stepped into the bath. He should be downstairs right now asking Balin to throttle him back to his senses.

Someone knocked. "Come," he called out and rested

the back of his head against the warm basin. When he heard the sharp gasp of his visitor, he opened his eyes and smiled at Gianelle.

"You are making a habit of coming to my room when I'm not fully dressed. Stop standing there gaping and shut the door behind you. You're letting in a draft."

"Do you not even have the decency to cover yourself?" She slammed the door shut and turned to face it, rather than him.

"What would you have me do? Take a bath fully dressed?"

She hated to admit it, but he made perfect sense. With a quick intake of breath, she decided she had best make haste and tell him why she was here.

"Balin just informed me that you knew it was me who took the wicks out of the candles."

"Oui." He settled deeper into the soothing water and closed his eyes again.

"And you said nothing to me? Why did you pretend I was innocent? Why did you take me to the sea when you knew I had done such a devious thing? Will you do anything to seduce me, my lord?"

Dante knew that nodding his head probably wasn't the best idea. He shrugged his wet shoulders instead, "I don't care about candles, *fée.*"

She spun around to face him. "Do you care about anything?" She knew she had no right to say such a thing, but her last query was the true reason for her condition. She should be grateful that he didn't punish her for stripping the candles of their wicks, and part of her was. But she was also so mortified that he knew what she'd done, and angry he didn't tell her. It proved that he didn't care what she did as long as it didn't interfere with his seduction of her. He didn't even ask her why she had done it.

"I care about many things, Gianelle," he said, his voice deep and full of meaning. "Now would you pass me the soap?"

In a habit born of obedience, she crossed the room, eyed his bed, and then looked at him. He pointed to the soap and smiled gratefully at her when she picked up the bowl.

"Enjoy your bath." She fought herself not to look at his corded arms slung over the sides of the tub, dripping wet. She handed him the soap and turned to go.

"Don't leave, Gianelle. Please." There, he thought to himself. That was done. He felt better. A little.

She stopped. Her hands trembled, and her heart lay slain in her breast at his plea. No one had ever uttered that word to her. "I think it's best if I'm not here while you bathe," she said quietly.

"I was referring to you leaving Graycliff." He tried not to let his smile widen into a grin when she looked over her shoulder at him, a flush of heat scalding her cheeks. "But now that you mention it, I don't see why you shouldn't be here in my chambers."

"It isn't proper unless I am here to bathe you."

He held the soap up to her and his gray eyes warmed to smoky quartz. "You're not afraid to touch me, are you?" he asked when she didn't take it from him.

She snatched the bowl out of his hand. "Don't be ridiculous. I've bathed men before."

"I'd prefer not to think of that."

"I know it's difficult," she snapped as she knelt beside

the basin and yanked up her sleeves, "but do try not to convince yourself that I cannot resist you."

"It's quite obvious that you can, *fée.*" His dimple flashed and he closed his eyes again as she began to work the soap over his arm.

She was daft, she argued with herself. She knew she was falling very neatly into the trap, but she didn't care. She was tired of denying the effect this man had on her. And what harm could just bathing him do? She'd done it for her lords hundreds of times, though she had to admit she hadn't wanted to touch those other men. They didn't make her blood rush through her veins just thinking about what hard, heated flesh felt like.

It felt wonderful. She bit her lower lip and looked around the chambers in an effort to draw her thoughts away from his sculpted body.

Dante could live in this room and be completely content. There were two small settees upholstered in lush blue velvet. One sat before an enormous hearth, and Gianelle imagined his long body stretched over it, enjoying the fire on a cold winter night. Every inch of wood in the room, from the ornate carvings on his chest of drawers to the thick cherry posts of his bed, was polished to a mirror finish. There was fresh fruit laid out on a table against a wall painted with unicorns and—Gianelle blinked and then smiled—faeries. She narrowed her eyes to examine the tiny winged creatures painted so delicately. She blushed, and then scowled at Dante while he relaxed beneath her skilled touch. All the faeries were naked. Which led her scrutinizing gaze to Dante's bed. It was massive, even bigger than the one she shared with Casey downstairs. She wondered how many women he had bedded there, cloaked within the indigo blue velvet that draped the canopy from the ceiling and flowed like waves when released from the small wooden clips along the posts.

With a sigh and a muttered curse, she chased away images of Dante in bed with a woman, and turned her attention, once again, to his bath. She rubbed the soap into his shoulder. He groaned deeply and she swallowed hard at the sensual sound.

"Who did you bathe?"

Gianelle looked up to find him watching her, and the flecks of green in his eyes stopped her heart. "I thought you preferred not to think of that."

"I don't. But who?"

"Bryce Dermott and his brother on occasion." She slid her hand over a muscle in his chest and felt it twitch beneath her fingers.

"Did either of them ever touch you?"

"There were plenty of servants who freely gave themselves to the Dermotts. I did not."

She massaged his arm, caressing muscles that were firm and hard to her soft touch. Fascinated by the fine contours of his body, she slowed her fingers, hypnotized by his strength, and ran them smoothly over the black crisp hair of his forearm. Her touch softened until just her fingertips glided like a whisper down to his fingers.

"That is not an answer, Gianelle."

"It is the only one I wish to give you. You're quite strong," she said, wanting to change the subject and saying the first thing that came to her mind. She realized then that she was touching him too softly, feeling him too intimately.

"Forgive me." She snatched her soapy hand away from

his and looked away, ashamed of her obvious enchantment with him.

Dante lifted his hand to her chin and gently brought her eyes to his. He spoke softly, quietly, touching her with his tender gaze. "Why are you sorry? For being curious about a man's body without the fear of him forcing himself upon you?" He took her small hand in his and laid it on his chest. "I would never hurt you that way." His words, the sound of his voice, and the steady beating of his heart against her palm touched her so profoundly she had to bite her lip to stop the rush of tears that threatened to overwhelm her.

He continued to shed her of the defenses that had taken her years to master as he moved her hand lightly over his chest, up to his strong neck, and then over his chin where he dipped his head and kissed her fingers.

"You are so big," she admitted breathlessly.

"*Oui.* But I shall use my strength to protect you from any danger, never to cause you pain."

She believed him. He had proved to her again and again that she could trust his temper. He allowed her to be defiant, rebellious, and saucy. He laughed with her and listened to her when she told him about her father. Oh, how could she tell him that it wasn't her flesh she worried about at his hands, but her heart? She couldn't tell him how happy he made her by asking her to stay, how happy he made her by asking her everything, not ordering, not demanding. His attention made her feel beautiful for the first time. His tenderness made her feel precious. And that was what she couldn't trust. He didn't mean any of it, and she wanted him to mean it. Suddenly, she wanted to weep for all the lost dreams of being treasured like fragile crystal by a man like Dante Risande, dreams that were torn from her heart until there was nothing left but numb submission and silent defiance.

"You must cease enchanting me, or I fear there shall be nothing left of me when you go away." She tried to laugh at herself, but the attempt was lost in a tight groan. "It turns out that I am the biggest fool of all."

She felt Dante's hand close around hers. He pulled her toward him and she went willingly, no longer surprised at the terrible yearning that burned deep in her heart. She hovered over him, suspended by the warm, unyielding rim of the basin and the heart-wrenching warmth of his gaze.

"I know what you're afraid of, Gianelle. I will not leave . . ."

"Non!" She pressed her finger to his lips. "Don't promise me such a thing."

Dante's jaw clenched, crushing words he wanted to say, but she was too delicate and too important to him to speak so casually. Needing her closer, he cupped his fingers around the nape of her neck and drew her mouth to his.

The sweet caress of his lips drew another sob from Gianelle's throat. She rested her palms on his hard, wet chest to keep herself from melting over him. But he made her feel it was all right to melt if she needed to. She longed to let go of the indifference she thought she needed to stay strong. She didn't want to be strong anymore. She wanted to feel the power in his arms and pretend that he would never leave her, that he couldn't live without her. Those arms closed around her now, reassuring her. In the nest of Dante's safe embrace, Gianelle felt the last of her defenses fall away. She clung to him while he dragged one kiss after another from her until she grew breathless.

He withdrew only a scant breath away from her mouth. "My sweet angel." The silk of his voice, the desperate demand of his mouth on hers, made Gianelle feel drunk with a strange desire of her own. He sat up in the water, pulling her into the bath with him until she was perched upon his steely thighs. "I won't hurt you." The truth of his whispered promise lit his eyes like diamonds under moonlight.

His gaze brushed over her throat and settled on the peaks of her nipples pressing toward him through her soaked gown. Her flesh tightened as if he had kissed the swollen buds with his mouth. The muscles below her navel quickened as he moved the pad of his thumb over the ripe tips of her breasts and lavished her face with slow, torturous kisses. Dante groaned into her mouth. His kisses grew hotter, more demanding. His tongue met hers in a sensual dance that drove her hands through his hair, pulling him even closer while his deft fingers moved over her flesh with ruthless mastery. Gianelle could do nothing but cling to him while his hands explored the perfect angles of her body.

Finally, with a ragged breath and hunger in his eyes that would have frightened Gianelle had he been any other man, Dante tore his mouth away from her and captured one luscious nipple between his lips. He sucked her right through the fabric of her gown. She arched her back, inviting him to take his pleasure. His palm fit perfectly over her rump, and he used it to move her against the rigid flesh raging for her beneath the water.

Dante was wild for her. The touch of her palms gliding over his bare arms, his chest, his face, drove him mad with desire. The way her body reacted to his kisses, his tongue, made him want to drive himself into her until they both grew too weary to move. He felt his control snapping, weakened by the fevered heat in Gianelle's eyes, the sound of her delicately feminine moans, the feel of her sexy bottom rubbing his erection. He slipped his hand beneath the hem of her dripping skirts and traced the sensitive curve behind her knee, then along her creamy thigh until he found the moist velvet hidden behind her undergarments. Gianelle's breath became a ragged whisper as his broad fingers tore away the barricade and began their tender yet thorough assault. He stroked the tiny jewel and captured her nipple between his teeth at the same time, making Gianelle cry out.

"What are you doing to me?" she groaned with pleasure that was almost agonizing, it felt so good.

"Nothing . . . yet." His rich baritone filled her ears and sent delicious quivers down her spine.

She clutched fistfuls of his hair and tried to bring her knees together, but Dante stroked and petted her until she purred not to stop. Never stop.

Cradled in his arms, against his chest, Dante gently probed and then caressed as her legs opened wider, allowing him entry into her delicate sheath. He laved his tongue over her lips, aching to do the same to the blossom in his fingers.

"I'm eager to discover how you taste."

Gianelle opened her eyes to find Dante staring at her, his gaze simmering with heat. He offered her a wicked, dimple-inducing smile that awakened a thousand butterflies inside her stomach. She smiled back at him. She could never have prepared herself for what happened next. She thought when a man took a woman to his bed it was for his pleasure alone. When Dante lifted her out of the water and set her rump on the edge of the tub, she thought he meant to do the same. But when he smoothed her skirts up past her thighs and coaxed her knees apart, her heart began to pound even more wildly. Dear God, he was so incredibly handsome and virile, she thought, gazing at him, with his long hair spreading over that great expanse of shoulders. Gianelle could scarcely believe how sexy a man could look on his knees. The delicious heat of his tongue along her inner thigh made her whisper his name in surprise and shock. But instead of stopping, he fit his hands neatly around her thighs to still her when she tried to squirm away. He placed a downy kiss directly on her and she clenched her teeth, aroused beyond endurance. His lips teased and his teeth nibbled. He spread his tongue and laved it over the scalding bud beneath her patch of golden curls, tasting her, branding her. Unable to bear his wicked ministrations, Gianelle held on to the edge of the tub, her grip tightening with each salacious lick of his tongue.

His appetite was insatiable, and he feasted on her until she tossed her head back and panted between convulsing tremors of pure ecstasy that made her groan and wrap her legs around his shoulders. And still Dante drank from her. When there was nothing left, he rose out of the water dripping wet and hard as steel, and kissed a fiery path up her body, to her neck.

"You are even sweeter than honey." His voice was a raw growl as he hovered over her. "Just as I always suspected."

Gianelle stared into his eyes and tried to slow her gasping breath. Before she could thank him for what he had done, he fitted his arms under her and carried her to the settee before the hearth fire.

He put her down for a moment to find his black trousers and Gianelle couldn't take her eyes off him. He stalked around the room naked, wet, and bigger than she ever thought possible. A rush of scarlet flamed her cheeks, and then the flame burned somewhere else, causing her to squeeze her knees together. She was somewhat mortified to find that looking at his naked body made her want to climb all over him. Mayhap, even taste him the way he had tasted her. He was not a man, he was—he was a sculpted statue of a Greek god she had seen once in a painting. Zeus, Hercules—it mattered not who. She watched in quiet fascination while he dried himself off. The small cloth traversed each sinewy angle that sculpted him.

"You have a mischievous look in your eyes, *fée.*" Dante smiled at her while he pulled his trousers over his legs. "Should I be worried?"

Gianelle shook her head. "I want to . . ." Her eyes followed his every move as he plucked a tunic from his wardrobe and stalked toward her. When he stood over her, she finally looked away.

"You want to what?" He lifted a curious eyebrow at her, his elusive dimple as frivolous as ever.

"I want to . . . you know . . ." Gianelle's suddenly timid gaze found his. "With you."

"Make love?"

Her breath exploded into a sigh. "Well, I never called it that before."

"But that's what it will be between us." He did his best not to smile at her loss of composure.

"When?"

Here she was, all flushed and breathless and ready for him, even asking him for it. Dante groaned as his need for her, still unsatisfied, knotted into a ball and almost doubled him over. He fought himself not to lunge at her. She was inexperienced, probably more afraid of the act than she was of escaping in the dead of night on a rope. He thought of Edgar Dermott touching her and anger coiled his muscles, curling his fingers into fists. Was it he who had made her afraid of what should have been wonderful? He was certain the release he brought her with his mouth was the first time she had ever experienced such sexual pleasure.

"I'm going to teach you how to enjoy a man's body first." Dante's silky promise made her belly spasm. "My body. Stand up."

Gianelle obeyed, but squeezed her eyes shut when he began to lift her soaking gown over her head. "Do you want me to close my eyes too?" he asked her, careful to keep the sudden rush of emotion he felt for her out of his voice. She nodded her head and he smiled, his heart melting within his ribs.

"Put this on. It's dry."

Gianelle opened her eyes and took the tunic he offered her. When she saw that his eyes were closed, she wanted to kiss him. Quickly, she changed out of her wet clothes and into his big, warm tunic.

"Done."

Merde! She couldn't have looked more tempting if she was completely naked. His tunic hung past her knees; the sleeves dangled over the tips of her fingers and she yanked them up, looking away from the heat in his gaze. Knowing she was naked beneath that thin muslin made him want to drag the hem over her thighs and have his way with her right there on the settee. Dante clenched his jaw to quench the fire she sparked in him. He had to go slowly, control his raging desire. He wanted to show her that sex was something she could grow to love. And he couldn't show her if he leaped on her and cleaved her in half. And if the excruciating, straining ache beneath his trousers was any indication, cleave her in half he would.

When he slowed his pulse back to some semblance of normalcy, he touched her. He reclined on the settee, bringing her with him to rest atop his body. He wanted her this way to help her feel like she was in more control. He circled her waist with one arm and tucked her honeyed hair behind her ear with his free hand.

Instantly, Gianelle was bombarded with the awareness of every hard muscle beneath her. She looked down into his magnificent face and swallowed audibly.

"That does not pain you?" she asked him, a little embarrassed to be speaking so casually about his manhood stiff against her belly.

A beguiling smile curled his lips. "Immensely."

She bit her lower lip and thought about it. "I thought when that happened, a man needed to be satisfied."

"I'm satisfied to have you in my arms."

She kissed him then. She had to. She kissed his hungry mouth, his chin, working her way with tiny nibbling sighs to his corded neck. Curiously, she bent her mouth to his chest and licked a droplet of water off his nipple. She felt his body tighten beneath her; the crisp dark hair dusting his flesh tickled her nose. She wondered how much of him she could explore before his control deserted him. She spread her palms over the rolling planes of his chest and allowed herself the pleasure of touching him. Emboldened by the sweet caress of his hands sweeping down her back, she wiggled her hips. He groaned and spread her legs with his large palms so that she straddled him fully.

"Oh, my," Gianelle practically panted. "You feel very nice . . . there."

Beneath her, Dante smiled and clenched his teeth at her intoxicating heat that gloved his throbbing flesh. "I'm pleased you like it."

"Ummm, I do. I've never done this before. Your size seems"—she closed her eyes and smiled, rubbing herself against him—"perfect."

Dante almost exploded. He slipped his hands beneath her tunic and clutched the sinfully tempting mounds of her bare buttocks. He knew she was close to release. He knew he was as well. He cursed between his teeth and pressed her hard and slowly down the entire length of his erection, then back up again. Gianelle's eyes opened wider at the fullness of him an instant before she shuddered with a great raptured spasm that made her cry out so loud Dante had to cover her mouth with his to keep Balin and Talard from kicking the door in and rushing to her rescue.

Chapter Thirteen

MANY HOURS LATER, Gianelle opened her eyes. She didn't move, feeling the warmth and power of the body beneath hers. She basked in the luxury of Dante's arms, the strange feeling of belonging there. She listened to the breath that left his body, then filled it again, felt his chest expand and contract beneath her cheek. She would never move again.

"Dante?"

He stirred and opened his eyes. The caress of her hair as it fell over his face brought memories of what they had shared earlier rushing back to him. He lifted his hands to her head and tunneled his fingers through her thick tresses up to her scalp. Then he moved under her. He could have been stretching, Gianelle told herself as she caught a languid groan before it escaped her parted lips. But the gentle shift of his body was so provocative it made her ache for him again.

"The fire is dying out." She smiled at him and he bent his head to kiss her.

"Are you cold, *fée*?"

She nodded and he closed his arms around her, then

rose from the settee, bringing her with him. He carried her to his bed and laid her down on the furs. He went to the hearth and poked at the embers until they sparked to life again. He tossed more wood into the fire and turned back to her. She looked so beautiful in his bed, shrouded in the rosy candescence of firelight, that the sight of her nearly halted his heartbeat. Her hair flowed around her like a golden veil; her eyes were wide and luminously lit with a fire he knew he had ignited in her. He didn't feel victorious, but infinitely grateful. He moved toward her, toward his bed that had become a reminder to him of how alone he was. "Are you hungry, lovely?"

"*Oui,* my belly is rumbling."

Dante was tempted to tell her that her belly was always rumbling, even after she filled it with food. He laughed instead, delighted with her and her ravenous appetite. He crossed the room and picked up the tray of fruit and strips of mutton that Talard had brought him earlier. "Don't eat the meat. It's been sitting too long." He sat next to her on the bed and lifted a blackberry to her lips. "Taste this."

Her lips brushed his fingers. He leaned his body closer to her, drawn by the sight of her tongue when she accepted his offering.

"Umm, sweet," she murmured as his scent covered her.

"Now try this one." He closed his lips around a ripe grape and crooked his index finger at her. Gianelle smiled and bent her mouth to his. She tugged on the succulent fruit with her teeth, but Dante's lips molded to hers, kissing her with a need that could only be met by her passionate response.

They fed each other in much the same manner until the fruit was gone, kissing and laughing when Gianelle tossed a grape in the air to show him she could catch it in her mouth. Her aim was poor and the grape hit Dante in the eye.

She traced her fingers over the dozen scars that marked his back and side and asked him how he'd received each one. He touched her intimately in places she never thought could feel so profound: along the slightly curved arch of her nose, in the tender hollow at her throat. He ran his finger inside the sensitive curve of her elbow and behind her knee with such tenderness that her flesh quivered. His lips explored her earlobes, her chin, the satiny softness of her flesh just above her breasts. He wanted to make love to her, and he told her the ways he wanted to do it.

Every salacious word that poured from his mouth produced another titillating tremor in Gianelle's loins. She pulled him down on top of her, astonished at her own boldness, but not caring.

"You can't keep your hands off me, can you, woman?" His voice was husky with sexual longing, his arrogant smile adding a depth of heat to his already smoldering eyes.

She laughed and he kissed her, delving deep into the sumptuous sweetness of her mouth. He tangled his hands in her hair and drew her head back, exposing her throat to his hunger. He nibbled her flesh with excruciating leisure while his hand slipped beneath her tunic and then up along her outer thigh. Caressing her bare bottom, he pressed his substantial arousal, straining against his trousers, to the hot nook between her legs.

A knock at the door lifted Dante's mouth from her neck. "What!"

"My lord, is Gianelle with you?" Talard was on the other side.

"*Oui,* go away." Dante went back to kissing her.

Silence, and then, "Forgive me, but Casey is beside herself with worry. She seems to think that her friend has run away."

Gianelle pushed Dante off her and sat up. "I would never leave without her," she said to the door. "She knows that."

Dante gave his body a few moments to relax, then left the bed and strode to the door. He swung it open, offered Talard a quick glare, and then slid his gaze to Casey, hiding behind his vassal's shoulder. Christ, even if she didn't resemble his sister, she would have melted his heart standing there looking so afraid of him. "Thank you, Talard." The vassal nodded and turned to leave with Casey hot on his heels. "Casey."

She froze in mid-step, then turned around and smiled meekly. "I'm sorry for . . ."

"Come in here." He moved aside, offering her a path into his chambers.

She skittered past him and looked around. When she saw Gianelle lacing her gown, she paled. "Oh. I truly am sorry, then."

Dante walked around her and sat down on the bed. He offered Casey a seat on the settee by the window and winked at Gianelle as she hurried to finish dressing.

"Casey, no one is leaving Graycliff."

"They're not?" Her huge blue eyes cut to Gianelle.

"Not unless they want to," Dante answered. "But it would break my heart if you and Gianelle left."

"That is very kind of you to say, my lord. But . . ." She eyed Gianelle and the wrinkled gown she squeezed into.

"You won't grow tired of her, will you? And if you do, will you still want us here?"

"Casey." Gianelle closed her eyes and sank to the bed. She didn't need to look at Dante to know that he must be furious. Surprisingly, though, when he spoke his tone was quite mild.

"Casey, who told you that I would grow tired of Gianelle?" Dante remembered Balin accusing him of that very thing with the women who slept with him, but surely Balin would never tell Casey the like.

"I told her," Gianelle said faintly. She also remembered Balin's words and didn't want Dante to suspect his friend.

"I see." Dante rose from the bed and took Casey by the hand. "I will always want you and Gianelle here. No matter what happens between us." He kissed Casey's hand and led her to the door. "Gianelle will be down shortly."

Dante shut the door and leaned against it. He looked at Gianelle sitting at the edge of his bed. He folded his arms across his chest. "I don't want to know where you got the notion that I would grow tired of you. But I'm asking you now if you believe it."

"Have you been with many women, Dante?" she asked him.

He closed his eyes and cursed in French. Pushing himself off the door, he stalked to the settee and fell into it. "*Oui,* Gianelle, I have."

"And where are they all now?"

"I don't know," he admitted honestly.

"How do I know that I won't be one of them?"

He shook his head and, without looking at her, said, "I don't know that, either."

He rubbed his hands down his face, but didn't stop her when she left his bed and walked out of his room.

～

Dante dined in the great hall that night with Balin, Casey, Simone, Lady Dara and her husband, and some others. There was no dais in Graycliff, assuring that the lord sat with anyone who shared the bounty of his larder. Brand Risande had designed the hall in that manner when he was lord here, and Dante saw no reason to change it when the castle was given to him. Still, one only had to glance at him to know he was lord here. His formidable stature proclaimed him the mightiest among his men, the way his gaze swept over every table revealed his careful vigilancc for any sign of dangcr if a passing bard or juggling troupe entertained here. Normally, his laughter rang out deep and true, softening the angles of his rugged features. But tonight the Lord of Graycliff barely heard the conversations going on around him. He smiled when one of his men elbowed him, following a good round of laughter. He greeted those who touched his shoulder in passing, but his thoughts were once again preoccupied with Gianelle. She hadn't yet arrived for supper, and he found himself eyeing the entrance between every sip from his cup.

She was angry with him, or hurt. Either one, he understood. He *was* a rogue. But each time he heard her voice calling him such in his mind, it made him grind his teeth and brood more fiercely. Did she expect him to lie when she had asked him if she would become like the rest? How was he to know the true answer? He had never given his heart to one woman; fancying them all had served him well in the past. But he knew Gianelle needed more than a lover. He'd known it since she told him about her father. He tried to let her go, but his own base desire got in the way. Her beautiful smile and glorious tawny eyes got in the way. Her hair, the feminine sway of her hips, her small hands and coral lips, her temper brewing just beneath the surface of her timid obedience—Christ, they all got in the way. But he didn't want to hurt her. He knew he cared about her more than any woman in his past, but was that enough?

He studied Simone sitting across the table and wondered if he'd hurt her when he turned his attention to Fiona, the daughter of Kennit of Derry. After that came Patrice, sister of his friend Geoffrey the Swift, and then Bridget, Anne, and Aubrey. He was a rogue, and Gianelle was right to be angry with him. But there hadn't been anyone since Katherine's death the past winter. No one had been able to pierce the fire of revenge that drove him. No one but Gianelle.

He looked up and saw her stepping through the entrance. He almost smiled at her fragile beauty that never ceased to mystify him. She was so delicately formed, as though faeries had spun her together with gossamer gilt thread. Her long hair was swept up to bare the graceful curve of her neck. She wore a gown of pale yellow linen with tapered sleeves that tempted Dante to recall the alluring curve of her slender arm. The neckline was trimmed in dark blue lace, and a matching cord dipped over the slight swell of her hips, accentuating her narrow waist that fit so perfectly in his hands.

She looked around the hall and their eyes met. Dante counted breaths waiting to see if she smiled at him or turned away. She did neither, but waved to Dara, who called her over.

When she reached the table, Dante stood up, prompting the men around him to stand as well. There were empty seats to Dante's right, beyond Balin and Casey. When Gianelle passed him to go there, he closed his fingers around her wrist. "Sit with me, please."

To his surprise, she nodded. He asked Balin and Casey to move down, and then beckoned to one of the servers to bring her a trencher and some wine.

"We thought you weren't going to join us." Balin offered her a carefully concealed smirk beneath his whiskers. "I was afraid Dante's eyes would remain permanently fixated on the doors, even after supper ended."

Dara smiled and subtly nodded when she caught Gianelle's eye.

"Balin." A slow, murderous grin danced across Dante's features as he turned to his captain. "Gianelle doesn't want to hear how I was pining for her, do you, *fée?*"

It was clever of him to make a jest at his own expense rather than smash his cup over Balin's head as the lethal glint in his eyes suggested. But Gianelle was not about to let him off so easily. "*Oui,* I would." She tossed him a purely innocent smile and blinked her huge eyes at him.

"Very well," he drawled lazily. "I have been spending the evening cursing my ill fortune at having to listen to Balin's half-witted droning. I was, most eagerly, awaiting a woman to sit beside me with the wits to challenge me and my ego." He leaned back in his chair and flashed her a grin, lifting his goblet to his lips.

"Gia." Balin laughed and scooped an oyster into his mouth. "There is no winning with him."

"That is true," she said. "And winning all the time can leave you with empty victories."

Simone patted her mouth while she yawned, swept her inky hair off her shoulder, and rose from her seat. "My lord," she said to Dante before she left. "You look hungry, yet you haven't touched your food. It doesn't surprise me, though." Her dark eyes slid to Gianelle. "Your appetite craves something with a bit more flavor."

"Simone." Dante's voice was an octave above a growl, but the raw demand it carried halted Simone's exit. "Certain spices leave me with a bitter taste on my tongue."

Dara giggled as Simone stormed off. "It's a wonder she doesn't clear the table and offer herself up to you on a trencher."

Gianelle looked up at Dante. "She still cares for you?"

"Simone cares for no one but who can best serve her," Dara said. "She would love to have the lord of this castle under her thumb."

"She certainly is beautiful," Casey remarked.

Balin took a swig of his ale and swiped his hand across his mouth. "You are more beautiful than she."

Gianelle and Dara exchanged smiles while Talard appeared at Dante's side. "Conrad Lowell, emissary to Lord Edgar Dermott, has just arrived and seeks an audience with you."

"Bring him to the solar and wait with him there, Talard," Dante said. He turned to Gianelle and leaned in close to her. "I'll return in a moment." His lips brushed her nape in a beguiling caress before he rose to his feet.

Balin followed him out of the great hall. "What do you suppose he wants?"

"I'll ask him," Dante promised, and made good when he pushed open the door to his solar a few moments later. He looked at the two men surveying the cozy room.

"Who's Lowell?"

A tall, lanky man, pale in complexion, a stark contrast to his dark hair, raised his palm. He looked sallow and pasty, with a sharp nose and pinched lips. "What do you want?" Dante asked him coolly.

"I've come to deliver a missive to you." Lowell reached his hand beneath his mantle and pulled out a folded parchment with the king's stamp. The seal was broken, and the message was addressed to Edgar Dermott.

Dante looked at it, and then at Lowell. So this was the brother of Trevor the Black, the man Gianelle and Casey had recognized when they were ambushed in the woods. Dante was certain the order to attack him that night had come from Edgar Dermott. There was a way to find out for certain. "Your eyes burn with hatred. Is it because of your brother's death?"

The emissary blinked. "I didn't know it was you who killed him," he said through clenched teeth.

Dante snatched the missive from his hand. "Then you have already found his body?" He turned to Balin as he unfolded the letter. "What has it been, Balin? A se'nnight?" He offered Lowell a challenging smile. "How did you know where to look? You must have had men combing every inch of the woods, and you must have known he was missing even though he didn't visit Devonshire often, *oui*?"

Without waiting for the emissary to answer, Dante switched his attention to the missive. It was written in William's hand.

Dermott,

    While I am certain the Earl of Kent had every good reason, and used fine judgment in leaving your brother's murder unresolved until I return to England, I am taking the matter you brought to my attention regarding your servant, Gianelle Dejiat, into careful consideration.

    Even though you have sworn to your king to having witnessed the woman entering your brother's bedchamber, cup in hand, I must confess I find it odd that Lord Risande would remove her from your service without punishment if he suspected her of committing the deed.

Dante looked up from the missive to set his glare on Lowell. "Lies. Dermott never saw her enter his brother's bedchamber."

Lowell said nothing, but dipped his eyes back to the note, waiting for Dante to continue.

    Still, I will grant your request and order that she be returned to you to await my arrival. But this I charge to you, vassal of the Sovereign, that no harm come to her while in your care. And if Lord Risande has taken her as his wife, you shall not claim her.

    As for the other accusation you made against her, I trust Lord Risande entirely to find out if she . . .

Dante's expression darkened with rage as he read Dermott's last accusation. He handed the missive to Balin, and in a single stride, clamped one hand around Lowell's throat and yanked the man's own sword from his scabbard with the other. Before Lowell's companion had time to comprehend what had just taken place, the sword was pointed at his throat.

"He lies! Do you hear me?" Dante raged at Lowell. "Tell that bastard you serve to come here if he wants her and get her himself, and I will cut his lying tongue from his mouth." He tossed the emissary in Balin's direction, then did the same with Lowell's sword. "Show them the way out."

He stormed out of the solar, but he did not return to the great hall.

Chapter Fourteen

2

GIANELLE'S FEARS HAD COME TO FRUITION. Dante did everything he could to avoid her in the following week. He ate alone in his chambers. He either locked himself away in his solar during the day, or he left and didn't return to Graycliff until nightfall. She watched him from the battlements on some nights as he rode his snowy white mare across the narrow ledges, beneath a sky frosted in pewter, racing toward the sea with the salty air whipping through his hair and snapping against his sleeves. So wild and untamed did he look that Gianelle imagined him part of the landscape.

She tried to tell herself that she didn't care if Dante ever returned. But she waited for him night after night, missing his cocky smile, his eyes ever on her, and his voice speaking her name.

He abandoned her, and it made her angry at first, and then as the days wore on, it broke her heart. The feeling was all too familiar, had taken her years to lock away. She told herself that it was her own fault. She was a fool to expect anything more from him than what he was doing to her. She knew he cared for no one, and still she had fallen weak into his arms. She wouldn't weep over him, though. She held on to that vow if nothing else. But at times, when she watched his dark form racing away, she wished she were with him on his horse made of mist.

On the sixth night, Dante finally returned to her.

She was sitting with Casey and Dara in the great hall, pretending interest in a conversation about sewing, when he appeared in the doorway. He looked dangerously handsome with his mane of dark hair thick and wind-blown, and days of shadow covering his jaw. He cut a direct path to Gianelle without stopping to greet anyone. When he reached her, the fragrance of wind and sea covered her.

"We need to speak."

"You'd best go," Dara urged her while Dante strode back toward the entrance. "I've rarely seen him this way."

Gianelle wanted to defy him, but when he turned to look at her upon reaching the doorway, she snapped to her feet and followed him.

He led her to his chambers, where he opened the door and allowed her entry first.

"Edgar Dermott wants you back," he said and slammed the door shut behind him.

Gianelle spun around, gaping at him. "What? Why?"

"Because he has a death wish." Dante crossed the room and threw himself on the settee. He kicked his boots off and tossed his leg over the side. He looked like a brooding prince on his throne. "My guess is that he misses you in his bed."

Gianelle walked right up to him and slapped him hard across the face. "How dare you say that to me?" There was no scorching venom in her tone; there was no anger, just disgust. "I told you I was never willing."

Dante rolled his jaw around a few times before he spoke again. "And I'm to believe he sent a request to the king for your return because he enjoyed your cold responses?"

"Why not? You do," she shot back at him. Her lower lip began to tremble. She couldn't believe how cruelly he was treating her. She choked back a sob and glared at him. "Just send me back then."

"Never. But I want the truth from you."

"You deserve nothing from me." She whirled on her heel. She heard him leap to his feet behind her and she ran for the door. He reached it before she did and lifted his arm over her head to smash the door closed when she opened it.

"I thought Dermott was going to kill you," Dante spoke into her hair. "That's why I took you from him. He sent his men to attack us, and I couldn't understand how he could want to harm you. I thought it was because I shamed his brother for you. But he cares for you, doesn't he, Gianelle? He knows you and the things you do when you're angry. That's why he believes you murdered his brother."

"He doesn't know me. I was just something he wanted." She pressed her forehead against the door and shut her eyes. "You know me."

Dante buried his face in the honey folds of her hair and inhaled her. "Does he love you?"

"If love is trying to force his will on me, if it means causing me pain, or if it's selfish and controlling, and demanding, then *oui*, he does. But I don't know for certain,

Dante. I don't know what love feels like, save for what I feel for Casey." *And you,* she wanted to scream at him. *And you before you left me.*

"Do you think I loved him in return?" she asked him. "Is that why you stayed away?"

Dante turned her around to face him. No matter what he thought anymore, he had to look at her. He missed her face.

"I tried to escape, Dante. Have you forgotten that?"

"Non," he said quietly.

"Then why do you care if he loved me? I don't understand."

"Because he told the king that you and his brother were followers of Hereward the Wake. I can only believe that Edgar Dermott would place you in that much peril if passion drove him. He has no proof, only suspicion that you killed his brother. He would not go to these lengths to see you punished over a suspicion. He is scorned."

Gianelle stared up into his eyes, disbelief and horror widening her gaze. "So if I told you that Edgar didn't love me, or that he was indifferent toward me, you would have believed that I am one of those you hate?"

"Gianelle, Hereward has been able to infiltrate William's own army with spies no one would ever suspect."

She lowered her gaze, and tears spilled down her cheeks like liquid crystals. "I thought you knew me. I was wrong."

Dante turned away from her and raked his hand through his hair. He knew he deserved every ounce of disgust and loathing she felt for him, but still, it drove him mad. "I'm sorry I doubted you, but I can never take a chance when it comes to these people."

"I understand."

"You don't." He went to the window and looked out. "You don't know how I fought this. I refused to believe it. Every instinct I have told me Dermott lied. But I don't live by instincts, Gianelle. I trust logic, and I realized that an emotion like love or jealousy had to be behind this for Dermott. I had to know for certain, and at the same time the thought of him loving you made me angry."

"You couldn't simply ask me instead of leaving?"

"There were other things on my mind as well. Things I needed to figure out."

"Well, I hope you did." She wiped the tears that kept coming no matter how hard she tried to stop them.

"I did." Dante walked back to her, his arms at his sides, his despairing gaze fixed on her face. "I decided that I wasn't sending you back to him even if you were involved with Hereward. And I knew once I questioned you, you would never agree to this."

"To what?"

"The king has ordered you to be returned to Dermott. The only way to keep you here with me is to make you my wife."

Gianelle didn't say anything at first. She tipped her head back to meet his gaze and swiped her eyes. "And you are willing to do this?"

"*Oui,*" he replied without hesitation.

"That had to be a very difficult decision to make."

"None of it was as difficult as standing here right now and not holding you, Gianelle." He raised his fingers to her mouth and smoothed his thumb along her lower lip. "I've been insane over you, without you. I will never be cruel to you again. On my life I swear it to you. Be my wife."

She shook her head and took a step away from him when he tried to grasp her hand. "Dante, I cannot marry you because you want to protect me from Edgar Dermott. I cannot marry you for any reason."

"Why?" His voice was a harsh whisper. He moved toward her, and this time he captured her face in his big hands and stared deeply into her eyes. "Tell me why you can't."

"Because I think I have fallen in love with you, Dante. And it's frightening. I am helpless against my own emotions, held prisoner by a man who needs no locks or shackles to keep me, just his smile"—her eyes shimmered in the firelight while she pressed her fingertips to his lips—"his kiss, his kind words. I'm a prisoner to this land that is also you. For I love it here, and even if I have to suffer your cold indifference, I never want to leave. You feel the same way about love, Dante. You will not be bound by it. It ties you up, and you have tied yourself to no one." She bit her lower lip and turned away from him. "I think the only thing worse than love is loving alone," she said quietly and stepped out of the room.

The moment the door closed behind her, Gianelle felt the well of tears, like a rushing spring, rising up within her. She covered her mouth and squeezed her eyes shut, but the well finally erupted. She ran to her room cursing every bard's inability to describe this kind of pain.

⌒

Gianelle woke the next day to find that Dante had gone to Lord Richard Dumont's keep. He didn't return to Graycliff that night or the day after that. She refused to think about him. That decision was not born of pride, or denial of her feelings, but a need to keep her eyes from swelling shut. She couldn't understand it, really. For years she had been able to control her tears, but now nothing could stop them. There did seem to be one consolation to her unconstrained emotions, though, and it was the most peculiar thing of all. It felt good. As good as giving her anger a voice. Good like a fit of hearty laughter. It was as if releasing her feelings, whatever they were, had some magical effect on her, because even though she was miserable she felt freer than she could have ever imagined.

She realized last night during a bout of unabashed sobbing, followed by an hour-long spasm of hiccups, that she might not be able to control her emotions at present, but she was free to express them. This morning she decided she wouldn't even mind being enslaved to Dante's smiles and heated kisses if he loved her. She had been wrong to tell him that love tied people down. Even though it hurt, look what it was doing for her. She blinked her burning eyes, rubbed her raw nose, and hiccupped.

She met Balin and Casey on her way upstairs after breakfast. They were heading for the sea and invited her to come along. Casey hugged her and begged her to change her mind when Gianelle declined.

"Come and take your mind off things," Casey pleaded. Her own eyes didn't look any better than Gianelle's after staying awake for the last two nights weeping with her.

"*Non,* I must speak to Douglan. I am fine, Casey. I swear it." She smiled to prove that she was, and Casey finally relented and left with her captain.

Gianelle found Dante's steward rummaging through a

stack of parchments in the solar. She cleared her throat and he peered at her over his shoulder.

"Douglan, you know how to write, *oui*?"

"What on earth happened to you?" He hurried toward her and pressed his palm to her cheek. "Are you ill? You look dreadful."

"I'm not ill. I just need you to write something for me." She walked around him and settled into a comfortable chair. "I would like to send a missive to King William." She folded her hands in her lap, ready to begin.

Douglan stared, stunned. And then he laughed and went back to his parchments.

"It is most urgent." Gianelle sniffed and tears welled up over the rims of her eyes.

Yielding to the pleading look she gave him, the steward sighed, then nodded and picked up his quill. "Of course, I will have to show this to Lord Risande before it is sent."

"There is no time, Douglan. You will understand once you begin.

"Dear Your Majesty . . ."

Douglan looked up and smiled at her. "'Sire,' or just 'Your Majesty' will do."

Gianelle nodded and continued. "My name is Gianelle Dejiat, but Douglan is quilling this correspondence for me since I don't know how to write. I was a servant to Baron Bryce Dermott of Cambridge before Dante rescued me . . ."

"Lord Risande," Douglan corrected without looking up this time.

"*Oui,* Lord Risande." Gianelle sniffed and swiped the back of her hand across her nose before continuing. "He is the reason for my . . . Douglan's writing. Lord Risande is a very stubborn man, and quite determined to have his way in whatever he sets out to do. I don't mean to say that he is anything like my former master. He is even-tempered and fair, kind and"—she dabbed the corners of her eyes with her knuckles—"tender. Save for a few nights ago, but that was because Edgar Dermott told you I was a follower of Hereward the Wake."

Douglan dropped his quill. Gianelle glanced at the fallen plume, waited for him to retrieve it, then went on.

"But Dante figured it all out. You see, King, Edgar Dermott thinks he is in love with me. I say 'thinks' because now that I know what love is about, I understand Dermott only wanted to possess and control me. And herein lies our dilemma.

"Dante told me that he will never return me to Devonshire, and as I said, he is a man who will have his way. He even asked me to become his wife to avoid sending me . . . Douglan, you are not writing."

The steward gaped at her, openmouthed. When she pointed her chin to the parchment, he snapped his lips closed and went back to writing.

"Of course, I refused, which was most difficult because I believe if Dante loved me, he would be a wonderful husband." She paused while Douglan handed her a handkerchief. "Your Majesty, I don't think Dante will send me back, and I worry that you will be angry with him, since you ordered him to do it. You simply don't know the powers of persuasion this man possesses. He is clever and so very disarming. I know he would not deliberately defy you, for he speaks of you with the love a son has for his father. He only wants to protect me from Edgar

Dermott. He will not concede, of that I am sure. He even won my heart, and though I know you have probably heard that from many women regarding him, let me assure you, my affection was hard to surrender to him. Please show him mercy when the time comes.

"And if you are persuaded to allow me to remain here, I ask you to consider sending Edgar to his brother's estates in Ely. They often enjoyed visiting there, so I don't think Edgar would protest overly much. Otherwise, I fear he will send more men to try to kill Dante.

"If I might beg your ear for one more moment, I would have you know that I am not one of Hereward the Wake's followers. I would never follow a man who refuses to face his enemy, but prefers instead to hide and let others do it for him."

Gianelle stood up and handed Douglan back his handkerchief. "You will fix it for me, won't you? I'm afraid I'm not as eloquently spoken as you or Dante."

"It's perfect," Douglan answered with a whole new respect for her.

She graced the steward with a grateful smile and left the solar.

Chapter Fifteen

DANTE RESTED HIS ARMS across the wooden fence and gazed at the trees in the distance. All around him summer flaunted its splendor. Birds chirped within the canopy of an old oak tree, flowers blossomed along the edge of the fence, a cloud drifted lazily across the vast sky. But the colors that should have burst forth seemed gray and dull to Dante's eyes. Even Tess, the woman who had thrown him a kiss the last time he was here, had lost her beauty. The spark of her eyes, the deliberate sway of her hips, went unnoticed by him. Only when he thought of Gianelle did the spectacular colors of sunset blaze to life.

Enfer, what was he doing away from her?

He wanted time to consider what she had said to him. And she was right. Love does bind you to another person. It does indeed tie you to them, and he may not have wanted that with anyone else, but he wanted it with Gianelle. He lived his life with a world of women at his fingertips. But the world lost its appeal without her in it. He had tried to win her to his bed, and in the process he fell in love with her. It seemed so simple, yet he had tried to deny it. The thought of her returning to Dermott, the thought of any man besides him loving her, drove him mad.

Christ, he loved her, and it felt wonderful.

"Dante." Lord Dumont appeared at his side, interrupting his thoughts. "This is the first time I've seen you smile in days."

"I'm a fool." Dante laughed and shook his head at himself. "But love does that to a man, *non,* Richard?"

"Love?" The older man quirked his eyebrow at Dante. "You?"

"*Oui,* I know. And it consumes me. She consumes me. I've tried to deny it because I'm a fool, but I don't want to live without her."

Richard scowled. "William is to blame for this. He raised you and Brand, and you are both as stubborn as he is."

"I'm going home, *mon frère.*" Dante patted Richard's shoulders, opened the gate, and whistled for Ayla.

"Go, go," Richard called out as Dante vaulted to the mare's back. "Make her your wife and have a dozen babes."

The ground trembled beneath Ayla's hooves as she thundered toward Dover. When she reached the rocky slopes, she soared over them, her glorious mane billowing against Dante's hands. She already knew every path, every dip and hollow that would bring her and her rider home.

The portcullis rolled upward at their approach, but Ayla never slowed, nor did Dante want her to. He bent his body low over the long column of her neck and flew beneath the gate's huge wrought-iron teeth. Finally the mare slowed. She rose up, fluid and beautiful, on her hind legs and pawed the air.

"*Oui*." Dante scratched her neck. "I'm happy to be home as well." He leaped from her back and headed straight for the doors.

Gianelle had gone to her window when she heard the portcullis being raised. She watched Dante's return with her hands clutched to her chest. The moment he separated from Ayla's back, she took off out of the room. She didn't know why he had gone to Lord Dumont's, and she prayed it wasn't to see the bold serving wench. Something deep in her heart told her it wasn't. He had to care a little for her if he was willing to marry her. It didn't matter. He was back, more brutally handsome than when he left.

She reached the top of the stairs as he came racing up them.

He slowed at the sight of her, his gaze a profound caress she felt all the way to her bones.

"Forgive me for being a fool."

"Have you been a fool?" She smiled delicately, breathlessly. "I hadn't even noticed."

He took the last three steps in a single leap and swept her weightless into his arms. Gianelle opened her mouth to the desperate demand of his kiss, clutching his shirt in both hands.

His mouth fell to her throat as he lifted her off her feet and carried her to his room. Kicking open the door, he brought her to his bed, and bending over her, laid her down on the soft furs.

"You have stolen into my heart and made me want to be a better kind of man, and yet when I look at you, I feel like a savage. You think I am afraid to love you, *ma fée*?" He kissed her eyelids so tenderly Gianelle began to weep again. "I would give my life for you." He raised his knee to the bed and tilted his head to capture her mouth with his. He withdrew slowly, caressing her face in his hands. "Do you think I am able to deny falling in love when the air I breathe is snatched from my lungs by a mere smile from you cast my way? *Non,* my heart cannot deny that." His lips molded to hers, caressing her. "How easy is it to love one who touches you and makes you feel like you have been born anew? Who awakens every nerve and ravishes the soul with the rose of her lips? Look at me, my only love, and see how you hold my heart in your hands, see how much I love you when you look into my eyes."

If the shutters had burst open and she could have flown out the window and soared toward the heavens on wings given her by God, Gianelle knew she would stay right here with him forever.

"I want you to be my wife. I want to be the father of your children. I will never leave you, Gianelle." His eyes gleamed with the passion that burned his blood.

"And you will have your way." She took his full, lower lip between her teeth and traced her tongue over it.

"*Oui,*" he groaned with pure pleasure. "I will." His eyes darkened with emotion and moved over her like a searing flame while even darker intentions moved through his thoughts.

For a brief instant, Gianelle worried that this hungry wolf might be too wild, and would ravage her completely. Dante's body was large and strong, but there was no darkness in his eyes, only sweet, beautiful light and curious fascination. His fingers were long and calloused from wielding his sword, yet tender when he smoothed a stray lock of hair away from her cheek.

She closed her eyes at the sound of the wolf's whispers,

quivered at the longings he told her plagued his heart. Each softly spoken word was a caress to her soul as he revealed his own fear of losing control and taking her too roughly.

Oui, this man was different. He was afraid of his power, aware that she was weaker than he. And for Gianelle, his knowledge made him that much stronger. But there was something else. Something he had taught her in his bath, and stretched out over his long body on the settee. She had power with this magnificent warrior. Always defenseless against men, powerless by her station as a slave, she'd had no idea what it meant to be able to bring a man such as Dante Risande to such a vulnerable place. She had the power to make his body ache. Power to make him lose control, to make him afraid of his own desire. He made her feel like a woman, not only when they were intimate, but every time he laid his eyes on her. The thought made her stretch under him like a cat and close her eyes so languidly he groaned and tore her gown from her body as though it were nothing more than old parchment.

She lay bare beneath him, defenseless. But he didn't devour her. He simply stared at the pure glory he had revealed.

"God's mercy, *ma fée,* your beauty wrenches at my heart."

She sat up slowly, using her palms to push him up so that he was kneeling over her. She pressed her cheek against his chest while he loosened her braid and lifted her long tresses to his nose. She could hear him inhaling her, feel him filling himself with the scent of her. Her fingers worked delicately, patiently to untie the laces of his shirt. Above her, Dante inhaled sharply again and his hard chest expanded beneath her lips. She ran her palms over his defined contours.

Impatient to be out of the garments that confined him, Dante lifted his shirt over his head with one great stretch that made Gianelle tremble at the sight of his massive arms over his head. She kissed the bare flesh of his belly and then sighed with delight when his fingers tunneled through her hair. He drew her head back until their gazes met.

"I can't wait any longer to have you," he whispered hoarsely, his breath uneven, racked with need for her, wild to be inside her warmth. He slid his hand down the back of her thigh, caressing the soft curves and mounds of her buttocks with gentle restraint. And then before she knew how, his boots and hose were peeled away and tossed across the room.

And there he was, naked, dark and so very beautiful as he brought her back down on the soft bed. Dante covered her completely from her head past her toes, and Gianelle reveled at the dominant strength that pinned her. She trembled in his arms, not from fear, but from a need as primitive as his. When he tore his mouth from hers she tried to pull him back, needing him, wanting him to take her, to quench the flame that burned unmercifully within her. But he slid down her body, his lips lingering over her flesh like scorching brands. He caressed the soft mound of her breast and laved his tongue over the tiny crest of her nipple that tightened and grew beneath his silken touch. Every touch was a caress, a sigh, enflaming her until she writhed beneath him.

Dante straddled her, rising up on his knees, so dominantly big and volatile, poised over her. He slid his hands behind her back and lifted her breasts to his ravished appetite, sucking, tasting each tender bud in turn. Gianelle twisted beneath him as sharp, glittering sparks ignited every nerve and set her afire. She clawed at the tight, sleek muscles straining his arms. She whispered his name and the sound floated on a heated breath. Shockingly, wantonly, she arched her back, straining to find the silken sword that rested upon her thigh. She wanted to be claimed by this man. She needed it.

His tongue, his lips, his mouth, moved over her, back up her neck, wildly finding the mouth that ached for his. When he lifted his head to gaze down at her, Gianelle gasped, for truly he was a wolf. His black hair fell over harsh, carved features. Smoky lightning passed over the surface of his eyes like a warning. A warning that he was about to take her, and take her hard. No longer was there a thread of fear in his eyes, only the fierce need to finally have her. And she wanted it more than anything else in her life.

With his hand cupped behind her neck, Dante lowered her. He balanced himself on one hand while the other stroked the hollow of her neck. He whispered her name and parted her thighs with his knees.

He entered her smoothly, groaning with fevered restraint until he realized that she was able to take him fully. And then sweet thunder filled Gianelle to her womb. Light cascaded over her like stars falling from the sky, shaken from their foundations by Dante's powerful thrusts. Gianelle closed her eyes and threw her head back with quick, convulsive sighs. What was he doing to her? He felt so sinfully good that she coiled her legs around his thighs and lifted herself farther to meet him, take him deeper.

He rose up on his palms and she smiled and held her breath at the majestic sight of him. His hot, achingly hard flesh impaled her, his strong thighs gave power to each seething, slow plunge. He withdrew slowly, then sank deep inside her again, over and over until the delicious friction drove her to lift her head and bite his shoulder.

The passion he pulled from her only made Dante more wild for her, as though even this joining were not enough. He stared into her eyes. His gaze was deep, startling, and intense. It brought her hand to his face. Why was he looking at her as if she might fly away and he needed to hold on to her? He was possessing her, and she didn't care; marking her, claiming her, and she wanted more.

His ecstasy rocked her, made her legs close tightly around his waist while his hands cupped her buttocks, stroked her thighs, bringing her closer so that she could feel every long, titillating stroke. His thrusts became more furious until he drove her to the edge of madness. She panted and clenched her teeth not to scream with delight. God's mercy, she was the one grunting!

But the sound of her passion was joy to Dante's ears and he smiled down at her. Which was her undoing. Suddenly, frighteningly, light burst forth like an explosion in Gianelle's body. Liquid passion drenched her. She cried out his name as the sweet agony pulled her taut, made her twitch and convulse beneath him.

"I'm yours," she whispered, giving herself up to him completely.

Dante moaned and his body tightened as if a whip had been snapped against his back. His body raged into her, hard, long, full. Gianelle raked her fingernails over the bulging muscles in his arms, down his back, and then over the tight swell of his buttocks, delighting shamelessly in the power of his thrusts. He slowed, and a harsh guttural cry broke forth from his lips. He advanced like a great, dark animal and then retreated once more, clenching his jaw when he plunged within her again. She felt him explode deep inside her body. She reached up to touch his jaw, clenched with the spasms of his release. Gianelle thought she heard him curse as his seed erupted into her, his fingers closed tightly within the thick folds of her hair. He was binding her to him forever while he filled her to overflowing.

Later they rested. Dante's long leg was tossed over her hips while he held her wrapped in his arms.

"My love," Dante whispered against her cheek. "Edgar Dermott had his way with you, didn't he?" She hadn't given him a proper answer the first time he'd asked if the bastard had touched her. She had merely told him that she wasn't willing. When he'd accused her of sharing Dermott's bed and she slapped him, she'd told him again that she wasn't willing. Why hadn't he realized then what she meant? He hadn't wanted to. Even now the thought enraged him. "I should have killed him."

"*Non,* Dante. I never shared Edgar's bed."

"But you were able to take me."

"He wanted to, but I belonged to his brother, and although my lord took many servants to his bed, he refused to share any of us." She smiled into his stricken gaze. "You saved me. And then you freed me, even from the confines that I built around myself. I shall spend my life thinking of ways to thank you."

Dante's lips curled into a curious grin. "You will?"

She smiled and nodded, knowing her promise would distract him from her past.

He rose up on his elbow, resting his head in his hand. "Have you come up with any ideas so far?" When she giggled, it made him laugh softly with her while he drank in every beautiful angle of her face.

"Well, I was thinking I might begin by . . ."

"My lord?" Douglan called from behind the door.

The flurry of venomous oaths that issued from Dante's mouth did nothing to prevent Douglan from rapping on the door next.

"I'll kill him," Dante growled and flung his legs over the side of the bed. He seized one of the furs from the bed and wrapped it around his waist, then trudged to the door. Before he swung it open, he looked at the bed and smiled. Gianelle's entire body was hidden beneath the coverings.

"Do you mean to tell me that you have been up here all day?" Douglan plunged into the chamber, shaking his finger at his lord. "I didn't even know you returned until just . . ." He slanted his gaze to the bed and watched the mound of fur shift a little to the left.

"It's Gianelle," Dante told him.

"Oh." The steward grinned wider than Dante had seen him do in years. "Greetings, Gianelle."

A creamy hand popped out from beneath the covers and waved at him.

"What is it, Douglan?"

The steward wheeled around and glowered at him. "'What is it, Douglan?' That is all you have to say?"

"*Oui.*"

"Well, for your information, while you were up here without bothering to tell me you were back, a missive arrived from the king. He will be returning to England before the next full moon, and wants you in Winchester when he arrives. I have also received word informing me that your brother is but a meager twenty leagues away, and should be here by morning."

"Wonderful, he will be just in time for my wedding."

"Your wedding?" Douglan near swooned in his spot. Behind him, Gianelle pulled the covers off her head.

"How am I supposed to know who to invite to your wedding or even have the time to invite them at all if . . ."

"Is a se'nnight enough time to make all the preparations?"

"Well, I . . ."

Holding up a finger to Douglan, Dante motioned him to wait a moment while he went to the bed.

Gianelle looked at him and felt a river of heat color her cheeks, thinking how alluring he looked wearing nothing but a fur and a warm grin.

"Will you be my wife, Gianelle?"

"I don't want you to do this because you are gallant and fear dishonoring me after . . . ," she whispered, "you know."

Dante nodded and his firm lips curved into an indulgent smile. "That would be a terrible reason to make you my wife."

"Or because you want to protect me."

"But I do want to protect you." His eyes locked with hers and seemed to control her every movement. She couldn't look away.

"You are an earl and I am a ser . . . a commoner," she reminded him, giving him an excuse to take back his offer.

Dante brought her hand to his lips. "My love, I'm not worthy to marry you."

That was all he said, but it floored Gianelle until her thoughts spun so fiercely she had to bite her tongue to keep from fainting. She opened her mouth to speak, but no words came out, only ridiculous utterings that widened his charismatic smile. *"Oui?"*

"Oui." She laughed and threw her arms around his neck.

"Douglan?" Dante called out, his voice husky with the last shred of restraint he possessed while Gianelle whispered in his ear.

"Aye, my lord?"

"What are you still doing here? You have wedding plans to make."

"If I may say so, my lord, you have made a very wise choice."

"Thank you, Douglan. Now get out." Dante swooped down on his bride-to-be before the chamber door quietly closed.

Chapter Sixteen

CASEY WOVE THE LAST STRAND of emerald green thread into Gianelle's hair, then pinned it, along with two other plaited strands, around the top of Gianelle's head to form a braided crown. A few more brushstrokes to the long, honey bronze locks floating down Gia's back and she was done. She had been working since the sun rose, carefully dressing Gianelle in a gown of deep golden Byzantine silk with a matching quilted overcoat embroidered with fine emerald ribbon. Now she moved to stand in front of Gianelle to admire her hard work.

"What if Lord Brand hates me, Casey?" Gianelle was happy to finally be free of her friend's meticulous fingers and stepped away from her to pace before their bed. "What if his wife thinks . . ."

"That you are far too beautiful to wed an ungainly oaf such as I?" Dante leaned against the doorframe, trying to appear casual, but in reality he feared his poor heart might thud right out of his chest. For a moment, he couldn't move. If his body didn't ache so to have Gianelle in his arms, he would have been content to simply stand there letting his gaze wash over her, drinking in every facet of her delicate beauty. When she bent her head to hide the heat that colored her cheeks pink, Dante moved toward her. He was oblivious to Casey slipping past him and out of the room, wearing the grin of a satisfied cat on her lips. He saw only his wild faerie, transformed into a blushing princess. He stood before her, afraid to touch her lest she shatter into golden stardust before his eyes.

"Command me to fall upon my knees and pay you the homage you deserve, and I shall do it, fair lady."

"I am but a peasant, my lord," Gianelle answered him beneath the veil of her long lashes. His words made her want to weep with joy, and she feared if she looked at him she might be the one to fall to her knees with gratitude.

Slowly he touched her hand with his finger, and then another, until their fingers were entwined. "Soon to be my wife," Dante corrected in a low voice racked with feeling. He wanted to drag her into his arms and promise her his very soul. "Look at me, *ma amour.*"

Gianelle lifted her face to him, her large eyes shimmering with love and desire she'd never felt for anyone else before him. Her lower lip trembled and he lifted his thumb to trace its full outline. Then, without another word he bent his head to hers, and using his deft fingers, coaxed her lips apart to receive him.

Gianelle sighed into his mouth at the same time her body melted against his. He consumed her with muscles that ached to possess her, in a kiss that branded her his alone. Even when he widened his stance to haul her closer to his hardening desire, she didn't resist him but curled her arms tighter around his neck.

Slipping his hands beneath her overcoat, Dante cupped her buttocks within his palms. He angled his hips, a slow, unbearably sensual movement that forced the silken niche between her thighs to caress the full length of his manhood. His hold on her tightened. His kiss deepened into something more feral, more untamed, until Gianelle felt stiflingly hot in her heavy gown and wanted to rip it off and stand naked in his embrace.

"I hear babes in the distance."

The sound of old James's voice crackling against their ears almost tore Gianelle from Dante's embrace. But he pulled her back and turned to inflict his most deadly glare on the grinning servant. "*Damnez-le,* James, have you not heard of knocking before you enter a lady's chambers?"

James focused his sightless eyes on his lord for a moment, his bushy gray brow creased in confusion. Confusion, Gianelle realized, that was meant only to avoid Dante's anger. "Aye, I woulda heard me knocking had the door not been gaping open for all to see ye locked in yer lady's arms."

Dante turned to frown at the open door and Gianelle suppressed the urge to giggle at the sly old fox now inclining his ear toward something no one else could hear.

"Yer brother comes," he said, then held up a crooked finger. "And one of his babes is howling something awful." He shook his head and covered his ears. "There will be no peace in Graycliff with all that screeching. I tell ye, none at all."

Dante pulled Gianelle toward the door, but she shook her hand free of his and raced to the small table beside her bed. She grabbed a jar resting there and tossed Dante a smile.

"What is that?"

"Fireflies. I collected them with James last night," Gianelle told him, and then went with him to meet his brother.

~

James's sharp hearing proved to be correct, although the Earl of Avarloch and his family hadn't yet reached the drawbridge when Dante and Gianelle stepped outside the castle.

The sound of the wailing babe sent James running back inside and made Gianelle squint in the sunlight to see their guests in the distance. Clutching the jar to her chest, she took a step forward, answering the call from someplace deep within her heart to comfort the child as she had comforted Casey in the past.

Standing beside her, Dante turned and flashed his betrothed a smile. He was happy to see that her anxiety over meeting his brother had lessened. Why, she looked about to leap out of her slippers and race toward the oncoming entourage as if she had been waiting a lifetime to meet them. He should have known his little spitfire wouldn't be overcome by nerves. *Oui,* she would be able to withstand even the most vigilant scrutiny by King William himself. Dante's heart swelled with pride and he slipped his arm around her waist just as his family rode into the bailey.

"He is called 'Brand the Passionate' by some." Dante leaned down and whispered close to Gianelle's ear. "Be wary of his smile, my joy, for should he charm you overmuch I shall be forced to take my sword to him." He would have offered her a playful wink, but Gianelle was already tearing free of his embrace. He could only watch, somewhat stung, as she raced straight for his brother.

Lord Brand Risande was about to hand his squealing

three-year-old son to a squire when he found himself staring down into the enormous golden eyes of a beautiful woman instead.

"Oh, there, there, my precious one," she cooed, reaching for the boy. "Why all the tears?" She held him close and kissed the downy velvet curls of his auburn hair. Turning away from the child's father, she set the little boy down on his feet and knelt beside him, careless of the dust and dirt staining her gown. "If you keep this up you shall frighten all the faerie lights." She held up the jar filled with fireflies for his inspection.

The child sniffed and wiped his eyes. "Bugs." The word erupted from the aftermath of a sob.

"Oh, but they are not just bugs. Behold." Gianelle flipped the cork lid and dug inside the jar until she caught a firefly on her finger, then closed the lid again. She held the insect up to the boy's face and smiled when its rear lit up and the babe gasped with surprise. The firefly flew away but landed an instant later on the nose of a little girl, only a few years older, who laughed and crossed two beautiful green eyes in an attempt to see the insect.

"May I keep them?" she asked Gianelle.

"Heavens, no," Gianelle said. "I caught them only to show you. We must set them free. Would you like to help me let them go?" The crying boy's sister smiled at her, exposing an enchanting dimple very much like her uncle's, and nodded. At first, Gianelle felt so overwhelmed by the child's beauty that she near sighed. "What is your name, little one?"

"Tanon Elizabeth Risande." The girl grabbed a blue-black curl that was resting on her shoulder and popped her thumb into her mouth.

"All right, Tanon Elizabeth Risande, we will need your thumb to set the fireflies free." Gianelle turned on her haunches to the boy. "We will need your assistance as well. When your sister opens the lid and shakes the jar, you must shout as loud as you can, 'Fly away!'"

"Fwy away!" the boy squealed.

Gianelle laughed and helped Tanon pop the lid, clapping while the child shook the jar and the insects tumbled out, first to land in the grass, and then to wonderful, glorious flight. "Fly away!"

"Fwy away, bugs!"

"I miss them." Tanon's eyes filled with tears and she popped her thumb back into her mouth.

Immediately Gianelle was at her side wiping her tears and smoothing her curls. "There now, they will return tonight just before you and . . . what is your brother's name?"

Tanon released her thumb long enough to give his name. "William Robert Risande."

". . . just before you and William Robert Risande go to sleep to bring you pleasant dreams. If you look out your window you will see their lights."

"You are wonderful."

Gianelle looked up at the man offering his hand to her.

"Who are you? I beg you to come back to Avarloch as the children's nurse."

Gianelle accepted his hand and rose to her feet. Her eyes scanned the bailey for Dante. She was not comfortable with her new station as the soon-to-be lady of the castle and had no idea what was expected of her.

She found her betrothed an instant later in the arms of a breathtaking woman who carried in her arms another babe with dewy red hair. "Lord Brand," Gianelle said, turning her attention back to the man who hadn't let go of her hand. She bent her head and her knee at the same time, as was befitting a servant. "Welcome to Graycliff. I am Gianelle." When she felt his lips press against her knuckles, she lifted her gaze to him.

And then the Earl of Avarloch smiled at her.

Gianelle had never trusted any man before she met Dante. In fact, there were very few men she even liked. But Lord Brand Risande's smile was so captivating, so completely guileless and beautiful, Gianelle found herself smiling back, completely at ease. He was an irresistibly handsome man, though he didn't resemble Dante as much as Gianelle thought he might. While their hair was the same luminous shade of black, Lord Brand's was shorter, with satiny curls that fell around his face and gave him a softer look. His eyes were such a radiant combination of blue-green they reminded Gianelle of her beloved sea.

"Anyone who can stop my son from crying . . ." He laughed at himself then, and his laughter, like his voice, was as soothing as a warm breeze on a winter day. "I'm tempted to ask you if you have wings hidden behind your back. You're as comforting as an angel, and as lovely as one."

"*Enfer,* I leave you with my betrothed for a moment and you have already made her blush."

Gianelle turned her head to watch Dante walking toward her with the stunning redhead at his side and Tanon and William cradled in each arm.

"Your what?" Brand asked, sincerely astonished. "Did I hear you right?" He looked at Gianelle again in a whole different way. "What magic have you wrought on this rake to make him agree to marriage?"

"Agree? I had to practically beg her." Dante kissed his niece and nephew before setting them back on the ground.

Gianelle watched, smiling while Dante swallowed his brother up in his arms and the two men exchanged greetings. Then Dante introduced her to the woman still standing beside him.

Everything about Lady Brynnafar Risande was exquisite. Her thick copper locks were pulled into a tail that fell over her shoulder in wavy splendor. Her striking eyes were the same color as her daughter's. She was tall and so very elegant that Gianelle felt like an awkward child in comparison. "Sister," she said, pulling Gianelle into a delicate embrace. "It was a very thoughtful thing you did with the fireflies, and quite clever too!"

"Children are a blessing." Gianelle touched the babe's cheek while he slept in his mother's arms. "And you are richly blessed."

"Aye, but there are days I consider moving into a separate bedchamber and bolting the door from my . . . Ouch!" Brynna spun around and swatted her husband's hand away from her derriere. "That pinch hurt, you knave!"

"Then you will think twice about ever saying such a detestable thing again." Lord Brand merely winked at his wife, but Gianelle was certain the lady looked faint.

"Rake," Brynna mumbled under her breath after she regained enough of her breath to speak. She offered Gianelle another brilliant smile, then snatched up Gianelle's arm as if they had known each other for many years and began walking with her toward the castle.

Still not quite sure what her duties were now that she was to be Dante's wife, Gianelle looked over her shoulder, desperate for Dante's aid. He smiled at her while he strode with his brother a few steps behind the women.

"What brings you to Graycliff?" Gianelle heard Dante ask his brother.

"You know we usually spend the summers in Winchester with William," Brand told him. "I wanted to stop here first. I've been very concerned about you, Dante. Katherine's death was difficult for us all, but I know it was hardest for you."

"I'm well, brother. Gianelle has brought new life to my heart."

"You must tell me all about this woman who has tamed your wild heart."

Gianelle looked over her shoulder and met Dante's ravenous gaze.

"We have a silent agreement never to tame each other."

"Hmm." Brand smiled at her, and then his aqua gaze settled on the luscious curve of his wife's derriere. "I've always said there's nothing better than a good dose of savagery between a husband and wife."

~

That night there was a grand feast in the great hall in honor of their guests. Beef stew and baked black bread whet everyone's appetite while they waited for fresh baked cod, shark, and seven roasted pigs Ingred had sizzling on enormous spits. There were pear tarts, pies filled with sautéed fowl, and enough wine and ale to keep all the men at Graycliff drunk for the next se'nnight.

Gianelle ate with young William in her lap, making

certain that his food was cooled enough so as not to scorch his mouth. Tanon sat beside her, chatting endlessly about fireflies. Seated at Gianelle's right, Brynna whispered something into her ear that made Gianelle toss her head back and laugh.

Dante and Brand sat together opposite the ladies and discussed Casey and her incredible resemblance to Katherine. And while Dante tried to concentrate on their conversation, he found his gaze returning to Gianelle throughout the evening. Seeing her with children pleased him and made him eager to start their own family. When she laughed, so carefree was the sound, so astoundingly beautiful did she look to him, that he longed to snatch her from her chair and carry her to his room. He was quite satisfied to discover her dreamy gaze drifting to him on more than one occasion. When their eyes met, Dante curled his mouth into a smile of pure contentment.

"She's beautiful," Brand said, pleased to see his brother so happy. "But I must admit from what you've told me, William might not be as convinced of her innocence as you are."

Dante turned to cast his gaze on his brother. "I will convince him."

"She is accused of murdering a baron, Dante," Brand reminded him, and then caught his daughter's eye and blew her a kiss. His gaze moved to Gianelle. "I admit she looks more like an angel than a murderess."

"Brother." Dante's tone drew Brand's attention back to him. His molten gaze was as lethal as it was in battle. "She didn't murder anyone."

"I'll be damned." Brand slammed the cup he was about to bring to his lips back down on the table. "You're in love with her. Brynna almost had me convinced that no woman could ever snare you. Don't look so shocked, *frère*. Brynna's handmaiden, Alysia, has been wed for two years now, yet if I pass the kitchen at the right moment I can hear her breathless tales of how adept you are at . . ."

"I think a good thrashing in the list should ensure your mouth staying shut." Dante glared at him, and then cast a nervous glance at Gianelle.

His brother only laughed. "She's done nothing to lessen your arrogance, I see."

"What is arrogant about me knowing I could best you in a fight?" Dante asked, lifting one corner of his mouth in a taunting half-smile.

"Ah, so you've been practicing, then?"

They laughed together, and then Brand announced, loudly enough for his wife to hear him, that it was late. "We've journeyed far and I ache for a warm bed." He smiled at Brynna, who nearly leaped from her seat to gather the children. The way her cheeks darkened to a heated rosy hue made Brand rise from his chair even faster.

"May I put the children to bed?" Gianelle asked Brand from across the table. "I'm certain Lady Brynna is weary from such a long day, and I promised William a story."

Brand gave his consent, then smiled at his brother while he reached for Brynna's hand. "Whatever your reason is to believe in her innocence, I trust your judgment, Dante. And I'm more than happy for you."

Gianelle watched the couple leave the hall whispering into each other's ears and smiling as though they were newly wed and off to spend their first night together. Unwittingly, her gaze slid back to Dante, who had arisen from his seat and was coming toward her. Gianelle couldn't help but smile. Just looking at the man clouded her good sense. Tempted her to leap from her chair and into his arms where she felt treasured for the first time in her life.

"Gianelle?"

"Hmm?" She looked up at him when he stood over her. And, oh, that smile of his, laced with such tender affection. She gazed into his eyes and felt her belly knot and burn at the way they deepened in color to a smoky, smoldering gray, reminding her that he could, in fact, make her cry out, not in pain but in pleasure.

She heard him laugh softly above her and she blinked, scattering her wanton thoughts of him. Completely mortified at being caught admiring him, she stood up and brushed past him. "Come, children."

Dante allowed her a few steps while he watched the sensual sway of her hips. He mumbled through a tight jaw at what she was doing to him before he strode up behind her. Staying close enough to tilt his head to her nape, he inhaled the clean scent of her hair. "Shall I follow you like a servant before my entire castle?"

Gianelle nearly stopped in her tracks. Her heart pounded wildly against her ribs at the feel of him behind her. His warm breath against her neck made every nerve in her body react. "If you wish," she said haughtily, fighting the intense urge to turn around and kiss him. She tried to resist the effect he was having on her, but she failed miserably when his hands settled on her hips. He pulled her backside against him, though his gait never faltered.

"What I wish," he began, his voice hard and husky with desire as he nuzzled his face in her hair, "is that we were on our way to my chambers at this moment." Dante felt her body tremble at the meaning of his words and slipped his arms around her waist.

"We still have a se'nnight before I am your wife," Gianelle said tersely, but she could barely think straight. His body covered hers, dominating her.

"And you think that will stop me?"

She should pull away from him, but she lifted her hand to cover his instead. "You're going to make me fall, Dante." What she meant to sound like an admonishment came out sounding more like a languid purr. She even found herself angling her head so that her cheek rubbed against his chest.

Then she remembered the children and her eyes sprang open. Tanon stared up at her and smiled when Gianelle met her gaze. William had fallen behind and was rubbing his sleepy eyes with his fists. "Look what you've done!" Gianelle snapped at Dante. She snatched up Tanon's hand, gathered William under her other arm and huffed all the way to the stairs.

Dante watched her, a wide grin spreading across his face before he caught up with her.

Chapter Seventeen

BRYNNA, CASEY, AND DARA DRESSED GIANELLE in a pale blue wedding gown that had belonged to Dante's mother, Lady Andrea Risande. Handed down to her by her mother before her, the Gaulish lace dress was to have been saved for Katherine on her wedding day. Gianelle wept when Dante asked her to wear it, adding that one day he hoped she would give him a daughter and carry on the tradition.

The old workmanship was extraordinary, Gianelle thought, looking down at herself. The neckline rose up high on her throat and the long sleeves' cuffs dripped low from her wrists. The snug bodice dropped to below her waist in a rich, creamy tapestry encrusted with crystals that reflected the soft golds and silvers in her room. Layer upon layer of the sheerest linen, also embroidered with crystals, fanned out from her hips and fell in a sparkling cascade to the floor.

Sighing dreamily behind her, Casey wove long, single strands of pearls through Gianelle's thick braid. "I simply cannot believe this is happening." She shook her head behind her friend and pulled one lock of hair through another.

"Nor can I," Gianelle murmured.

Making last-minute adjustments to the hem of the gown with skilled, quick fingers, Lady Dara glanced up at the bride. "Goodness me, you sound unhappy, Gianelle."

"Oh, Gia, are you?" Casey leaned over Gianelle's shoulder to look at her. "Lord Risande is wonderful and handsome, and so kind. Everyone loves him."

"*Oui*, that's the problem."

Brynna looked up from smoothing the wrinkles out of Gianelle's veil.

"I'm not unhappy." Gianelle took a deep breath and closed her eyes.

"Then why all the sighing?" Dara asked her.

Biting her lip, Gianelle thought about the answer for a moment. She met Brynna's gaze. "Your husband is a very handsome man. His smile is . . ."

"I know." Brynna agreed with Gianelle's loss for words and smiled at her.

"Do you not worry that other women will . . . that he might . . ."

"Nay." Brynna went to her and clasped Gianelle's hands. "And neither should you worry. Brand and Dante both value loyalty above all else. They don't just expect it. They give it as well."

"But everywhere Dante goes women throw themselves at him. And he's a man, you know."

"Aye, I've noticed." Brynna laughed.

"We all have," Dara agreed, tying off a piece of thread.

"There, you see?" Gianelle sighed. "Even Dara noticed!"

"Oh, for heaven's sake, of course I have." Dara swatted Gianelle's leg. "I'm not blind. But I have never thrown myself at him, nor would I. Malen makes me very happy."

"What if he tires of me?"

"Oh, not that again." Behind her, Casey rolled her eyes heavenward.

"*Oui,* that again." Gianelle turned to toss her friend a dark scowl, causing Casey to lose two strands of pearls.

"Hold still." Casey snapped her tongue and slapped Gianelle's shoulder.

Gianelle sighed. Then, with a pensive expression drifting over her eyes, she said, "King William's brother is the bishop, is he not? Dante could tire of me and have the marriage annulled easily enough."

"You need the pope for annulment, dearest," Dara pointed out, barely looking up from the hem of Gia's dress.

"You don't know him!" Gianelle argued in defense of her worries. "He has naked faeries on the walls in his bed chamber."

Casey snickered, smoothing out the twisted ends of hair at her friend's temples.

Dara squeaked, piercing herself with a pin, and shoved her finger into her mouth.

"I know him," Brynna said, crooking her finger and slipping it under Gianelle's chin. "I know his reputation with women, and I understand that it frightens you. I was quite honestly stunned to hear him call you his betrothed. But Gianelle," she coaxed in a soft voice when Gianelle looked away, "it was because I never thought he would marry. You have done what no other woman before you could. You've won his heart. And you must believe me when I tell you that once you have won the heart of a Risande, it is yours forever."

Gianelle's shoulders relaxed, and Brynna's emerald

eyes sparkled with happiness. "I have no sisters. You will come visit me often?"

"*Oui*," Gianelle promised and threw her arms around Brynna. "Thank you," she whispered, and said a silent prayer that Brynna was right about the man waiting below stairs for her.

~

Hundreds of flaming candles faceted Dante's diamond eyes as he surveyed the small chapel. He shook his head in disgust and turned to his brother. "We won't be able to fit all the guests and villagers in here. They still arrive as we speak. Blast Douglan. The little twit managed to invite everyone in the whole damned country!"

To his left, Balin scratched his closely clipped beard and nodded. "And to make matters worse, Conrad Lowell has just arrived."

Dante scanned the many faces standing in the back of the chapel. He scowled when he found the tall, pasty-looking emissary entering with an entourage of men at his side. "I don't see Dermott. Keep your eyes on them, and if he arrives and makes a move to stop this wedding, kill him."

Balin glanced at Brand with disbelief widening his dark eyes, then he turned back to Dante. "Do you not think that would be a tad disruptive on your wedding day?"

Dante shook his head. "*Non,* I don't."

"It's never disrupted any wedding I've attended," Brand offered nonchalantly. "But I do think my brother spent one too many years in William's service."

Dante smiled for the first time that morning, then inhaled sharply before he stormed off to find the friar.

Watching him leave, Balin mumbled under his breath. Kill a man for trying to stop his wedding? God's fury, Dante truly loved the girl. It was about damned time!

No one could be happier for his lord than Balin was. He had seen the terrible change in Dante after Katherine died; when the sun fled in the sky and Dante wandered through the castle, plagued with guilt and grief, to the turrets overlooking the harsh sea, cursing the wind and the earth and all who lived in it. Gianelle brought happiness back to Dante's life. Still, killing a man over her was quite a statement. Balin wondered what would be next, defying the king?

He eyed Dante while the Lord of Graycliff huddled with the friar who would give the benediction. Both men smiled, and Dante patted the older man's shoulder and then headed back toward Balin and his brother.

"Lead the guests outside to the cliffs and then go see what is keeping my bride."

Balin was afraid to ask, but his curiosity got the better of him. "The cliffs?"

"*Oui*, the cliffs." Dante beamed and started threading his way through the crowd. He turned on his way toward the doors. "It will make her happy," he called out with a joyous grin.

Balin stared at him, an incredulous look spreading over his rough features. He turned to Brand and shook his head. "Lord help us all, he's gone completely over the edge."

"Let's hope not." Brand patted the captain's back and

flashed him a smile. "Remember where we'll be standing in a few minutes."

~

"The cliffs?" Gianelle's face lit up to a healthy pink when Balin entered her chambers and gave her the news a few minutes later. "We are getting married on the cliffs?"

With a long sigh and a slight smile tossed to Casey, who was also ready to burst, Balin nodded. "The church is too small for all the guests, and Dante is bent on making you happy, even at the risk of losing a few guests to the sea." This was a hard business Dante had set him to, Balin thought gruffly. Every noble in the castle mumbled through tight, gossiping lips about how such a wealthy lord could marry a commoner. He loathed hearing the mocking whispers of those who thought his friend had chosen poorly. Seeing the wee maidservant now, quite beautiful in her flowing gown and rose-dusted cheeks, Balin knew Dante could not have chosen anyone more perfect. Indeed, Casey melted his own heart every time he looked at her. Well, he thought, if he heard a single word against any of them, whoever uttered it would have to deal with him.

"If you are ready, my lady, I will escort you to your joyful groom."

With a nervous smile, Gianelle laced her arm through Balin's and let him lead her out of her chamber with Casey, Brynna, and Dara following close behind.

"Tell me, Balin," Gianelle asked, glancing up at him as they descended the stairs, "is he truly joyful?"

Balin smiled, keeping his eyes fixed straight ahead. "Only enough to make me worry that he might cast himself into the sea thinking he can fly."

Behind her, Lady Dara sighed. "I tell you, love is divine."

Gianelle never thought she would agree with a statement like that one, but the bards had been right, and the smile it brought to her lips illuminated the corridors. Walking at her side, the tall captain of Dante's guard squeezed Gianelle's arm closer and held his head up a bit higher as he led the future Lady of Graycliff to the sea.

~

The only thing Gianelle saw when she reached the massive white cliff was Dante. She passed hundreds of guests sitting along the rocky crags, some teetering uncomfortably upon the jagged hills that overlooked an ocean as serene as her betrothed's wonderful face when he turned to look at her. But she saw no one, heard no whispers as Balin aided her up the steep stone. Only the man who waited for her at the top captured her attention. Standing against a background of billowy clouds and an azure sky, Dante looked like a warrior angel. The wind riffled through his hair, snapped at the sleeves of his scarlet surcoat, making him look as though he had just landed there from God's perfect paradise. She sighed at him. He took a step toward her, his hand outstretched. A lock of raven hair blew across his eyes. He smiled. He radiated light from within, and Gianelle closed her eyes, thinking this was all a dream.

"Greetings, *belle fée*." His voice was like the waves, deep and tranquil in its power. He took her hand and brought it to his lips, where he kissed her so tenderly she was sure she would faint and tumble into the water below.

Everything after that was a blur to Gianelle. She barely

heard the friar's nuptial benediction or Dante's softly spoken promises to her. She hardly remembered his kiss or when it ended, save that he made her tingle from foot to crown. All she knew was that now she was his wife.

Dante led her back to the castle with one arm carefully placed around her waist so that she wouldn't slip off the rocks. All around her were faces, some smiling, others turned toward the person closest to them with mutterings she couldn't hear. She searched amid the masses for Casey but didn't find her. She saw Balin, though, and Brand and Brynna and even old James, each grinning from ear to ear as she passed them.

When they reached the castle, Douglan led everyone to the great hall where the festivities were to begin. Tables groaned under the weight of silver bowls filled with soups, breads, and rose water for hand washing. Plates overflowed with pheasant, venison, and swan, as well as tarts and pies, candied fruits, and barrels of fine wine. There were dozens of freshly cut roses strewn along the tables and velvety petals sprinkled on the floor to cushion the delicate feet of the bride as she made her way with her husband to a high dais that had been set up for the day.

Gianelle's head reeled when she took her seat beside Dante. Was this real? Was it all for her? She turned to the man at her side and swept her gaze over his profile while he smiled at their guests. She wanted to touch him, trace the carved angles of his jaw, smooth his velvet hair off his shoulders. She wanted to touch every inch of his face and imprint it on her soul forever. Vaguely, she heard Brand making a toast. His words made Dante begin to turn to her. He seemed to move in slow motion. Gianelle held her breath, knowing that any moment he would see her, set his dazzling gaze upon her and somehow make it all real.

Dante lifted a goblet to his lips. She watched him, her fingers trembling in her lap. He next held the cup to her mouth, offering her a drink, as was the tradition. She accepted, and while she drank, his eyes penetrated her very soul until she lowered her gaze in defense of his power. She could feel him coming closer, leaning into her for a kiss that would fill her and make her even more heady than the wine.

"You look flush, my love," he whispered against her ear after he kissed her. His breath was sweet and warm and hungry for more of her. "I pray my kisses always make you so fevered."

"I feel as if I'm dreaming," she replied, unable to lift her gaze from his lips.

"Then I shall never wake you." He kissed her again to seal his vow, and then captured her hand and greeted Lord Dumont with her.

There was music and entertainment after everyone ate. Dante excused himself for a moment, promising Gianelle that he would return to her in a breath.

When he was gone, Gianelle scanned the happy faces of their guests. Lord Dumont proudly showed off his youngest grandchild to anyone who would look. Brand and Brynna were laughing together in one of the more dimly lit corners of the hall while William chased his sister around Brynna's skirts. Gianelle sighed, hoping that she and Dante would always be so happy together. Her gaze moved around the hall and she spotted Casey laughing with Balin. Gianelle rose to her feet to go to them and mayhap have a word with the handsome captain about another wedding day in the near future. She hit a brick wall when she turned for the dais steps.

She hadn't seen the man who stepped in front of her. But she looked up now from his hard chest and into eyes she would never forget. She gasped and stepped back, reaching behind her for something to hit him with. He lifted a perfectly manicured hand to aid her from falling. Gianelle jolted her arm away.

"Forgive me for frightening you," he crooned with a smirk that told her he wasn't sorry at all.

"Stay away from me," Gianelle warned.

"Gia, is that any way to greet me?" Edgar Dermott's smile was like a grotesque mask concealing the fury that raged within. "Nobility has soured you."

"What are you doing here?" She almost lowered her gaze from his, but then grit her teeth and looked him boldly in the eye.

"Why, I'm here to see you, my dear. Why else would I come to this godforsaken place but to face my brother's murderer?"

Gianelle searched the faces in the hall for Dante. When she couldn't find him, she lifted her eyes again to the handsome face of the tall man who blocked her path.

"Your brother's demise was not my doing, and neither is the fact that he is rotting in hell at this very moment."

Edgar Dermott's lips widened into a grin that was every bit as ruthless as his brother's had been. His eyes devoured her, drank her in until she wanted to scream and run for her life. "Let me pass."

He held up a finger. "In a moment."

"You will let her pass now." The voice behind him was so lethal that it frightened Gianelle even more than the sudden appearance of the man she had prayed she would never see again. "You will move *now,* or die before you take your next breath. And I would hate to soil the floor that so pleases my beautiful wife."

Dermott turned his face to a force so deadly, he stepped back and almost landed on Gianelle's toes. With more grace than his bulkier brother had ever possessed, he quickly gained his composure and offered Dante a kind smile and a gracious bow. "I only wanted to offer your wife my blessings on her marriage, my lord."

Dante's eyes were sharper than daggers following the man as he bent. Then he lifted them to Gianelle. "Come here."

She couldn't move. Her feet were rooted as firmly as a tree to the rose-covered floor.

"I see she is still as obedient as she was in my brother's care," Dermott mocked, straightening to toss her a smooth grin out of the corner of his mouth.

Angry that his wife hadn't come to him, Dante's face darkened staring at her. He called Balin over his shoulder, meaning to escort Dermott and his men out of Graycliff. The captain moved toward him immediately, tugging Casey with him.

When Casey saw Edgar Dermott her steps halted so abruptly Balin nearly lost her in the crowd. She resisted Balin's gentle tug and shook her head at him, her eyes wide with fear. "He's come for me."

"*Non,* my joy," Balin assured her. "He is simply a fool who obviously doesn't care about seeing another dawn. Come, Dante beckons me." He smiled and pulled her forward.

When they reached the dais, Dermott turned his eyes on Casey and she cringed against Balin's arm.

Perhaps, the captain decided, feeling Casey tremble beside him, killing the man wasn't such a poor idea after all.

"Balin, escort Dermott out of my castle," Dante ordered.

"Nay." Dermott shook his head slowly and pulled a parchment from inside his surcoat. "Since you did not return Gianelle to me as the king ordered, I have permission from the bishop to remain here . . . safely, until your marriage is consummated and my brother's murderer is claimed your true wife by the king. She isn't fully under your protection until this marriage is consummated."

Casey moved to Dante and tugged on his arm.

"And how will you know when it is?" Gianelle snarled at him. "Your brother made sure that there would be no blood on my marriage bed."

Dermott's gaze darkened at the thought of Bryce's hands on her, and then he aimed that deadly glare at Dante. But the Lord of Graycliff had turned to Casey when she tried to pull him away.

"I must have a word with you," she pleaded.

"In a moment, Casey," Dante replied impatiently.

Brand appeared at Dante's side and ripped the parchment from Dermott's hand and read it, then passed it to his brother. "The decree is worthless. It's not signed by William."

Dermott shrugged his shoulders vaguely. "A murder has been committed. It will take a bit more time, but King William is aware of my charges, and I am certain I will have his stamp soon enough."

Dante crumpled the parchment in his fist and threw it at his unwelcome guest. "Justice was already served in your brother's defiled bed. You made a dreadful error involving the king in your schemes, but if I see you near my wife again, even the king's stamp will not matter when I kill you. I warn you to leave my hall while you can still do so on your own two feet." He reached his hand across what seemed a distance wider than the ocean, snatched Gianelle's wrist, and pulled her to his side.

Casey tapped Dante's shoulder while he watched Dermott leave the dais. When he turned to look at her there were tears pooled over the rims of her eyes.

"There is something I must tell you, my lord. Please give me a moment in private." She turned her stricken gaze to Gianelle and her tears spilled over her dark lashes. "I'm so sorry."

Chapter Eighteen

CASEY WEPT OPENLY by the time she reached the solar with Dante, Balin, and Gianelle. The captain ushered her to a chair with Gianelle at her side, trying desperately to comfort her. Dante watched with quiet anticipation of what Casey might be about to tell them.

"Oh, Gia, you must believe me. I had no idea Dermott would come after you. I thought we were safe. Oh, please forgive me."

Gianelle wiped her friend's cheeks with her sleeve. "There now," she said softly. "It cannot be as bad as that."

"Forgive you for what, Casey?" Dante asked, stepping toward her.

"I was afraid he would come to our room and catch us trying to escape. He would have blamed her. He always did," Casey cried. She snatched Gianelle's hand and pressed it to her cheek. "I didn't want him to hurt you again, but I didn't mean to kill him. I swear it. I didn't mean to kill him."

The solar grew silent save for Dante's footsteps treading to where Casey sat, pale and trembling at his approach. He almost smiled at her, wanting to comfort her, but also because he had suspected her when he'd questioned the servants of Devonshire. She had been nervous and anxious to end her interrogation. Her large, frightened eyes had darted to the door the moment she sat down to face him. He had questioned enough people in the past few years, since the Conquest, to recognize guilt, but his instincts then had told him she was too meek to commit such a crime. Which, he reminded himself now, was the reason he didn't put much faith in his instincts.

He squatted beside her now and covered both of her hands with one of his. "Why didn't you tell me the truth before this day?"

"I was afraid," Casey told him. "And then we left and I tried to put it from my mind. But I cannot let Gianelle be punished for what I did. I didn't mean to kill him. I only put a small amount of mandrake in his wine, just enough to make him sleep. But I must have put too much."

"*Non.*" Gianelle stepped away from them and went to stand by the hearth. She gazed into the flames and drew in a deep breath before she spoke. "I wanted to ensure our safe escape as well by adding some mandrake to his drink. I was surprised the small amount killed him. But truly"—she turned to them—"I didn't care."

Dante stared at her, dumbstruck. He wasn't sure if he should be angry with his wife or just simply amazed that she had managed to deceive him so effectively.

"Wife, you're a much better liar than I had initially given you credit for."

She lowered her gaze from his stunned expression. "If you recall, I never denied the charge."

An indulgent smile hovered at the corners of Dante's lips and he rose to go to her. "I will handle this," he said, cupping her face in his hands. "No one knows the truth but the four of us."

"You cannot live this deceit with us, Dante. I will not ask it of you. I never intended to tell you."

"That's quite obvious," he replied with a gentle quirk of his brow.

"You're angry with me."

"We will discuss it later," he promised in a voice meant only for her ears, "when we are alone." The glint of naked male intent in his eyes made her tingle all the way to the soles of her feet.

He swung around to Casey, his tone authoritative but tender. "Dry your eyes. Stay here until you calm your nerves. Balin and Gia will remain with you until then. I don't want Dermott or his men to see you like this.

"Casey," he said after she nodded and wiped her nose, "I will not let any harm come to either of you. But I want you both to promise me one thing. Stay the hell out of the kitchen."

~

Candle flames flickered in their sconces as Dante whipped past them down the stairs on his way back to the wedding feast, his boots beating a steady litany against the floor of Graycliff. When he entered the large wooden doorway of the great hall, he ignored the questioning faces of his guests and set his eyes on Edgar Dermott, seething that the bastard had the boldness to remain. Here was the man who'd sent word to William risking Gianelle's very life. Here he was standing like a proud peacock, his head bent to Simone's ear, whispering things that made him smile.

Dante wanted to kill him as he marched toward him like a warrior entering the battlefield.

Brand took one look at his brother and rushed forward, stopping what he knew would be a swift slaughter. "Pray, brother, it is your wedding day. Whatever revenge you seek can wait. Think of your wife."

Dante stared into Brand's eyes for a moment, then nodded before he continued on toward Dermott. The knave's hand rested on Simone's shoulder, and when Dante reached them, he snatched the scoundrel's wrist and grasped it firmly in his hand. His eyes were the color of smoky quartz. He lowered his head a fraction and looked up from under dark brows. "Never let me see your hands on anyone that lives in my castle again." His voice rumbled like the warning of a coming earthquake. "You live and breathe this very moment only because of that parchment you carry. But I vow this to you, the moment I hold King William's seal, I will make certain your brother's name is cursed throughout England for how he mistreated his vassals. As for you, you will be fortunate if you can scrape a pennyweight from a passerby while you beg for food on the side of the road."

"Do you stand here and threaten me?" Dermott asked in amazement. He tried to pull free of Dante's viselike grip, to no avail.

Dante's slow smile was a chilling promise of what was to come. "I make no threat. It's a vow. The choice is yours. Stay here and I will most certainly kill you, or flee and wait for my revenge. But it will come. It will come because you accused my wife of being in league with the highest enemy of the king. And because you accused her of murdering a man who should have died at the end of my sword rather than in his bed."

Dermott studied him for a moment and then his lips snaked into a warning grin. "Mind what you drink, Risande. Your wife knows her poison."

"Pity then that she didn't use her knowledge on you." Dante rubbed his fingertips together at the hilt of his sword. He knew that if he had to look at this man for one more moment, he would kill him and to hell with the law. He called Talard, who was never too far away, and two of his guards. "Escort this swine to a room." His eyes burned into Dermott's. "The sight of him sickens me."

He was about to turn away when Sir Conrad reached for his sword. Dante smiled at him, but there was only ruthless violence in the curving of his firm lips. "Come." He beckoned Dermott's guard with a slight wave of his fingers. "What are you waiting for?"

Brand stepped forward and blocked Conrad's path, although Lord Dermott's emissary already looked as though he was having second thoughts about attacking Dante. "Lift your sword against my brother, and before you swing it your head will be rolling across the floor."

Conrad backed away and then followed Dermott and his men out of the great hall.

"Well, this has been an interesting wedding." Brand scowled at Dante when the guests began to murmur quietly to one another. "I must say, you make a terrible host."

Dante looked around at the questioning faces of his guests and raked his hand through his hair. "If you have any suggestions on how to salvage this day, I would love to hear them."

Brand tossed his arm around his brother's shoulder. "I

would suggest you go fetch your wife and bring her back here. You need to show your villagers that all is well with their lord."

Neither man had noticed Simone hovering around them while they spoke, but Dante glanced at her when he felt her hand slide down his arm. "Your wife seems to have deserted you. Let us strike up the music and show your people that their great lord will not be alone in his bed tonight. They care not who makes you happy."

"She has not deserted me." Dante cast Simone an impatient look. "But you may dance for the guests, Simone. I'm sure you can distract them for me until I return." Simone turned to motion to the bards to play her favorite tune, and looked straight into a pair of stunning blue-green eyes. She smiled like a cat that had just spotted its morning meal.

"Careful." Brand smiled back at her. "My wife's claws are even more dangerous than yours, Simone."

Dante left the great hall just as Gianelle entered. The two nearly collided with each other.

"I was just coming for you. Dermott and his men have been removed," Dante told her as a strange, darkly sensuous melody began behind him. "How is Casey?"

"She's better, but don't expect them to return soon. When I left the solar, Balin was kissing her."

Dante smiled and lifted his fingers to her cheek. "And how are you faring, *ma fée*?"

"I'm sorry I lied to you." She meant to sound more repentant, but the music drew her. She looked around Dante's arm to see inside the great hall. She had never heard anything like it. It was not Celtic in its origin, nor Norman as most of the music was, nor were any pipes used to create the soft exotic tones that sounded like a woman moaning in ecstasy. The erotic chords had a lulling effect, and yet Gianelle felt her blood pumping through her veins in a beat as primal as war drums.

"What is that sound?"

As if he had only just become aware of it because she mentioned it, Dante turned and looked over his shoulder. "Simone is dancing." He only looked for a moment before turning his attention back to Gianelle. But she was already pushing past him to get inside.

The entire atmosphere of the great hall had changed. When Gianelle had left earlier, the hall was brighter, she was sure of it. The air seemed thicker now as well, charged with scents of musk and sweat as Simone, twirling in the center of the room, shed the long silky wrappings of her gown to a rhythm that made Gianelle feel heady. She watched in stunned silence as the dark beauty's hair whirled and fanned out around her shoulders—down her back, her eyes closed in some languid sexual fantasy while she danced. The music droned and rocked her and Simone fell to her knees. She threw her head back and washed her hands down her neck and over breasts that were barely concealed now save for the last few layers of emerald gauze that covered her. She fell backward on her thighs like some pagan goddess and arched her back, gyrating to the building crescendo that halted the breath of almost every male in the hall.

Behind Gianelle, Dante was drawn to the sound as well. The melody coursed through his veins like ancient heat, burning flames that licked his flesh and made even the tips of his fingers ache. But it was not Simone's seductive dance that halted his breath. His wife had stepped back, as if startled by the hunger in their guests' eyes. The back of her small, soft body touched his. Like a breath, against his chest, his hips, his thighs. Passion ripped him like a blow to his gut as her scent drifted up to his nostrils. He bent his head, drawing her in farther still, closing his eyes for a moment to savor her. She was so close, her skin so pale against the soft glow of the firelight. He wanted her. From the beginning he had ached for her. The idea of thoroughly ravishing her made him draw in a harsh breath just as Simone groaned, finishing her dance like a spent woman on the rose-covered floor.

Gianelle spun on her heel and glared at her husband. "Are you all right, my lord? Does the sight of Simone still heat you so that I should fetch some cold water to toss over your head?"

Dante impaled her with his striking gaze, watched her lips as they moved and her chin lifted in defiance, her cheeks flushed dusky pink. Even the quick flutter of her long lashes didn't go unnoticed by him, but heated his passion further. His wife was fire and innocence. Her eyes, so large and round, sparked golden from within. He drenched himself in the sight of her breasts rising and falling in anticipation of the hunger she saw in him. He could control his need for her no longer.

He lifted his broad hands and slipped one around the back of her neck and the other around her waist and hauled her against him so fiercely she nearly gasped on her own breath. Dante grew hard immediately and smoothed his hand over her buttocks, pushing her in closer to the place that ached for her. His mind rebelled against the force he used, but the music played on his blood like a sexual caress; the scent of his wife so close nearly drove him mad.

When he felt her arms close tightly around his neck, Dante knew they wouldn't be spending much more time with their guests.

He withdrew only slightly, enough so that his breath fell onto her lips. "You make me feel like a madman. Only you," he whispered and licked the seam of her lips, coaxing them apart with his tongue. She groaned, and the sound halted Dante's heart. He felt as if he were going to burst and pulled her in closer until his body completely covered hers. She tilted her head back, exposing her neck. He bent with her, biting her gently, as gently as his body would allow, for he wanted to plunge into her, mark her as his with the force of his thrusts. And she wanted it too. He could smell it all over her: wild, heated passion that ached to be released. Her fingers curled into his hair, guiding his mouth over her throat. She gasped and moaned and lifted his face to hers for a kiss that ignited explosions of fire and vivid color that burned every nerve from her fingertips to her toes. He made her forget her past, her very name.

The music stopped and their kiss continued until every eye settled upon them. Some guests stared slack-jawed while Brand smiled and nodded his approval at his brother and his new bride locked in an embrace of delirious, heated passion.

Dante felt the burning stares first and opened his eyes, but still he couldn't release his wife. He smiled while taking her lower lip between his teeth, which made her groan again. When their guests began to clap and the sounds of men hollering for more reached Gianelle's ears, her lids finally lifted slowly. She blinked as if waking from a dream.

With cheeks the color of the deep red rose petals on the floor, Gianelle pushed herself away from her husband. But his chest was hard and strong against her palms and she trembled with the memory of him.

He smiled at her. Not just any smile, but one of such heated anticipation she went weak in his arms.

The great hall rumbled with the sounds of plates thumping against tables and cheers of approval. They wanted him to take her, carry her off the way a husband was expected to do. And they expected to follow the blushing couple to the marriage bed and witness the blessing. The thought of it paled Gianelle until she swooned. But her husband's strong hands were there, gently pulling her against him. He quieted the crowd and announced in a deep, rough voice that he was taking her to bed. Another roar rose up and he smiled and waited, then warned them that whoever followed would have to meet him in the lists the next morning. Tradition or no, he wouldn't have men gaping at the beautiful jewel in his arms. Bidding them all good night, he took his wife's hand and led her out of the great hall.

Part of Dante wanted to lift Gianelle off her feet and get her to his room faster, but he enjoyed the rush of his blood as it coursed with anticipation like fire through his veins. He turned and climbed the stairs, watching her, his back almost pressed against the rough, torchlit wall.

"I cannot wait to have you." His voice pulsed with arousal. His eyes appeared to be forged from fire as he lifted her hand to his mouth and spread his tongue over her palm, and then upward between the sensitive creases of her fingers.

His tongue felt like a flame. The sight of it could not

have been more seductive if he laved it across a more intimate part of her body. Gianelle moaned with regret when it withdrew behind his teasing lips.

"More?" he whispered, taunting her with a smile of forbidden temptation that heated her blood and hastened her steps. He drew her finger into his hot mouth and sucked softly, flicking his tongue over her flesh. "I intend to lick every delectable inch of you."

Gianelle's eyes closed with the fevered memory of just how masterful his tongue could be. She opened them slowly, her breath heavy on her lips. She gazed at his chiseled angles made even more sultry against the flickering torchlight. "I might do the same to you," she told him, tempting him to the edge of his endurance.

His jaw tightened as they reached the landing. He dragged her into his arms and Gianelle shivered at the hard tightening of his muscles and the dark sensuality of the smile that curved his mouth. Pinned against him, she could feel every rock-hard inch of him: his chest, his thighs, his fierce erection. He didn't kiss her but cupped her bottom, and with an almost brutal possession, drove her up his body, giving her a wicked idea of where he might want to be licked. He let her go with a gentle slap on her derriere and followed her to his room.

The hearth fire blazed, illuminating his bed. Gianelle stepped inside and turned around when she heard Dante bolt the door. She wasn't afraid or timid, though he looked like a hardened warrior on the verge of pillaging a wife he hadn't seen in months. He reached down and unhooked his belt. His slow, wicked smile curled her toes, and her heartbeat hastened at his awesome strength, the coiled energy that made him look like he was about to lunge at her. His eyes moved over her, hungry with desire, hard with the restraint of his rigid control. His gaze brushed over her throat and settled on the peaks of her nipples that tightened as if he had kissed them. He advanced on her, peeling off his surcoat and shirt. Gianelle bit her lip, wanting to do the same to his bare shoulders, his chest, his hard belly. She was so wild for him, she almost couldn't fathom that this was her. But here was another part of her that Dante freed. Her breasts felt swollen and heavy at the sight of him, the scent of him. She wanted to be free of her gown and feel his warm skin against hers.

He was there, hovering over her. He fit his hands around her waist and turned her around. His fingers swept her hair away from her nape and he dipped his mouth to the throbbing pulse just beneath her flesh. Molding his powerful body to hers, he encased her in his arms while he nibbled and kissed her throat. Beneath his hose, he was hard, swollen, and throbbing for her. He untethered each button of her wedding gown with deft fingers, pressing kisses over every inch of flesh he exposed. When she stood naked in his arms, he guided her to his bed and sat down.

A thick cord of bronze muscle twitched along his arm as he lifted it to her, inviting her to sit—not atop his thighs, but between them. She went, willingly, unable to resist him. She never truly could. With her back pressed against his chest, he cupped her breasts in his palms, caressing, and then kneading her erect nipples in his fingers. Lower, his heavy arousal pushed against her, aching for release, aching to be deep inside her.

Splaying her across his unyielding muscles, he laved

his warm tongue over her lips. She dug her fingertips into his shoulders to hold on while he dragged her nipple between his fingers. Throwing her head back, she exposed her throat to his fevered gaze. Her hair spilled down to the floor in a golden puddle, and Dante slipped his arm behind her and clutched a handful in his fingers. He pulled, making her arch her back even more, lifting the glorious peaks of her breasts to his mouth. He closed his lips around her and sucked. His hand was big enough to cup her entire breast while he raked his teeth over the other. He hauled her in closer, needing her near him. He groaned deep in his throat, a feral growl that set her nerve endings ablaze. His muscles flexed to steel slabs as he parted her legs and stroked the dewy nub between them.

Dante's mouth covered hers with supreme domination, that masterful tongue plunging into her while his fingers explored her below and within. She cried out, begging him to cease his torturously erotic ministrations and have his way with her. She was so warm and wet in his hand, ready to receive him.

That was all the provocation Dante needed. Lifting her with his hips, he tore his hose away. He closed his hands around her waist and lifted her once more, this time to straddle him. His gaze was smoldering and fired with a need so wild, so untamed and uncontrolled that finally Gianelle felt a little frightened. She pushed her meager palms against his chest as he set her down, impaling her with a grunting thrust that drove her upward. Widening his fingers over her back, he moved her over him, gyrating his hips to pleasure her more fully. She traced her palms over the sleek sinew of his arms, then clutched his shoulders, straining against his long, rigid flesh. His hands slid to her rump, and he groaned as he lifted her up and down, felt her tight body enfold him from stem to tip. He suckled her and she trembled in his arms. Tearing his mouth away, he whispered how much he loved her. Clenching his jaw, he tossed his head back. Gianelle descended on his thick neck and kissed. She had to taste the salty flavor that filled her lungs, and when Dante felt her tongue glide over his Adam's apple he nearly erupted. He flipped her over, and without releasing himself from her, laid her down beneath him. He angled her thigh higher over his back and plunged deeply, his gaze so hot on her Gianelle dragged his mouth to hers and bit his lip.

"You fill me so fully." Her voice shuddered along with her body, and her heart took up the rhythm pulsing around his thickness.

He cupped her buttocks, driving against her harder, and then withdrew only to slide his velvet lance over her crest. He watched his seed spill out over her belly, then he sank inside her again. When he rose up on his knees, Gianelle ravaged him with her gaze, knowing that he was as majestic and beautiful as the finest stallion, and as big as one. She stiffened and clutched the furs beneath her, ready to lose herself all over him, but he withdrew again and lifted her to his hungry mouth. Gianelle rocked and pitched in his hands, grabbing fistfuls of his inky hair, and drenched him in her passion.

When it was over, she lay there panting, weak, and quivering. Dante climbed up alongside her and held her in his arms. "Rest, *ma belle fée,* we're not done."

Later, Talard brought wine to the room, but Dante didn't drink his. He dipped his fingers in his cup and let the nectar drip onto her nipples, her neck, her belly, then licked it off her. He did the same to her lips, kissing and drinking from her sweet mouth. When he dabbed his wet fingertips along her inner thigh she giggled and he smiled hearing her. He tickled her some more and laughed with her, but their playful fun led to more lovemaking; standing up with her legs wrapped tightly around his waist, at the edge of the bed, her body atop his while he pushed her up, off his heavy thighs. She answered with slow caressing dips that pulled the hot seed from his body and into hers.

They slept, drained and exhausted. But the next morning when she woke, Dante was hard for her again. She shook her head at him when he pulled her closer. He watched her with hooded eyes as she rose from the bed and beckoned him to the settee. He went to her and she pushed him down, then stepped back to admire the wickedly sexual sight of him sprawled out so dark and powerful in front of her.

She knelt before him and took his fullness in her hands, then into her mouth. She stroked him with long, provocative licks up his entire length. He cursed in French and cupped the back of her head to take him more deeply. Finally, he pulled her up into his lap and took her again.

Chapter Nineteen

"DON'T TOUCH ME." Gianelle held up her palms to ward Dante off as he approached the bed. The fact that he was fully dressed meant little, knowing how quickly he could get his clothes off.

He laughed and held up a tray of food that he had retrieved from the great hall.

It was late afternoon and she hadn't been out of bed yet. "You're a brute," she murmured, and picked at a poached egg when Dante sat next to her. "I hurt everywhere."

Satisfaction cast a steely spark in his smoky gaze and Gianelle sighed. "You have turned me into a shameless trollop, Dante. I hope you're happy."

"I am." He winked at her and bit into a slice of pork.

Gianelle pinched herself after watching his tongue move over his lips, wiping up the juice from his food.

"Stop that!"

He cut her a curious side glance. "Stop what?"

"Licking your mouth."

Dante stopped eating and grinned at her. "You're crazy about me. Admit it."

"You make my skin crawl."

He laughed. "Liar."

Reaching her hand out, she brushed a black strand of hair off his shoulder. "I love your laugh. You look . . . cute."

"Cute?"

"*Oui,* like a boy who is a man."

"When you laugh, you look like a sexy harlot." He laughed when she punched his arm and threw herself on top of him. "Forgive me, I meant angel. I was thinking of last night. It is not my fault."

She swatted his arm again and he caught her hand and kissed it. "I love you."

"Will you always?" she whispered, gazing deep into his eyes.

"*Oui.*"

"Do you promise, husband?"

"*Oui,* I promise."

"And you will never leave me?"

"Never," he vowed. "Never."

"Because if you did, I would find you and put hot coals in your breeches . . . while you wore them."

"*Enfer,* you're dangerous, woman."

She gave him a cheeky smile and blinked her wide eyes like an innocent puppy, then she pushed off him and reached for the tray that teetered on the edge of the bed. She looked around the room after eating a pear tart. "You forgot the wine. I'll go get it."

"*Non.* I don't want you roaming the castle while I'm up here and Edgar Dermott is walking about."

"Did you see him?" she turned to ask him, finishing off another pear tart.

"Do you see blood on my shirt?"

She shrugged and went back to eating. When she struggled to get the dry pastry down her throat, Dante rose from the bed. She watched him, loving how he looked. He wore an ivory linen shirt belted to flare over his lean hips, and loose-fitting black gauzy breeches tucked into low kid-leather boots.

"You can't take your eyes off me," he called out without turning around.

"I would rather look at a fly-infested turd."

His deep, throaty laughter filled the chamber, and then the hall.

~

Dante almost tripped over a clucking chicken that scurried across his path with old James in hot pursuit.

"Good day, milord. Sleep well, did ye?" James stopped directly in front of Dante and offered him a sly wink.

"Very well. *Merci,* James." Dante flashed him a wide grin. "James?" he asked a moment later, narrowing his eyes, suddenly trying to figure out why the old man harbored a desire to rid the castle of its chickens. "Why are you chasing a chicken around my castle?"

Inclining his ear in the direction the hen had taken, James scowled and knit his bushy eyebrows. "She kept me awake all night with her constant yapping, milord. I aim to eat her."

"Eat her." Dante nodded as though he understood perfectly well now.

"Aye, Sir."

"And how do you know it was that particular chicken

that kept you awake all night?" Dante asked while laughter colored his eyes.

"Well." The old man raised a bony finger to Dante's face. "She has a particular cluck, different from the others—well, the truth of 'tis they are all different, much like a woman's voice. I may not be able to see who is chatting, but I can tell who 'tis by her voice. Take last eve for instance, when I was passing Lord Dermott's room. I couldn't sleep because of that blasted chicken." His almost sightless eyes wandered aimlessly through the corridor for the white feathers he couldn't see, then he turned back to Dante. "I heard a woman's voice in there with him. *Ye* wouldna have known who 'twas, but Simone has a sweet foreign ring to her voice and I . . ."

Dante's eyes opened wide and then smoldered dangerously. "Simone was in Dermott's room?"

James nodded and proceeded to explain the many subtle tones to her voice that differentiated it from the other women's voices in the castle.

"What was she doing in there?" Dante interrupted, his tone biting the air like an early frost.

James gave him a knowing, semi-toothless smile. "What do ye *think* she was doing in there?"

Dante remained silent for a moment, letting James's words sink into his head. "Blast her!" he cursed. "She cannot keep her legs closed to any man."

"None but poor old James." The old man snapped his tongue against the roof of his mouth in self-pity. He heard a sound and tilted his head to the right.

"Here, chicky, chicky," he sang and bent forward to listen. He pulled a large ax out from behind his back and swooshed it past Dante's horrified face. And then he was gone, hurrying after his clucking supper.

Dante watched him and shook his head. He had to figure out somewhere to station the menace before he killed someone.

He smiled, feeling happier than he had in months. He found Talard and asked him to deliver more wine to his chambers.

A few moments later, he caught his wife at the bottom of the stairs. He grinned into her face and slipped his hand around the small of her back. "What are you doing out of bed?" He pulled her closer until her back was arched so that he could run his warm lips down her neck. "Was I gone too long, *fée*? Did you miss me already?"

Gianelle laughed softly against his ear, forgetting everything else but the wonderful ache in his touch as his hands drifted over the soft mounds of her buttocks.

"I didn't even know you were gone," she lied, giddy with the thought of teasing him. "I came down because I am still hungry."

He breathed huskily and nibbled her neck. "Amazing. So am I."

Gianelle was melting quickly against his hot breath and wicked cravings, but she was not ready to face defeat just yet. "If you release me, I will lead you to our room and let you taste the sweet rose of my breasts."

Dante's head came up from her neck and he cast her a smile of such sensual intensity her knees went weak. She doubted if she could continue.

He released her, rendered speechless by her sensual promise. But instead of turning back up the stairs, Gianelle laughed and raced away toward the castle doors.

Dante's smile darkened moments before he took off after her. He reached her just as she began to pull the heavy doors open. He threw his palms against the cool wood, slamming the door shut again. He stood behind her, his hands over her head. She could feel his breath in her hair and turned to face him. "Where are you going, wife? Hmm?" He tilted his lips to hers and kissed her mischievous grin.

Before he could grab her, Gianelle slipped under his arms, twirled on her heel and yanked on the door. Ancient, extremely hard wood smashed into Dante's nose, but Gianelle never slowed, even when she heard the venomous string of oaths mumbled through his hands while he held his wounded face. She laughed and bounded over squawking chickens and squealing pigs. Her feet carried her as though she were flying on the salty wind toward the lowered portcullis. When she reached it, she spun around, knowing Dante was close behind her.

With her thick hair tumbling around her face and her cheeks rosy pink from running, Gianelle faced her pursuer and inched backward until her back nudged against the cool wrought iron. "Give the order to raise the portcullis or I shall never sleep in your bed again," she warned with sunlight sparking her eyes.

Dante shook his head slowly and closed in on her like a male lion stalking his mate.

"Do it. I warn you. I shall lock myself away in my room and laugh while you pine for me."

"Pine for you!" Dante stopped and chuckled. His eyes devoured her from her head to her toes. "I would break the door down and take what is mine. Never would I pine."

Giggling at his cocky pride, Gianelle waved him away

with a slight brush of her hand. "Step away, or I shall never smile at you again."

"Ah, now that would be hell." Dante turned and called up to Roland to raise the portcullis. When his gaze returned to his wife, the excitement that gleamed in his eyes reminded her of a predator poised for attack. "I warn you, fiery maiden, when I catch you, and I will—I will take you wherever we fall, so you better return to our bed now while you have the chance."

"And admit defeat to you?" Gianelle called out as the great iron gate lifted behind her. "Never!" She ducked and slipped under the gate to freedom. Knowing he was hot on her tail, she ran.

Dante's gaze followed her for a few minutes, soaking in the splendor of her hair as it bounced and glimmered over her shoulders and down her back, set afire by the sun. When she hiked up her muslin skirts, he admired her lean, shapely legs leaping over rocks to escape him. She laughed and the sound filled his heart. He allowed her a generous lead and then gave chase, following her path past the gatehouse. Then he darted to the left with a wide grin of victory already spreading over his face.

Gianelle sped past rocky slopes and around huge jagged walls that led down to the path to the ocean, her heart pounding madly in her chest. If Dante caught her while she was still in sight of the castle, she had no doubt he would throw her to the ground and claim his victory while whoever was outside watched. She risked a quick look over her shoulder but didn't see him. Had he stopped chasing her? She couldn't stop now to find out. Not when the sea was such a short distance away. She could smell the brackish scent of the waves and hear their crashing fury as she ran. Overhead, gulls soared and screeched and dipped into the liquid blue horizon in search of food. She was so close. If he caught up to her there she wouldn't protest.

She was thinking how delightful it might be to join with him in the sand when she crashed straight into him. Stunned momentarily, she stared up into his molten gaze, wondering how he had come to be in front of her.

He grasped her wrist so that she couldn't flee again. Both of them gasped for every breath they took into their lungs, but Dante managed a sensual smirk. "This victory shall be my greatest. Perchance even spoken about in centuries to come. See? We have witnesses."

Gianelle hated to do it, but she looked around and saw at least a dozen fishermen watching them. "*Non,* you wouldn't." She breathed heavily, her chest rising and falling as feverishly as the swell of the sea.

"I would. And I will." Dante regarded her with a dark look of such naked intent that she could do nothing but believe him.

"Fine," she retorted, determined that no matter what it took, she wouldn't lose. "I will help you get this over with." With eyes that never left his, she offered him a challenging grin and began to unlace her kirtle.

Folding his arms across his chest, Dante watched her with eyes that burned. "I am going to enjoy this."

"*Oui,*" Gianelle purred. "And so will they." She smiled and waved to the fishermen, who stopped folding their nets to gape at her.

Dante's eyes darted toward them and his triumphant smile faded, but he didn't stop her when she dropped her overskirt to her ankles.

Their eyes locked in a battle of wills as Gianelle tossed

her slippers aside like the half-eaten chicken bones thrown to the dogs in the great hall. She stood there, a tiny goddess about to shed her wings and expose her soft womanly beauty to the whole world. Dante's pulse ticked furiously in his neck, aching to gaze upon the magical creature, but not willing to share the vision with anyone else.

She crossed her arms over her head and began to lift her underdress. Dante watched, his breath rapid, his eyes hooded and burning dangerously. When he saw the golden treasure between her thighs, he cursed and snatched her hands away from the fabric.

In one fluid motion he lifted her off her feet. "You are mine alone," he told her and carried her to a small cave set in the cliffs on the shore.

His words were spoken with such power, such authority that Gianelle's body quivered in his arms. She had been owned by many men, but none of them had possessed her. None of them had claimed her the way he had last night. She belonged to him. And held against the indomitable strength of his chest, Gianelle knew she wanted to be his.

His fingers delighted her as he peeled the remaining underdress from her body. His smoldering gaze and feverishly uncivilized passion thrilled her while his lips devoured her. And when he positioned her on her knees and palms in the white, warm sand and knelt behind her, she knew that he was about to lay claim to so much more than her body.

By the time Gianelle finally made it to the great hall later that day, she was ready to eat a seven-course meal.

Dante sat next to her at the long trestle table with his chin in his palm, watching her while she shoved honey-soaked cakes into her mouth. She barely swallowed before popping a slice of mutton in next.

With cheeks bulging, she reached for her goblet and caught her husband's amused appraisal.

"What?" she asked with wide eyes of innocence caressing his heart.

His smile widened into a warm grin, not knowing which was larger, her eyes or her mouth. "You have a ravenous appetite for one so small."

Gianelle shrugged and took a generous gulp of wine. "I wouldn't be so ravenous if you had let me eat this afternoon instead of chasing me through the countryside."

Dante was about to protest, but laughed instead. The sound brought a smile to Gianelle's lips.

"Besides," she said merrily, and then bit into a juicy pear, "I imagine if I get good and fat it will give me some rest from *your* ravenous appetite, my lord."

His eyes delighted in the soft curve of her lips while she spoke and the thin golden brow that lifted impishly. "It wouldn't work," he proclaimed. The deep, low tone of his voice was like a flame licking every inch of her flesh. "I would still adore you."

Gianelle stopped chewing and looked at him while his words settled over her heart. Did he mean what he had just said? Did he adore her? Or did these heart-wrenching declarations simply fall from his lips the same way he congratulated Ingred on the wondrous feasts she prepared for Graycliff? She wanted him to say it again, tell her that he cherished her, that she meant something to him. But the moment was gone when Brand appeared before them.

Dante looked up from the dreamy gaze that had fallen upon his wife.

"Sorry to interrupt." The thin smirk that clung to Brand's lips said otherwise. "I just thought you might like to know that Dermott and his men left about an hour ago." Brand's smirk grew wider. "I guess he decided to wait for your revenge in Cambridge."

Dante flashed him a grin that shredded Gianelle's defenses altogether. Her husband's rugged beauty fascinated her. His eyes were like clear, shimmering crystals against his olive skin and ebony hair, crystals that sparked with verdant life. They could cut through flesh as sharply as finely honed swords, piercing and intensely powerful, but when he looked at her they softened and then burned, devouring her with emotions.

Dante was still smiling when he turned back to his wife. Brand had left the table, but Gianelle hardly noticed. "You have been wearing that same heavenly expression for the last five minutes," Dante spoke with a curious curl of his lips. "What are you thinking about?"

Hypnotized by him, Gianelle gazed at the play of muscle that corded his throat when he swallowed. She let her eyes drift over his face.

"I'm on the shore of a beautiful sea strewn with silver moonbeams," she whispered. "The power of this tumultuous sea calls to me, and though it frightens me, I must go."

Dante lifted his fingers to her mouth and brushed his thumb over her lower lip. "Why does it frighten you, most beloved faerie?"

She closed her eyes, keeping silent, and Dante pulled her into the warmth of his body, caressing her tenderly in his arms. "God's teeth, Gia, I would never hurt you," he swore into her hair, unable to even bear the thought.

Gianelle wanted to cling to him forever. She wanted to tangle her fingers into his hair and never let him go.

She pulled away from him just enough to lift her gaze to his. "The waves of this sea are not cold. Nor do they seek to pull me under their murky depths, but rather they caress me like heavenly hands, safe and warm. This wondrous sea does not roar, though its might is so great it could suck the life from me as if I were nothing. But *non*, its thunderous waves gently whisper the sweetest sounds my ears have ever heard."

Dante smiled at her tearful gaze. "What is so bad about that?"

"It's easy to fall so deeply in love with such magnificence and tenderness. But where there is so much power, one as insignificant as I may become lost, forgotten."

She felt him stiffen under her touch and hoped that she had not said the wrong thing.

"My love." He lifted his hand to stroke the silky tumult of her hair. Gianelle blinked into his smoky gray eyes. "A sea is merely a lake without the wind to stir it." He smiled and took her hand, drawing her to her feet.

"Come, let's go for a ride."

Dante led her out of Graycliff and to the stable, asking her to wait outside for him. When he exited a few moments later atop his wild white mare, Gianelle lifted her hand to her chest.

He rode toward her, this lord of the cliffs who had given her the sea, like a vision taken from the dreams of mermaids. Without breaking stride, he leaned forward, snaked his arm beneath hers, and lifted her to his lap.

His strong hand clamped to her waist thrilled her. His warm breath against her nape made her heady with desire, and when he drove his heels into Ayla's flanks, he set her heart to pounding.

They rode over low ridges and rocky crags without slowing, and for the first few breaths Gianelle kept her eyes sealed shut, afraid Ayla would lose her footing and send the three of them over the cliffs. But soon they reached the sea and finally slowed at the shoreline. Ayla snorted and kicked her hind legs, creating a cloud of sand behind them.

"She wants to run," Dante whispered close to Gianelle's ear. Then he pulled up her skirts and lifted her leg over the mare's sleek back so that she was better balanced. "Ride her," he said and placed the reins in Gianelle's hands.

"She frightens me," Gianelle answered, but she took the reins from him, her heart thudding wildly in her ears.

"And since when has that stopped you?" Dante laughed.

"Ayla," he called out. The mare's ear twitched. "Show Gianelle what it's like to fly." He reached behind him and slapped the mare's haunches.

Gianelle clutched the reins while the wind snapped her hair off her shoulders. The rolling waves to her left became nothing more than a gray blur as Ayla's legs soared over wet sand so fast she barely disturbed a single grain. Tears were whipped from Gianelle's cheeks, her breath snatched away the instant it left her body. She was flying, as free as Dante was when he rode Ayla. "Do you feel the wind, *ma fée*?" He held her, his voice as deep as the sea behind her. "It is as powerful as the ocean, *oui*?"

"Oui," she cried, understanding why he gave her this gift. She was not insignificant to him, but as vital as he was to her.

She put the reins in his hands and leaned her body against his chest, and then she spread her arms wide, trusting him not to let her fall. She tilted her face to his and her smile grew into laughter.

"Thank you, Dante. Thank you for setting me free."

Chapter Twenty

EDGAR DERMOTT PULLED OFF HIS GLOVE and tapped it against his other hand. The old, deserted shed smelled like decaying wood and manure. He stalked toward the window for fresh air, and to see if the man he waited for was anywhere in sight.

Dark clouds rolled across the sky, boding rain. Something squeaked behind him and he spun around. A large rat scurried into the shadows. He swore, stomping his boot to frighten the rodent back into its hole. He began to pace, feeling trapped in the dilapidated shed. His lungs ached from trying not to breathe too deeply.

He'd been waiting for an hour, but it felt like a se'nnight. He should just leave and carry out his plans without his lord's approval. But the last time he had done so had nearly cost him and his brother their heads.

His brother, he thought with contempt hardening his features. He was glad that fat old fool was dead. Of course, it was difficult keeping up the pretense of mourning his dearly departed sibling. But it was worth it. Devonshire would be his as soon as he showed King William the missives he carried from Hereward's loyalists to his brother.

He would plead complete ignorance to his brother's alliance with the notorious rebel. And then he would take care of Gianelle.

He'd been furious when he learned Risande was going to marry the wench and she would not be returned to him as he had hoped. But seeing her again changed his mind about wanting her imprisoned. He wanted her dead, and he wanted to be the one to do it, after he took her to his bed, of course. That cold bitch's days of rejecting him were over. A change of plans was all it would take to ensure that he would finally get his hands on her. His brother could no longer stop him, and soon there would be no one else to keep her from his bed.

He heard a horse approaching and peered out the window again, his hand poised at the hilt of his sword. He whistled at the hooded figure riding toward the shed. The man was alone, but Hereward the Wake needed no entourage of men at his side. He was a big man with a quick, brutal arm, and an even faster horse.

Edgar watched him dismount and walk his steed to the doors. Once inside, Hereward drew back his hood to reveal pale green eyes and a mane of deep red hair. He looked around with disgust carving his wary features.

"Is that stench coming from you or the rotting hay?" the hefty Saxon rebel asked.

"Unless I'm suddenly so frightened by the sight of you that I soiled my breeches," Edgar snarled, "I feel it's safe to blame the hay."

"It wouldn't be the first time you did the like, Dermott," Hereward replied coolly and slid his fingers over his sword's hilt.

"You will not be so eager to kill me when you hear what I have to say."

"Then say it and let us discover if you're correct." Hereward leaned his powerful shoulder against the door-frame and waited.

"King William is back in England. He arrived two days ago."

Hereward's eyes focused somewhere in the vicinity of Dermott's neck. "I think I shall slit your throat, though I'd rather hear you scream. Alas, I have other matters to attend to and a quick death for you would serve me better." His voice dropped to a deadly pitch. "I already know the bastard is back."

"Do you also know he sent his command for all his higher vassals to meet with him at court?"

"Go on."

"I myself have been summoned."

"No doubt you will cower at his feet and pledge fealty to him the moment he asks it."

"Never," Dermott lied. "I fully intend to prove my loyalty to you by killing the man who so fervently hunts you."

Now Hereward raised a sardonic brow at him. "Let's not forget the reason for Risande's fervor. If you and those other daft lackwits hadn't killed his sister, he would not have sworn his life to finding me. You owe me your life for that."

"I will give you Lord Dante Risande's life instead."

Hereward tossed his head back and laughed, careless of the rage gleaming in Dermott's eyes. "How do you propose to kill him, eh? If you had a dozen sword arms and a pair of eyes in the back of your head, you still couldn't fight him and win."

"I don't intend to fight him," Dermott replied woodenly.

"Oh, of course you don't. An arrow in the back is more your style."

"He will be dead. What do you care how it's done?"

"I don't," Hereward said, pushing himself off the wall. "I admit I want him off my tail, though a warrior like Risande deserves a more honorable death than an arrow in his back."

"How can you say that after he has killed so many of your loyal sympathizers?"

"You killed his sister, Dermott," Hereward growled. "An innocent who had naught to do with the king's war, just as my brother had naught to do with it. I understand his rage. Now tell me of your plan. My patience grows thin."

"Very well," Dermott said. "I have enlisted the aid of someone in his castle who knows the day Risande is planning to travel. I know how many men will be with him and we will follow him. I will kill him unseen, and then travel to Winchester and meet with the king. No one will suspect me, as I plan to ambush Risande's party far away from Dover. You have many followers who are as eager to kill him as I am. You yourself may take credit for the killing if you like." Dermott offered him a cool smile.

"Nay, I don't kill men from behind. No one would believe it."

"Of course. Forgive me."

"I will think about forgiving you after Risande is dead. Only, make certain you kill him, Dermott, or we will have an even angrier madman on our hands. And then I will kill you myself."

Hereward yanked the door open and left the shed without another word. He didn't worry about what Dermott would say to the king when he met with him. The traitor would never reach Winchester.

Inside the shed, Edgar Dermott touched the small stack of missives beneath his mantle. He would prove his loyalty to the king, but first he had a castle to storm, and a slave to take back.

~

"How long will you be gone?" Gianelle watched the strength in Dante's shoulders dip in a sigh that seemed to render him weak as he searched his wardrobe for his tabard.

"Not long. A few days." He gave up his search and turned to her, his face shadowed by the weight of duty that made him have to leave her. "I will make haste."

Sitting at the edge of the bed, Gianelle clutched her skirts, trying to calm the coils that had become her nerves. Any moment now she would spring from the bed and rush into his arms. "Don't rush the king, Dante."

"Come with me, Brynna and the children are going."

Gianelle lowered her eyes and shook her head. "I think it's best that Casey and I are not there while you speak with the king about us."

Dante stared at her for a moment longer and then turned away. He didn't want to leave her.

"I will make haste, Gianelle."

She nodded and left the bed. She paced the room while he folded clothes into his leather bag, glancing over to watch the strong angles that contoured his jaw as he bent his tall body to the sack.

She stopped pacing. "I will miss you," she blurted, twisting her fingers together. Her breath ceased when he looked up and cast her a beguiling smile.

"You will be relieved to see me go," he teased.

Shrugging her delicate shoulders, she took up her pacing again. "Just your foolish sense of humor," she retorted. "But I might miss arguing with you." Oh, she would miss so much more than that! His eyes always on her, the silky roughness of his hands when they touched her, his husky, sexy voice telling her how much he loved her.

Dante left his packing and snatched her wrist, stopping her anxious movements. He pulled her into him and slipped his arms around her waist. "Make love to me before I go." His voice was hoarse against her ear.

"I knew you were a ravishing beast the moment I first saw you." Gianelle huffed, but then closed her eyes and threw her head back in delight when he carried her to the bed.

~

Gianelle roamed the castle, left ominously quiet after Dante and his men were gone. She bristled on her way toward Casey's room. Who did King William think he was, anyway? Living in France for months at a time and then ordering his knights to his side on a whim?

She found Casey brooding in her room and wasn't surprised when her friend mentioned Balin's name a dozen times in one sentence in defense of her sour mood. Dara joined them a little while later, just as sullen over the absence of her husband.

"You never get used to them leaving," she told Gianelle. "It's much worse when they go off to battle and you don't know if you'll ever see them again."

Gianelle shivered in her skin. "I don't know if I could do it."

"What choice is there? They are warriors. We pray that the Lord protects them and brings them back to us. That, and trust in their skill. It is all we can do."

Gianelle felt sick. She hadn't thought about Dante fighting battles. She didn't want to. Ever.

She left her two friends when Dara pulled out some embroidery and began sewing. Gianelle couldn't think about practicing her needlework now. She made her way down the stairs, praying that Dante would always return to her from any battle. Gianelle thought of his eyes and the way they soaked in her face before he left.

"I will miss you," he had whispered minutes before Balin called that they would never get to Winchester if he bid her farewell one more time.

He loved her. She could see it in the smoky, dazzling haze in his eyes. He would never leave her the way her father had. She sighed long and slow and almost fell into James on her way to the kitchen.

"I'm sad to see him go as well, milady," the old man agreed and smiled blindly into her face.

"What?"

"The Earl. 'Tis what happens when the one ye love so very much journeys afar. Ye sigh as if yer heart is about to break free from yer throat and go after him."

James left then; just picked up his steps and left her there to gape at his back, wondering if his hearing was so sharp that he could hear the longings of her heart.

~

The setting sun spilled its rays through the intricate web of branches overhead. The filtering light created tall columns of golden fire where damselflies could be seen dancing to a melody played on the slight breeze.

And then the ground shook and the damselflies scattered as Dante's troop drove their horses through the quiet forest. They didn't ride as quickly as Dante would have liked, for Lady Brynna rode with them, cradling baby Richard in her arms while Tanon enjoyed the view from her father's lap. Young William insisted on riding with Dante, and having the boy nestled on his lap reminded Dante to ride with caution, even though every league that took them farther away from Graycliff was like a stone upon his heart. The faster they got to Winchester, the sooner they could go home.

Merde, how he missed Gianelle already. He loved her more than his heart could endure. He loved her beautiful, innocent face, her willful spirit that had been set free, and the passion that made her dainty hips sway when she knew he was watching her. The very thought of her brought fire to his nerve endings and made him close his eyes, fighting the savage urge to turn his horse around and race back home. The memory of her upturned face when she looked at him with those eyes of beaten gold set his heart to soaring.

He was still thinking of her when an arrow sailed past him and landed in the back of Sir Armond, a knight who had come to England with Dante years before.

"Break! Break!" Dante shouted, bending over his nephew to shield him from the arrows. He reined Ayla to the left and dug his heels into her flanks as his men broke formation and scattered throughout the dense wood.

"Balin!" Dante yelled toward him. "Take twenty men and scout those hills. You, Gerald, cut through that ravine with Robert and the others and close in on the other side of Balin's troop."

"Brand!" he shouted to his brother. "Take William and your family and go! Go!"

Suddenly, four more arrows whistled through the air and landed in the dirt before Dante and into the tree trunks around his men. He reined in, steadying his agitated mare, his eyes blazing like lightning against a charcoal sky.

He practically tossed his nephew to his brother. "Go!" His warrior blood scalded his veins. He watched his brother grab the reins of Brynna's horse and thunder away. Then he snapped his reins and drove Ayla into the wooded curtain of trees behind him. When he heard a sound to his right, he lifted his hand and motioned for one of his men to take position. He advanced, unsheathing his sword at the same time.

Someone called his name. It was a female voice. He kicked his feet and dashed through a maze of ancient oak and chestnut, forgetting caution, forgetting everything he had ever learned. He heard his men calling somewhere behind him, but he didn't answer. Reasoning told him that the voice he heard couldn't belong to his wife or Casey. They were leagues away in Dover. But he raced on as memories of his sister's body returned to him. He had left her alone, and when he returned to her . . .

Dried, fallen leaves rustled to his right. He turned. And then the arrow that broke through his chest shattered the images that haunted him.

"Dear God, you said you wouldn't kill him!"

"I lied."

Simone glared at the tall, handsome man beside her, but there was no time to argue with him now. Dante's men would be getting closer. All around her the forest was ominously quiet. Even the birds and critters seemed to sense her betrayal, and as she gazed down at the beautiful face of the man who had once been her lover, she felt the weight of that treachery and groped at her throat. Suddenly she couldn't breathe. "What have we done?" she gasped.

"Shut up!" Edgar Dermott commanded and bent swiftly to retrieve Dante's sword. He would have liked to take Risande's horse, too, but the beast took off back to Risande's men.

For a moment, Simone thought Dermott was going to slice her neck with that sword. But he only smiled, holding the amber-studded pommel up to his face. "Aye, this will do."

"For what?"

Dermott's hand snapped forward and closed around her cheeks, bruising her soft olive skin. His eyes were like blue fire singeing her flesh; his voice was chilled with the promise of violence. "My dear wench, if you ever question me again, I will cut your heart out and eat it for breakfast. Understand?"

Simone nodded her head, trembling at the cruelty newly revealed in her present lover. When he marched back into the deep thicket where a group of his men waited, he called her. She hesitated, gazing back down at Dante. What had she done?

Someone called Dante's name. Someone very close. Just beyond the trees. "Forgive me," she whispered to the still body lying at her feet. And then she ran.

~

Gianelle was just about to settle into her bath when she heard Roland shouting from the tower. She paused with one leg in the warm water. Was Dante home already? Her heart clattered madly in her chest and she nearly raced to the terrace naked. It couldn't be Dante, she told herself. He had left only three days ago and couldn't possibly have reached Winchester and come back already. She slipped into her soft woolen robe, one of the many gifts her husband had hidden in various places in their room with little notes attached for her to find. Of course, he had no way of knowing that she couldn't read, but Dara and Douglan were happy to read them to her.

She leaned over the edge of the terrace. Her thick hair snapped around her face like a pennant. From Dante's room she could see the bailey below and the outer court-yard, and Simone, alone and perched upon her horse, awaiting entry to Graycliff. The dark beauty looked up and Gianelle met her solemn gaze for a moment before Simone turned away and the portcullis was lifted.

With disappointment settling over her, Gianelle sighed and was about to go back inside and finish her bath when she heard the low rumble of distant thunder. She looked up at the clear sky. And then Roland began to scream.

Gianelle could hardly remember what happened in the minutes that followed. All she saw was Edgar Dermott's face, a mask of evil, firing an arrow toward Roland and killing the tower guard before he could lower the portcullis. Dermott led at least one hundred mounted men into the bailey. Like a river bursting through a dam, they advanced, cutting down Dante's men before they even had a chance to draw their swords.

Gianelle was quite familiar with violence, especially the kind bestowed by the Dermotts. Still, she couldn't move, watching the destruction that took place beneath her. He was coming for her. There was no denial clouding her thoughts. No shock or disbelief that what she was seeing was really happening. She knew how to deal with fear. She could think under extreme circumstances, not like the noble ladies who screamed and fell to pieces when danger struck. But this was Baron Bryce Dermott's brother, not some brutally handsome stranger with a kind voice and shimmering eyes.

She bolted out of the room and raced down the stairs. Just outside the castle doors she could hear the shouts of the rest of Dante's men. Some tried to stop her and lead her to the safety of the castle's bolt-holes, but she yanked free from their grasps and plunged into the kitchen where she had left Casey before retiring for her bath. "Casey?" she screamed, but no one was there. She searched the great hall, the solar, then raced back up the stairs to Casey's room.

Below her, the heavy castle doors burst open and silence, as foreboding as the terrifying quiet that used to still her heart moments before Bryce Dermott found her after an attempted escape, clung to Graycliff like a suffocating mist.

"Darling! Gianelle, where are you, my sweeting?"

Her knees almost buckled beneath her, but Gianelle sucked a great gulp of air into her lungs. She had been afraid of him once, but no more. She left Casey's room and ran to the chambers she shared with Dante. He had a dagger hidden in his wardrobe. She'd seen it when he was packing. She found it now, hid it in her robe, and walked quietly out of the room.

"Ah, what a vision of loveliness to behold!" Dermott grinned up at her as she slowly descended the stairs. He struggled for a moment, clutching one of Dante's men firmly under his arm. Edgar Dermott was a brawny man, and though the poor soldier fought with every ounce of strength he had, his captor barely moved.

"Let him go," Gianelle demanded, but her voice was only a whisper.

"Oh, I wish I could." Dermott pouted. "But—" He let the word linger in the air for a moment while he produced a long broadsword from behind his back. Without even blinking an eyelash, he plunged the blade into the soldier's back. "I'm not here to make friends," he said as the guard's body slipped from his arms and fell to the floor at his feet. Dermott stepped over him and marched to the bottom of the stairs. He held the amber-studded hilt up to Gianelle's face.

"Recognize it, my dear?"

Gianelle had learned long ago how to stop her tears. But seeing Dante's sword waving before her face made her stumble. "Where . . . where did you get that?"

Standing just below her now, Dermott's eyes narrowed into slits. "I thought killing you would bring me the greatest pleasure, but killing your husband and having you for myself is much more satisfying." He smiled at her and sheathed Dante's sword in the scabbard at his side.

"You are lying." Gianelle took another step down the stairs. "You could never kill him. He is a warrior and you are nothing but a filthy mound of scum."

Edgar Dermott took one step up the long staircase and

closed his fingers around Gianelle's throat. "That will be enough of that, dearest," he warned, squeezing her neck while his eyes seared into hers, daring her to say another word. She remained silent. In fact, she didn't even try to tear his hand away from her throat. She stood stock-still and stared into his eyes, defying him with her sheer strength of will. Dermott laughed and pushed her away from him with enough force to send her careening into the wall. As if touching her had soiled him, he brushed his palm over his quilted surcoat. "Your champion is dead," he sneered. "How else do you think I could disarm him of his sword except by killing him?"

He turned away from Gianelle when Simone entered the castle. He strode toward her. "It was quite an ingenious plan, if I may say so myself. We ambushed the troop far enough away from here to avoid suspicion. Risande's men think they were attacked by a small band of thieves." He laughed, quite pleased with himself. "Simone was there. Were you not, Simone?" He brought her hand to his lips and Simone closed her eyes, sickened with shame. "I think she regrets it now," he said, scowling at her. But then a chilling smile crept over his face. "But she was marvelous, calling his name. 'Dante! Dante!'" He mocked her in a high-pitched voice and then began to laugh, throwing his head back in delight.

Using the wall to help her stand, Gianelle stared at Simone in silence. "Is it true, Simone?" she finally managed to ask, dreading the answer. "Is he dead?" When Simone nodded her head, Gianelle removed the dagger from its hiding place and lunged at Dermott. She managed to catch him in the throat, but the wound was minor, a thin slice that he covered with his hand an instant before he swung at her.

Chapter Twenty-One

TWO DAYS OF LIVING WITHOUT HIM. Tomorrow would be three. She could do it. She could live another day without seeing Dante. She had done it before. But she hadn't loved him then the way she did now. She hadn't longed for him. She hadn't thought she would die without him.

He was dead. And it was only the second day.

She sat upon a brown gelding in Graycliff's bailey, watching a pale gray mist roll in from the cliffs. Fifteen of Dermott's men surrounded her, each mounted; some she had seen at Devonshire, some she had never seen before. None of them spoke to her. Their attention was turned to Edgar Dermott, mounted before them on a black destrier. The beast, along with some of the other men's horses, pranced nervously in the thickening fog that curled around its hooves.

"I've sent the rest of my garrison on to Devonshire." Dermott called out, and his voice echoed in the deserted courtyard. "Sir Lowell here and these ten men behind me will escort me to Winchester to meet the king. The rest of you will bring this woman to my brother's holding in Ely and wait for me there until I return. If she is touched, or if she escapes, you will all die by my sword."

"The king will have your head!" Gianelle shouted. She glared boldly at him when he turned his gaze on her.

"The king will kiss my arse when I lead him to Hereward the Wake."

Gianelle clenched her jaw. She should have guessed this swine was an associate of Dante's enemy. "He will kill you when I tell him that you killed Dante." Saying it made her choke on a sob. She bit her tongue, but it wasn't enough to stop the tears from gathering in her eyes.

"And who will tell him, Gianelle, you? Simone?" He chuckled softly and shook his head at her. "Simone is dead. She regretted helping me, and threatened to go to the king. It's you I wanted. I haven't yet decided if I am going to kill you. It pleases me to look at you. But trust that if I allow you to live, I will cut your lying tongue from your mouth. Either way, you will not be telling the king anything."

A few of the men around her shifted uncomfortably in their saddles at Dermott's threats to her and to them, but they kept their mouths shut and their eyes averted from Gianelle's.

"What about the ones in the cellar?" Conrad Lowell asked Dermott. "Shall I send in a few men to finish them?"

"You should have taken care of that yesterday, Lowell," Dermott snapped at him and then expelled a long-suffering sigh. He snapped his fingers at one of the men at Gianelle's side. "Raynard, come here," he called out impatiently. "Take care of the prisoners in the cellar after I leave," he said quietly when the guard reached him. "I want no one left alive who knows what I've done. No one.

Do you understand?" He let his gaze drift over his men waiting to leave with Gianelle. "When you arrive in Ely, kill them all."

"Aye, m'lord."

He raked his gaze over the rest of his company. "Now let's be off. I hate this gloomy place." He wheeled his mount around and called out over his shoulder as Conrad Lowell and his small troop followed him out of the bailey.

"Remember, all of you, keep my prize alive."

Gianelle watched him go and then looked up at the castle. She couldn't leave Graycliff. Dante was still here in the mountainous cliffs that rose up around it. He was here in the wonderful scent of the sea carried on the wind. Heedlessly, she wiped her eyes with her knuckles. Everything good that ever happened in her life happened here. Even if he was gone, she wouldn't leave him.

"I have some witnesses to dispose of. I will return shortly," Raynard announced and flicked his reins toward the castle.

Gianelle's heart pounded wildly. She knew that he meant to kill Dara and the others left inside. She couldn't let her friends die. She had to think of a way to save them, and fast. "Wait!" she shouted. "Please, give me just a moment to have a last look at my home."

"You've had enough moments to look at it."

"What's the harm, Raynard?" the guard who shifted around in his saddle earlier asked. "Give her a moment."

Gianelle blinked her topaz eyes at the guard who defended her, and he smiled. "Good people lived there, my lord," she told him and swept her tears off her cheeks. "Friends who died without the chance to bid them a proper farewell. I'm sure you've lost friends here as well."

When he nodded, she continued. "There is a small keg of my lord's finest wine just inside, in the kitchen. One of your men could fetch it . . ." She hastened her speech when the guard began to shake his head. "It would take but a scarce bit of time, and mayhap"—she offered him a soft smile—"we could share a toast to our fallen friends."

"Why would you want to share a toast with the men who killed your friends?" Raynard narrowed his eyes on her.

Gianelle turned to him and lowered her gaze meekly to her hands. "I hold no malice toward any of you. You were merely following your orders. We can leave the wine to spoil, though it would be a shame in my estimation. Lord Risande boasted many a night about his wine. Why, one sip and I was passed out cold without any remembrance of what took place the night before." She turned again to the first guard and smiled coyly beneath the veil of her long lashes.

"Albert, go fetch the wine. And be quick about it," the guard commanded.

"Albert," Gianelle called out to him as he went. "It's the keg on the long chopping table. You cannot miss it."

"It better be as good as you say," Raynard warned her. He swiped his hand across his lips while Gianelle assured him that it was. One thing she knew about castle guards was that they rarely turned away a drink, or the promise of an unconscious maiden.

She had already dumped the strychnine into the cask this morning while Dermott spoke to the men leaving for Devonshire. She had hoped to poison Dermott himself, but he refused any cup she offered him. The fool never bothered to search the kitchen for the keg.

She really hated having to think about these men dying,

but it was the only way to save her friends, and for her to remain at Graycliff.

When Albert returned hefting the small barrel under his arm, Gianelle remarked on how quick he was with yet another slight curl of her lips aimed at the first guard.

"What is your name? I don't remember seeing you at Devonshire."

"I'm Brody, my lady."

"Ah, Brody, I fear we shall all have to drink from the spout."

"Albert, damn you, you brought no cup," Brody admonished.

"Give me the bloody keg." Raynard snatched it from Albert's hands. "Since when do we need cups, eh?"

"Sir Raynard?" Gianelle stopped him as he popped the lip off the spout and tilted it to his mouth. "What about the toast?"

"Right, then. To the fallen," he offered, then took a long swig.

"The fallen." Gianelle let a tear slip down her cheek and whispered, "I shall never forget him."

"She's right, it's good." Raynard took two more drinks, and then wiped his mouth again. He handed the cask over to Albert, who guzzled a good amount.

Three more men drank before Martin, a guard who knew Gianelle from Devonshire, handed her the wine. "I recall you once poured a case of scribe's ink down Dermott's well. Sylvia told me it was you while she shared my bed one night. Here, you drink this before I do."

Raynard scowled and rubbed his finger across his teeth, then smiled to himself when it came away unmarked by ink.

Gianelle held the spout to her mouth and plunged her

tongue inside, stopping the liquid from coming out. She pretended to drink, even going into a fit of coughing.

Brody pulled the keg away from her and tapped her back. "Don't fight it, lady. Just let it go down."

She nodded and wiped her eyes. "It's strong."

Brody winked at her and began to drink.

"Were you with your lord when he killed my husband, Brody?" He lowered the keg and nodded, looking a little ashamed. "Well, then mayhap you might drink to him, *oui*?" Gianelle watched him while he drank, without any pity, without any feeling at all.

"Hurry with it," Raynard ordered as the keg was passed around to every man. "We've wasted enough time." He dismounted and drew his sword. "Brody, take her on ahead. I will meet up with you."

"You are not going to pilfer my lord's trunks, are you?" Gianelle blurted out. The strychnine needed a little time to take effect. She hoped rummaging around in Dante's chambers would be enough to kill the guard before he reached the cellar. "I'm certain Lord Dermott took all the gold already."

"Gold?" Raynard lifted his eyebrow at her, then spent another several minutes arguing with the others about divvying up the spoils. Finally, Gianelle's group and Raynard parted ways.

Ten minutes later, four of the men fell behind on their horses. They were crossing over a giant ledge with the sea battering below when Albert gripped his belly and fell from his saddle. Martin looked around and began to bellow, a little incoherently, that she must have poisoned them. Another man wheeled his horse around to have a look at her, but his mount lost its footing without its rider's careful hand to guide it, and tumbled over the edge of the grand white ledge.

Gianelle didn't blink as his screams rose to her ears. She tightened her grip around her reins and prepared to whirl around when she met Brody's glassy gaze. "You took my life. Now we are even." He blinked as if he couldn't understand her. "I'm sorry," she told him, and then she flapped her reins and fled away.

~

When Gianelle reached Graycliff, she vaulted from her horse. She landed hard on her rump, but sprang back to her feet and burst through the castle doors. She headed straight for the kitchen, searched for what she needed, found it, then barreled down the stairs that led to the cellar. She almost tripped over Raynard's body sprawled across the stairs.

"Dara!" she screamed. "Talard, where are you?"

"Gianelle? Here!" Voices beckoned her down a long, musty corridor, to a thick door with a tiny barred window.

"Is everyone well?" She rushed forward and peered through the bars.

"Aye," Talard whispered to her, his voice thick and rough with thirst. "But Lady Dara was ill this morn. Did you bring water?"

"*Non*, I brought something better." She shifted, trying to get a better look at Dara, but could only glimpse her friend's flaxen hair. "Dara, what is it?"

"I think I'm with child, Gia," she replied.

"God's mercy, I'm getting you out of here!"

"How?" Talard's dark eyes and the bridge of his nose stared back at Gianelle. "Do you have the key?"

"*Non*. But I have this!" She held up a thin filleting knife.

Talard knit his bushy brows. "What is it?"

"Cook uses it to cut the fish. It should work." She had already begun driving the metal into the large keyhole, working frantically while she spoke. "I have done this before, many times."

Another face appeared behind the door. It was Douglan. "Good work, my lady! Do it slowly."

She nodded, turning the metal in her fingers carefully.

"How will we get out of the castle?" Dara asked from somewhere behind him.

"Dermott's men are gone," Gianelle informed them. "Most of them left this morn, and I killed the rest."

She heard people moving around inside the holding room, confusion and hope filling their softly spoken whispers.

"How the hell did you kill them?" Talard asked her.

"Poison." She worked with steadfast diligence, trying to remain calm while her heart nearly burst through her rib cage. When she heard the sharp click of the lock, she nearly passed out. She took a deep breath and yanked the heavy door open.

Instantly, she was enveloped in Talard's arms first, and then Douglan's, and finally Dara's. She looked at the hollow expressions of the servants who were left alive. Beth was there and smiled at her. There were a small number of Dante's guards left. Many of the others had traveled to Winchester with him, but Dermott's men had killed more than fifty of those who remained.

"Where's Casey?" Dara shook Gianelle's shoulders. "Are there none left but us?"

Douglan took charge immediately, hearing the rising panic in Lady Dara's voice, and seeing the oddly calm look in Gianelle's eyes. He ushered everyone toward the stairs. He paled when he saw the dead guard, and asked Gianelle three more times if she was certain all Dermott's men were gone.

"Byron," he said to one of Dante's guards, "take Henry and Edward with you and get to Winchester. Ride on the wind. Inform Lord Risande of what happened here and . . ."

"You don't know then?" Gianelle turned to him, and her voice fell like a ghostly whisper to their ears, her huge eyes bleak with sorrow too powerful to contain any longer. "Dante is gone. Edgar Dermott killed him."

Dara's steps halted and she looked about to be sick. Talard and Douglan both denied Gianelle's words vigorously.

"Simone led him to Dante. I don't know why. She is dead also." While Gianelle spoke, there was no emotion in her voice, only emptiness. Vaguely, she was aware of people weeping. "One of Dermott's guards told me he was there when Dermott did it."

"Gianelle." Dara reached for her hand, but only wept when their fingers touched. "Come, sweeting. Let's get you into bed."

"Nay, we cannot stay here."

Now Gianelle set her wide gaze on Talard. "Of course we can. I told you Dermott and his men are gone."

"They may return, and we don't have enough . . ."

"I'm not leaving Graycliff, Talard," Gianelle said firmly. "He is here, and I won't leave him."

Dara draped her arm over Gianelle, but Talard climbed another step so that his eyes were level with Gianelle's.

"You are the wife of a man I swore my life to. Whether he lives or not, I will protect you. I cannot leave you here. We will return after we go to the king, my lady. Forgive me." Without another word, he tossed her over his shoulder and carried her out of her home.

~

The obvious place to seek shelter was the caves along the coastal shore. It was the only place in the world where Gianelle wanted to be. A place where she could live with the memory of Dante. She could smell him in this magical world. She could see his face carved in the cliffs; hear his voice in the rushing roar of the waves.

But the caves were *too* obvious. As much as Gianelle hated to admit it, Talard was right. When Dermott's men didn't show up with her in Ely, others would come searching for them. Still, it took two days for Talard to convince her that they had to leave. Two days of walking in the sand, gazing out across the glistening ocean as if she were waiting for her beloved to return to her from across the world. Oh, if it were so, she would stand there and wait forever.

Every day brought a deeper sorrow. Every moment spent without him was harder to endure than a lifetime of servitude. There were times when the depth of her love surprised her, as if her heart had to belong to someone else. She loved Casey, and cared deeply for Dara. But loving Dante had been entirely new and foreign to her. Needing his love in return was driving her mad. He had crept into her world, her heart, her soul. He was in her blood, her dreams, and in her tears.

"I miss your eyes on me," she called out to the sea. But there was no answer. There was never an answer.

She realized in her sorrow that she had never told him she loved him. She had only told him once that she might be falling in love with him. She had been afraid, so afraid to give him her heart. But he took it, and then he was gone.

"One more chance, God. Just give me one more chance," she pleaded, ripping at the sand with fingers that ached to touch his rough face.

That was where Talard found her each morning, lying in the sand, brokenhearted and silent as the tide washed over her.

"Dara needs help, Gia. We cannot stay here."

"I cannot leave," she argued numbly, staring into the waves.

She was the most beautiful woman Talard had ever known. He often looked at her with something close to shock creasing his brow. Why had he not seen it before? This fragile, lovely creature was falling apart before his eyes, and he could do nothing to help her. He watched her from the caves when she walked the shore alone, her arms wrapped around her chest in an embrace she longed for. He grew mesmerized by the way her hair cascaded down her back, catching light like fire from the sun. Soft, brilliant locks that obscured her sweet face and shadowed wide, tortured eyes. He smiled at the memory of her hiccupping throughout the castle, telling anyone who asked that she was coming down with a sniffle. But that was all

Gianelle was now. A memory. He could still see her, touch her, but she was as empty as the shells strewn along the shore. A home for the soul that had once resided within her.

"Come, my lady," he said, lifting her from the sand. "We must go."

"Non." A whisper as she clung to him.

Talard never expected her to vanish. But Gianelle was a master at planning her escape. And vanish she did.

Chapter Twenty-Two

JAMES STOMPED THE SMALL FIRE OUT with his boot, then popped his crooked index finger into his mouth and held it up in the air.

"Wind's from the east."

"So?" Casey sniffled and pulled the raggedy, tattered mantle James had given her tighter around her shoulders as she stood.

"So, me little chicky, Winchester is west. We go this way." He reached for what he thought was Casey's hand and yanked the mantle instead, twisting it on her neck.

"Ouch! Stop that, James. And cease calling me 'chicky.' It makes me think you might be trying to kill me after all."

"Ah." He shook his head at her. "Yer still brooding cause I took ye from Gianelle. But whose idea was it to go to Winchester and bring Lord Risande back to rescue her?"

"Mine," Casey reminded him.

James narrowed his eyes on her as if he could see her stern assurance. "'Twas yer idea?"

"Aye!" she scolded him.

He shrugged, mulling it over in his head, then turned his back on her and continued on through the thick bushes. "Well," he shouted over his shoulder, "ye wouldna be alive to think about saving her if it was not fer me. I told me lord that I could hear better than anyone in that blasted castle. Heard Dermott giving orders to his men from a league away."

"I know, James." Casey sighed, trudging behind him. "You've told me a thousand times already. I just . . . I just . . ." She began to cry again and James gave the heavens an exasperated look.

"Yer not going to cry again." He sulked, and then stopped and waited for her to catch up. When she did, he lifted his arm around her shoulder. "There, there."

"I should not have left her. I promised I never would." Casey sobbed.

"But yer going to save her, chic—lass." James tried to console her, but she only sobbed more loudly.

"What if Dermott's beating her? What if he is rutting her? Ohhhhh!" Casey wailed.

"Mercy be!" James gasped, shaking his head again while he stroked her hair. "If he is rutting her, Lord Risande will slice his peter right off."

He had meant to comfort Casey, but James guessed the only comfort she could find was in the vehement benediction that boomed from her mouth after he spoke.

James shrugged his slumped shoulders. "Come on, chicky. Let's go bring the master home."

They continued onward, exhausted and hungry. They had no horse, no water, no food, just sheer determination. For Casey, there was no turning back. She knew the evil that ran through the Dermott blood, and while she prayed

continuously for God to keep Gianelle safe, she knew the
only one who could rescue her beloved friend from Edgar
Dermott was Dante Risande. Still, every step that led her
farther away from Gianelle sparked another cry of guilt
until it became so heavy she had to stop twice when a
wave of nausea struck her. She didn't allow herself to
think that Dermott might kill Gianelle. Nay, that could
never happen. But there were things worse than even
death, and those were the images that invaded Casey's
thoughts over and over again and made her weep so piti-
fully that even James stopped to cry with her once.

Another day passed, and poor James's determination
finally gave out. He stumbled and held on to a thick tree
trunk for support while he gasped and licked his dry lips.
"We are not going to make it, lass," he breathed, more
weary than he could ever have imagined. "We need some
food."

Casey hiked up her skirts and ran back to him, tugging
on his bony arm. "Come on, James."

"I cannot."

"You have to. Please." She tugged again. "She would
never give up if it were me. Please, James." When he didn't
budge, Casey collapsed to her knees and began to cry. She
couldn't leave him here all alone. But she couldn't stop
either. She began to pray.

"All right, all right." James sighed, dreading another
long invocation. He used every ounce of strength he had
left to stand. "I'm coming. But while yer praying could ye
ask Him fer some bloody food!"

Shortly after that, they stumbled upon a small cottage
in the middle of the woods. A cottage with a window in
the kitchen, right above a spit where the most delectable

goose roasted and seared, and sent its sweet flavor on the slight breeze.

Casey elbowed James in the ribs. "You ought to thank Him now," she said before she took off toward the cottage.

Stupefied, James lifted his head to the sky as reverential fear enveloped him. "Thank Ye, kind Sir," he amended. "Now can Ye get us a horse or two?"

~

James wasn't a firm believer in the Lord, but that had begun to change after a good meal of succulent goose, and even more after he and Casey met up with a small group of men who offered to escort them safely to Winchester. The bandits sounded meaner than wild boars with arrows in their arses, but as soon as they learned who James's lord was, the leader seemed to take a liking to them. He gave them water and let them ride with two of his men.

"Have ye made our lord's acquaintance, then?" James asked the leader, who rode alongside him.

"Only once, and briefly. He is an excellent swordsman."

"Aye, that he is. And he'll use his blade to slice up Dermott once we inform him of what happened."

"Dermott, you say?" the leader asked. James couldn't quite make him out, but he was certain the man's ears perked up.

"Aye, do ye know him, too?"

"As a matter of fact, I do. He's the reason I'm on this very road. He was supposed to pass this way days ago."

Narrowing his sightless eyes on the stranger, James asked, "Ye aim to kill him then?"

"You're very astute."

"Thank ye for noticing." James tipped his head in the man's direction. "And might I know ye?"

"Nay, I don't think so. But tell me, if you please, what has Dermott done that Lord Risande's vassals rush to inform him with such urgency that they leave their castle with no food and no horses?"

"No time," James told him. "Casey? Are ye well, chicky?" he called out to the horse's rump in front of him.

"Aye, James," she called back from somewhere behind him.

"You were saying?" the stranger coaxed gently.

"There was no time, is what I was saying." James scratched his front teeth with his fingernail. "Dermott stormed the castle. Came for Gianelle, according to Casey."

"Gianelle?"

"Aye, me lord's wife. She used to belong to Dermott."

"I see." The man was quiet for a moment, and James heard several horses riding away behind him.

"Casey?" he called again.

"Aye, James. He has sent some of his riders away." She sounded nervous to James's hearing. He scowled deeply at the leader.

"Ye send yer men to Graycliff."

"Correct again. I surely hope Risande knows what a value you are, old man."

"He will when I bring him Casey," James announced. Then, "Did ye send yer men as friend or foe to me lord's home?"

"I sent them there to kill Edgar Dermott if he is still there."

"Hmm," James mumbled and thought about it for a moment. "Why did ye help us?" He didn't worry about not being able to see the man's expression. He could hear the slight sigh, the hesitation to tell the truth. When the leader spoke, James knew it was the truth he was hearing, laced with indifference and fearlessness.

"Dermott told me he was going to kill Risande and then ride to Winchester to meet with the king. But he lied to me and went for the man's wife instead. Of course, that part I did not know, hence my waiting in these woods for him."

"Why would he tell ye such a thing? Who are ye?" James demanded, angry now that this rogue spoke so casually about a plan to take his lord's life.

"It's best you don't know who aids you, old man."

"Very well then, thief. Tell me, what color is yer hair?"

"Thief?" The man bristled, but James could hear humor in his voice. "Have I tried to rob you?"

"Well, nay. But then it must be quite clear to yer good eyes that we have nothing to rob. Casey? What color is this man's hair?"

"Red, James."

"Aha," James said quietly and crooked his finger at the man to come closer. "Tell me now since ye didn't before why ye help us, and why ye mean to kill the man who threatened me lord's life, Hereward the Wake."

Casey gasped and James nodded proudly at himself.

"Well done." Hereward offered James a genuine smile. "We must speak of how your loss of sight has sharpened your other senses. But for now I will tell you this: I aided you for information. To my surprise I have found you quite pleasant to travel with, and mayhap for my kindness toward you and your lady friend, you will relay a message to your lord for me."

"Mayhap," James agreed, listening.

"Tell him I sought to kill the man who killed his sister. Aye, now that has shocked you, eh, old man? Edgar and Bryce Dermott, along with six other men who have since perished at your lord's hands, thought to avenge me while my men fought Risande in Peterborough, by killing his sister. Without my knowledge or consent they did this, causing your lord to make my life a living hell. I tell you, old man, I did not care if Dermott killed your lord. Dermott is a weakhearted fool who thinks he's going to win William's favor by turning me in. I meant to stop him before he did that."

"Dermott killed young Katherine?" James asked faintly. "Ye don't know what it did to Lord Risande losing his sister."

"Aye, I do," Hereward replied. "Battle claims many lives, but when the innocents die, it claims your soul as well."

"Ye are astute also, Hereward."

"I speak from personal knowledge. My brother was a simple farmer. The Normans killed him for naught after they seized my father's lands."

"I'm very sorry," James said. He fell silent after that, as did Hereward. Later, when the troop stopped for the night, they spoke about other, less heartfelt matters while Hereward shared his food and his fire.

Casey wouldn't speak to the Wake, knowing Dante didn't like him, but she did seem in better spirits now that she had James kneeling with her to pray, even though she scowled at him with each new request he begged from the Lord. The eyesight of a hawk, a henhouse filled with fat, juicy, *quiet* chickens, the agility of a leopard, the wealth of a king, the face of a Roman statue—the list was endless.

"It's not right," she tried to tell him while Hereward laughed, listening to them.

"Why? He saw fit to give us food when we asked, and He sent Hereward the Wake to us. Why not a few women to warm me bed at night?"

He was hopeless, and Casey finally stopped arguing with the old fool. Let him pray to fly on the clouds. All she cared about was reaching Dante in time to save Gianelle. She prayed it was not too late.

Three days later, they reached Winchester.

"This is where we part company." Hereward stopped his troop just outside Winchester and stuffed a few strips of dried meat into James's withered hand. "I have no horses to spare, but the king's castle is not too far."

"Thank ye." James nodded at him. "I know where it is."

Hereward turned toward Casey and bowed slightly in his saddle. She didn't want to like him, but his smile was friendly enough. She watched in silence as he and his men rode away. "Come, James," she said, sighing, and took his hand. "The faster we find Lord Risande, the faster we can rescue Gia."

James scowled and swore under his breath as they walked down the long, narrow streets of Winchester. This was not a small, quiet coastal village, but a large city brimming with wealthy lords and fine ladies. And every one of them halted their stately walks to gape at the two lowborn visitors.

James could hear their whispers as clearly as if they were shouting their insults at him. He didn't care one squat what they said about him, but Casey cringed in his mantle, growing smaller than she already was. James couldn't see, but he knew what the two of them must look like to these noble chickens. And his sense of smell hadn't abandoned him, either. A few times even *he* balked at the stink that issued from their tattered clothes. Their hair was matted and their faces were filthy.

"Just keep going, lass. We are almost there," he told Casey, straightening his shoulders and lifting his proud chin.

Casey nodded, keeping her eyes on the paved road ahead of her. She would have liked to look around at this fine city with its colorful banners snapping above her from the marvelous stone buildings. She would have loved to gaze upon the handsome men and beautiful ladies dressed in their fine clothes and imagine she was one of them, but they were just like Lord Dermott's guests, turning their noses up at her.

"Where is the blasted castle, James?"

"Fifty meters to the right ye should come upon a double row of ancient oak trees decorated with the lion rampant. Take us through that path, lass, and ye will see the finest castle ever built. Our lord is there."

"Well then, let's hurry. I don't like it here." Casey brooded and quickened her pace with newly heated resolve sparking her blood.

Knowing old James well after their journey together, Casey was not a bit surprised when, after exactly fifty meters, they came upon two neatly spaced rows of oak trees with lion pennants flapping lightly in the cool breeze of mid-afternoon. What she hadn't expected was the sight of the king's home. Stopping to gaze upon the magnificent castle before her, Casey inhaled sharply. Behind her, James chuckled. She had never seen anything so big in all her life. Great stone turrets topped by yellow banners decorated with the lionhead emblem impaled the clouds. Four separate towers cradled their ornately carved battlements against the sun. And atop those battlements were hundreds, nay, thousands of guards.

As they approached the lowered drawbridge, Casey's hands trembled and she paled under the shadow of towering walls so thick she doubted a battering ram made of solid iron could penetrate them. She sucked in the fresh air of newly cut grass and prodded her feet onward. Balin was in there, and so was Dante. She had nothing to fear, she told herself over and over, but nothing could calm the drumming of her heart. The King of England was in there as well, and she had killed one of his lords.

When they reached the gatehouse, James dusted himself off and squared his meager shoulders. "We have urgent business with the Earl of Graycliff," he called into the air with as much dignity as he could muster.

The guard standing watch just to his right took a step forward, and Casey was sure they were about to be tossed into the moat. "Why are you shouting when I'm standing right here, old man?" the guard asked, looking James over with a hardened expression creasing his face.

James turned his head in the guard's direction. "I cannot see well, young man. But I can hear better than you. Now, since I was shouting I'm sure ye heard me. We request an audience with Lord Dante Risande immediately. We have traveled afar with a most urgent matter."

"Off with you, peasant!" The guard scrunched up his face. "Before I take my sword to you."

James bristled like a cat who'd just had a bucket of water thrown at him. "We belong to Earl Dante Risande's house, and every moment that ye keep us from seeing him is another moment that may cost his dear wife her life."

The guard gave both of them a scrutinizing, lingering look, and then shooed them away.

"Casey?" A huge, hulking figure peered over a terrace and shouted down at them. "James?"

Casey looked up, and her face lit into a smile so dazzling James could swear he saw her glowing in the darkness that clouded his vision.

"Balin! Oh, Balin!" Casey called up, waving and jumping up and down.

Balin disappeared in the next instant and James tilted his head toward the castle entrance. A thin smile curled the tips of his crinkled mouth. "He's coming. I can hear him. Move aside, young man," he commanded the guard haughtily, "lest Sir Balin DeGarge cleave ye in half."

Casey never stopped jumping until the doors opened and Balin burst through the entryway, looking as tall and as wonderfully handsome as any man had a right to be. She stared at him for a moment, his face a mask of utter confusion and delighted surprise.

"What in blazes are you doing here?"

Casey ran into his arms as if shot from an arrow. She buried her face in his strong neck, kissing him and whispering how much she missed him. And then, as if she suddenly remembered why she was there, she pulled away from his tight embrace and stared at him.

For the first time, Balin looked her over completely. His face darkened at her tattered appearance. When her lower lip began to tremble, he looked at James. "What has happened? What are you doing here?"

"Where is Lord Dante, Balin?" James asked, and before

Balin had a moment to answer, Casey began to sob and fell back into his arms.

"Edgar Dermott has taken Graycliff. He has Gia and—"

"Oh, God," Balin breathed and broke away from her. "How? When?"

"Balin, where is Lord Dante?" James stepped forward and then around Balin and into the castle. "Where is he?"

Casey stopped sobbing long enough to stare at her brutish beloved, awaiting his response. Her hands trembled so fiercely she had to clasp them together to stop them from shaking.

"We were attacked in the forest on the way here," Balin began quickly. "Dante was shot with an arrow—"

"Nay!" Casey bellowed, bringing her hand to her mouth. "Is he dead?"

The next sound she heard stopped her heart and made old James wince and cover his ears with his hands.

"Balin!" The deep voice booming from a room somewhere above them resonated through the long corridors, bouncing like thunder off the stone walls until Casey thought the castle would surely collapse around her. "If you don't get this woman with her witch's brew away from me this instant, I'm going to come down there and make *you* drink it."

"My lord?" James tilted his head upward and called toward the sound. "Is that ye, my lord?"

The castle was silent.

"Keep up that hollerin' and I will find ye," James shouted, already on his way toward the stairs.

Chapter Twenty-Three

JAMES'S SLOW PACE WAS NO MATCH for Balin's, so even though the scrawny servant started up the stairs first, Balin reached Dante's room before him.

"Leave us immediately," Dante's captain told the old woman hunched over his dearest friend's bed.

She looked up. "But he has not taken his medicine."

"I don't care. Go," Balin demanded.

"Well, 'tis no skin off my back," she hurled at him, turning to gather her things. "He has been nothing but a pain in me arse since he arrived, always hollering and complaining. You would think his precious wife was home getting ready to leave him any second the way he carries on about her." Suddenly, she turned on Dante, her thin lips stretched across her mouth in a macabre mask of utter disgust. "You fool. If you are so concerned about getting home, take your blasted medicine!"

In three strides, Balin was in the room. He clutched her shoulders and ushered her as gently as he could out of the room.

"That is the last I want to see of her, Balin." Dante

clenched his jaw at his friend. "I don't need her potions. The fever is gone. I'm fine, and I'm going home."

"*Oui.*" Balin nodded and then lowered his eyes to his boots.

"*Oui?*" Dante looked at him as if he had just sprouted another head. "No argument? No running after William with threats of shackles to tie me to the bed?"

"*Non,* my lord," Balin whispered.

"Well, good. I'm glad to see you've finally remembered who is in charge here. I may have been shot through with an arrow, but I'm still your lord."

From the doorway, Casey peeked inside and caught her breath at the sight of Dante. Propped up against a huge satin pillow, lying in a bed that could have been carved from gold, in a room where the tapestries were so finely stitched they looked like enormous paintings dazzled by the afternoon sun drenching the room, he stood out like a lone wolf that had wandered into a golden meadow. Everything around him paled in comparison to his raw power and brutal beauty. Casey almost turned and ran back down the stairs.

But the wolf's eyes turned just in time to see her, and he rose from the bed as if about to attack. "Casey?" he managed as his gaze soaked in the full sight of her. Those eyes clung to James next and he swallowed, his dark brows falling over smelted silver. "What are you doing here?" Casey looked at Balin, and James cleared his throat. Now that they were here, facing him, how could they tell him?

"Dante." It was Balin. His normally rough voice was but a whisper now. "Edgar Dermott has attacked Graycliff."

Nothing more needed to be said. Dante knew what it meant. "Get the others. Saddle the horses, Balin. GO!

NOW!" He yanked his tunic from its place over the back of a chair, then ripped the flimsy shift he wore off his body.

Casey gasped and stiffened at the thick, bloodstained bandages wrapped over his shoulder and under his arm. But if he felt any pain from his chest wound, he didn't reveal it as he lifted his mighty arms over his head and slipped on the loose-fitting tunic.

His eyes met Casey's again, and for a moment she thought he would melt at the sight of her. Then he did indeed crumble against the wall as visions of his sister's body soaked in blood washed over him. His hands came up to cover his face, and Casey finally ran to him.

She wept as his arms came around her, begged him to save Gianelle as his strength covered her.

Stifling his own agony at what he might find when he returned home, Dante brushed his cheek against the top of Casey's head. "Don't cry, Casey. She will be all right. I vow it." He lifted her chin with gentle fingers and gazed down at her. "Now tell me everything that happened."

There was not much to tell, and when she finished, Dante went to James and rested his hand on the old man's shoulder. "Thank you for getting Casey out."

"I couldn't find Lady Gianelle, milord. Else I woulda taken her too."

"I know." Dante tried to offer him a reassuring smile, but his stomach churned and fury boiled down deep in his veins. "When we get back, you will be my head watchman, James. I will rely on your sharp ears to keep the castle safe."

Nodding happily, James bowed, finally getting the recognition he knew he deserved.

Balin bolted back into the room, carrying a large leather bag. He handed it to Dante, along with a new sword. "William wants to see you before we leave."

"*Non.* There's no time." Dante snatched his things and sat on the bed to pull his boots on. He winced slightly as pain radiated through his shoulder and down his arm.

"Dante." Balin stood over him. "He does not mean to stop you, but you must go to him. The country is in enough turmoil with Hereward the Wake still amassing small armies against him. The king's most loyal knight must not disobey him."

Clenching his teeth as he stood back up, Dante nodded and headed out the door. James followed closely behind him.

"Er, milord, speaking of Hereward the Wake . . ."

The throne room was just as Casey had imagined it. Rows of thick carved columns lined the entrance. A table the size of a Viking ship sat in the center of the cavernous chambers, and at the helm, upon a throne that barely covered the width of his wide shoulders, sat King William the Conqueror. He was a formidable man indeed, but he would have looked more imposing without little Tanon perched on his lap. Lady Brynna stood a few feet away and smiled softly when Casey met her gaze. Tanon's father, Lord Brand, was there as well, along with Lord Richard Dumont. He patted Brynna's hand when she whispered for King William to make haste. Casey slid her gaze back to the king. He wore no crown upon his head. He didn't need one to look towering and majestic. He was clothed in a military-style golden tabard with the bold emblem of a lion embroidered in black across his chest. His hair was dark with traces of silver over his forehead and at his temples. His closely cropped beard covered most of his face. His eyes were narrowed on Dante, who stood a few feet away from him. The king's long, broad fingers played with a loose curl that dangled over Tanon's ear.

When he saw Casey, the king smiled, exposing a row of bright teeth. "You must be Lady Cassandra." His deep, baritone voice drummed through Casey's veins. She squeaked and stepped farther into Balin, hiding under the shadow of his arm.

"Casey." Dante turned and held his hand out for her to come forward and join him.

She looked up into Balin's strong face and he smiled. "Go on, love." He ushered her to Dante and she finally stepped forward.

"I have heard much about you in these last few days." King William regarded her with kind, deep gray eyes. "I thought it strange at first that Balin would be so enamored with a young woman that he could forget what a cranky ox he is and chatter on so happily about her. But now that I see you for myself, I understand."

"William," Dante said, bringing the king's attention back to him. "I've just been informed by my loyal vassal, James"—he turned and beckoned James forward. Casey reached for the old man's hand to guide him close to her and Dante. He bowed in Lady Brynna's direction—"that Hereward aided him and Casey in getting here."

The king's expression turned deadly in an instant. "Richard, come take your granddaughter from me."

Lord Richard Dumont stepped forward and gathered his treasure in his arms. William stood from his chair after

Richard left the throne room, and while his darkened gaze frightened Casey, James merely tilted his head.

"You traveled with Hereward the Wake?"

"Aye, Sire," James replied. "And he was most accommodating."

William shot Dante an incredulous stare.

"He was quite forthcoming with every question I put to him."

"You understand he is my enemy?" William's voice rumbled low in his throat as he took a step closer to James.

"I do, Sire. But begging yer mercy, we didn't discuss you."

Dante closed his eyes for a moment and took a deep breath. "James, get on with it," he said before William lost his temper.

"Aye, milord. Well, he told me that Edgar Dermott and his brother killed young Lady Katherine, and . . ."

"What?" Brand broke away from his wife and nearly toppled the king in his haste to reach James. "Why would he tell you this?"

James would have recoiled at Lord Brand's harsh tone, but he'd just heard the same icy disbelief when he told his lord the news in the hall. "He wanted milord to know that he had nothing to do with it."

"And we are to believe Hereward?" Brand turned to the king, and then to his brother.

"Tell them the rest, James," Dante said, trying to remain patient and calm when he wanted to bolt from the castle and fly home.

"I believed him, milord. He was waiting for Dermott in the woods, bent on killing him when he found us instead.

Dermott told him that he was going to kill milord and then come to Winchester to win His Majesty's favor by turning him in. The Wake meant to stop him. When I told him about Gianelle, he dispatched his men to ride to Graycliff, knowing that Dermott had tricked him. We know now that the scoundrel did indeed try to kill Lord Risande."

"We had Dermott in our grips, Dante," Brand said to his brother. "And we practically threw him out of Graycliff."

"You may have him again." William went back to his seat and stroked his whiskered chin. "If what Hereward says is true, Dermott should be arriving here soon enough. If he makes it past the Wake, that is." The king released a long, drawn-out sigh. "This changes nothing, you understand. Hereward will still feel my wrath, and my mercy for this. When I find the bastard, that is."

"I did not ask where he might be hiding, Majesty," James let him know with a sheepish look.

William waved his words away. "I already know, thanks to Dante's wife." When Dante cast him a questioning look, the king explained. "She sent me a missive; had your steward write it. She didn't plead her case to me, but yours, Dante."

"Mine?"

"*Oui*, she begged me to understand what a stubborn bastard you are and not to treat you harshly when you refused to send her back to Devonshire. She asked me to send her former lord to his brother's holding in Ely, saying that they visited there often. Of course, neither of the Dermotts own holdings in Ely. Because of your suspicions about Dermott, I assumed their recurrent visits had something to do with the Wake. I've already sent an army there but so far they have not found him. Now I know why. He's been right here under my nose."

The king's steward entered the throne room and hurried to his side. He bent to William's ear, waited until the king gave his approval, then bowed and scurried away again.

"Well." William smiled at Dante first, and then at Brand. "It seems Edgar Dermott has arrived and seeks an audience with me on an urgent matter. Which one of you wants to end his miserable life after I grant his request?"

Dante ripped his sword from its sheath. His eyes sparked with a glint of something so brutal William almost smiled remembering the fierce warrior who'd taken down an entire regiment of Saxons his first day at Hastings.

"He is mine."

After the women were ushered out of the throne room and replaced with four of William's guards, Edgar Dermott was brought to the king. Conrad Lowell stood at his side, his dark eyes narrowed to slits while he scanned his surroundings.

"Your Majesty, it's a great honor." Dermott bowed low and then offered the king a polite smile.

"What is your urgent matter?"

The king's matter-of-fact tone quelled Dermott's eager anticipation to proceed. He threw a nervous glance to his emissary, then decided it was best to simply get on with the matter. "As you know, now that my brother has departed this world, Devonshire is without a lord."

"*Oui,* I've decided to give Devonshire to Sir Balin De-Garge and name him Baron of Cambridge." Dead silence fell over the throne room while William stared into Dermott's eyes, daring him to utter a word. But when Edgar's mouth fell open in stunned silence, William grew more impatient. "*Merde*, I hate gaping. Close your mouth before I have your head removed."

Dermott's mouth snapped shut, but then opened again a moment later. "I have missives giving the whereabouts of Hereward the Wake. My brother and he—"

"Tell me, Dermott," the king said cutting him off, "if your brother was alive, would you betray him easily?" William didn't wait for an answer. He couldn't. The man before him sickened him. He motioned for someone to his right. "Come, end this before I leap from my chair and do it myself."

When Dante stepped out from behind one of the thick columns, Dermott's blood turned cold. He took a step back, his eyes wide with disbelief. "You're . . ."

"Dead?" Dante finished for him, his mouth hooked into a menacing half-smile. "Not quite."

Conrad Lowell drew his sword, but an arm snaked around his neck from behind and spun him around, straight into Brand's sword. The emissary gazed into a raging storm of blue-green, opened his mouth to speak, and then crumbled to the floor.

Brand yanked his blade free and then snarled at Dermott, "You're next."

"Sire." Dermott rushed to William's chair and fell at his feet. "There's been a terrible misunderstanding. I've come to tell you that Hereward hides in Ely. He . . ."

"Dermott!" Dante's voice boomed through his ears and stilled the remainder of his words. "Where is my wife?"

Edgar spun around and held up his palms, as if that puny shield could stop the force coming toward him.

"Where is she?" Dante hauled him to his feet by his

throat. "You went to Graycliff for her. What have you done with her? Tell me, and I shall spare your life."

"I—I—she was sent to Ely with orders not to be harmed. I swear it."

Releasing him, Dante backed away, dragging the tip of his sword along the ground. "Unsheathe your blade."

"Nay." Dermott shook his head and began to turn over his shoulder to the king for help.

"You killed my sister." Dante's voice was low, ruthlessly detached, his features chilled with an utter lack of mercy. "Unsheathe your blade unless you wish to die whimpering."

With trembling hands, Dermott did as he was ordered. He held his blade before him in both hands and swung.

Dante parried easily, striking the blade and knocking it from Dermott's grip. He advanced with one step and sliced his blade neatly across Dermott's neck, killing him instantly.

"Hmmm, I would have made him suffer more." William stared down at the body.

"I have to go, William. Now." Dante sheathed his sword and shouted for Balin.

"Wait." The king held up his hand to stop him. "Tell me, Dante, did your wife kill Bryce Dermott?"

For a moment, Dante thought about denying it. He chewed on his words before he chose which ones to say. He trusted William's fairness. He could not lie to him. "She did, Sire. But she only meant to cause him sleep while she escaped his house. He . . ."

"Say no more." William stood up and went to him. "She saved me the trouble of doing it myself. Go," the king urged with a hand on his shoulder. "My men are at your disposal, *mon ami*. Go, save your lady."

~

Talard was the first to feel the vibration beneath his feet. He stopped and held his hand up to quiet Douglan. His eyes narrowed and scanned the empty forest, and then his face paled and his eyes grew wide as the thunder of hundreds of horses practically descended upon them.

"God's holy wrath, run!" Talard bellowed to the others.

Douglan, who was carrying Lady Dara, stood as still as death, unable to move save the frantic beating of his heart. He squeezed his eyes shut when the army grew close enough to mow him and Dara down.

Someone screamed for a halt and Douglan was certain that the living God had just descended from heaven itself to stop his death. Still, he was afraid to open his eyes to see how close he had come.

Someone was shaking him, quite violently, in fact. But nothing could prepare him for what he saw when he finally opened his eyes.

"My lord!" He nearly dropped Lady Dara to the ground when he recognized Dante hovering over him like a giant, dark cloud. "Talard! Talard! It's Lord Dante! He's alive!" he shouted into the forest.

Sir Malen yanked Dara from Douglan's arms and the steward stared at the reunited couple with a dumb grin plastered to his face until Dante clutched his shoulders and shook him again.

"Where is Gianelle? We met the guards you sent to Winchester, and they told me she escaped Dermott's guards and did not go to Ely. Where is she?"

Talard appeared from out of the trees but stopped again, stunned when he saw Dante. "You are alive."

Dante released Douglan and his broad shoulders fell, his face etched with fear as he turned to Talard. "*Oui*, I am. Please tell me that Gianelle is also."

Taking a cautious step forward, as if Dante and the hundreds of mounted knights behind him were not real and would disappear if he moved too hastily, Talard blinked and then cleared his throat. "Dermott told her that you were dead, my lord. She saved us all."

"Tell me she lives," Dante pleaded with him as his vassal took another step forward.

"She pined for you so," Talard told him quietly, dreading each word as he uttered them. "I never saw such sorrow before. She wouldn't come with us."

Behind Dante, Casey slipped from her saddle and walked slowly toward Talard. When she reached him, large tears slipped from the edges of her lashes. "Where is she? Please, tell me."

"I don't know where she is." Talard looked away and swallowed back emotions that had just sprung anew in the last few weeks. "She fled from us over a se'nnight ago. She is gone."

The low growl of distant thunder brought Talard's gaze back to his lord. He wished it hadn't. Dante had sunk to his knees. The terrible sound had come from him, a force of anguish that ripped from his lungs, stabbed his heart, and stilled the forest.

Chapter Twenty-Four

DANTE SCOURED THE ENTIRE COUNTRYSIDE, but Gianelle couldn't be found. He searched for days on foot and on horseback, days and nights with no rest, but she was gone. He spoke to no one; none dared go near him. Casey could only weep, clinging to Balin's strong chest while she listened to the sounds of Dante's torment after he stormed into the castle when his searches failed. After a se'nnight had passed, Dante finally called Talard to his room. He smiled hearing how Gianelle had rescued them from the cellar. But when Talard described her days wandering the shore alone, Dante covered his face in his hands and raked his fingers through his hair, aching to tear each raven strand from his head.

"She will return, my lord," Talard tried to tell him.

"*Non*. She thinks I'm dead. She won't come back. I must find her. I want every man we have to search every town, every village from here to the borders of Scotland if necessary," Dante agonized, and then stormed out of his room and out of the castle.

Gianelle walked along the edge of the shore, collecting seashells and placing them gently into the pockets of her overskirt. She walked barefoot through the wet sand, loving the feel of it between her toes. She hummed a song that she had made up about a beautiful man who had gone off to battle and then returned to his beloved. It comforted her. The sound of the ocean comforted her.

A gull hovered low in the sky and she tilted her head, squinting up at it. "Well met, bird," she called up. "Are you hungry? Come, follow me and I shall feed you." She turned on her heel and headed back to the caves. "I'm afraid I'm running low on bread, my little screaming friend. I haven't raided the castle in quite some time. Last time I went, some men had returned, talking to each other about Hereward the Wake. I cannot go back yet. But I haven't been very hungry lately." She looked up, but the gull was gone. She frowned as a wave of loneliness devoured her.

"Mayhap I should take a trip to the village," she said to no one. "I am in need of food." She nodded and disappeared into a well-hidden cave set deep within a wall of slate. A moment later, she appeared again, wearing her leather slippers and one of Simone's silky veils around her head and neck. She crossed a small, sandy path, hopped over a rock, and ducked when she saw a local villager hefting his nets toward the sea for a day's fishing.

It was not a long walk, really, and she enjoyed climbing the slanted slopes and jagged bluffs. She was quick on her small feet and agile as a cat, hiding when she saw another person or heard an unfamiliar sound. She had even managed to keep her footing on the steep cliffs and escape without being seen when she heard the canter of Dermott's horses returning from the village two nights past. She'd crept deep into the caves when Dermott's men began to search for her. The monster was quite tenacious, too, sending his garrison out almost daily. Gianelle was almost afraid to come out of her cave after a while. But this morn seemed quiet enough. She smiled to herself now, admiring her own prowess, and jiggled her pockets, listening to the tinkling seashells she would use to trade for food. She stopped when she came to the dirt path that would bring her to the village. This was the only place that was truly dangerous. The path was wide and open on two sides, and horses were constantly going to and fro.

The coast was clear, and Gianelle raced across.

Just before she reached the village, she adjusted the veil around her head, covering her face as well as her hair. Many of these people would recognize her, though she doubted any of them would notify Dermott. Still, she was not about to take that chance.

Barrels of herring, swordfish, and shark lined the cottages. There were buckets of oysters and mussels everywhere, making her belly rumble. Men worked outside repairing nets, and women boned large fish under the warm sun. Everywhere she looked, she saw families working together and children playing games along the rocks. Music flowed on the salty breeze while men drank and told stories of great, monstrous fishlike creatures they had seen on the sea. Laughter permeated the air and brought a smile to Gianelle's lips, but any joy she had found in these last weeks was but a shallow echo and always left her missing Dante even more, if that were possible. She guessed no one had told the villagers yet that their lord was gone.

Wading through a flock of geese pecking at the small grain scattered along the ground, Gianelle crossed to a small cottage and traded her shells with old Lizzy Somers for some fresh water and a loaf of bread.

Gathering her goods under her arm, she headed back for the cave, letting her tears fall freely again as they had every day.

She crossed the dirt path without looking first for any riders and was nearly trampled by a destrier the size of a cliff wall. Her bread fell to the ground, her water spilled and was soaked into the dry earth, and her scarf came loose and slipped off her head as she lay sprawled on her back. She sat up and shook the stars out of her head. Someone was screaming.

It was not a scream of terror, but one of sheer, unabashed elation.

"Gianelle! Oh, God's mercy! God's sweet mercy!" Casey leaped from her saddle, and beside her Balin followed, jumping from the destrier that had knocked Gianelle off her feet.

"Casey?" Gianelle rubbed her head, certain she was dreaming. "Casey? Casey! Oh! Oh!" she screamed as Casey lurched into her arms, crying like a babe who had found her mother. Balin nearly wept at the sight of them.

He helped Gianelle to her feet when Casey finally let her go. The two women touched each other's faces, feeling smiles they thought they had lost forever. Gianelle couldn't stop the flow of tears streaming down her face. When she turned to look at Balin, he grinned as wide as the ocean and gathered her up in his strong embrace.

"We have been searching endlessly for you," he whispered against her hair.

Oh, she couldn't believe any of it. Were they really here? Was this her Casey? She broke free of Balin's embrace and cupped her friend's face in her palms. "I have missed you so very much." She cried and laughed at the same time, and then pulled Casey into her arms again.

Suddenly her joy ended, her body stiffened. She turned her head to look over her shoulder at Balin and choked on fresh and familiar waves of sorrow. "Were you with Dante when he died?"

Still grinning like a fool, Balin shook his head. "He isn't dead, my dear lady."

She almost didn't hear him, caught up in images of Dante's broken body lying somewhere on the road, felled by Dermott's foul hands. She released Casey and took a small step toward the smiling knight. She blinked and then simply stared up at him. "Pardon?" she whispered.

"I said, Dante is not dead. But he will be if he does not lay his eyes on you soon."

Gianelle blinked again and a single tear rolled down her pale cheek. Did she dare believe him? It was too much for her heart to take. She stumbled. Balin caught her and smiled gently down into her face. "He has gone mad without you, and he's bringing us all there with him."

She clutched Balin's sleeves. For a moment she couldn't move a single muscle in her body save the one in her lower lip, which trembled on the brink of a screeching sob. And then everything awakened all at once and she hiked up her skirts and began to run.

"*Non*, not that way," Balin called out to her, laughing as she headed for the castle. "He is at the ocean."

Without turning her head to even acknowledge him, Gianelle bolted across the path and flew like a tiny sparrow, free and alive once again. Her heart quickened and gave her wings and her slippers barely touched the ground. He was alive! Colors burst anew before her eyes. He was alive! The gulls above her screamed, and she lifted her head and screamed back at them, "He isn't dead!" Tears whipped across her face as she flew down a steep incline. She jumped the rest of the way and smiled, spreading her arms wide as she fell.

When she landed in the warm sand, she barely stopped to pull the slippers from her feet and tossed them up at the gulls.

She scanned the golden shore from east to west but didn't see him. Still, she ran toward the roar of the white-caps. He was here, somewhere.

"Dante!" she screamed. Then she saw him, his power-ful arms raking the water as he swam in the deep depths that belonged to him. "Dante!" she screamed again, run-ning as fast as her feet would take her. "Oh, God, thank You, thank You, thank You."

Lost to the crashing of the thunderous waves, Dante hadn't seen her yet and swam toward the shore. Like a great, glistening beast, he rose from the waves and tossed his head back, flinging his wet hair off his shoulders. He heard a sound, like a gull screeching, and looked toward the shore.

"DANTE!" Gianelle's arms were waving over her head, her feet lifting her off the sand as she leaped. And then she was running again.

With faltered breath, Dante watched his beloved flying to him, her hair like golden wings snapping behind her back. His voice broke on an exhilaration of breath, his heart nearly burst in his chest seeing the sweet joy that graced her beautiful face. She had been free, free to fly, to soar away. And she was flying back to him. He laughed when she crashed through the waves, defying their power to stop her.

And then he moved and she was in his arms, crying his name over and over as if it was the only sound she ever wanted to hear again.

He swept his hands over her face and gathered her in his arms. "Ah, God, where have you been, my love?"

With her face pressed to the fierce beating of his heart, Gianelle wept at the feel of him touching her again, of being in his arms, hearing his voice, embraced by love she had denied for so many years. She tilted her head to gaze at him. For a moment, she couldn't speak, but stared into his eyes. Eyes that sorrowed and rejoiced, and soaked her in as if she were this salty sea air that was part of him.

"My tenderest love, I've been on the shore of a beautiful sea strewn with silver moonbeams. And I wasn't afraid of its power anymore. But I was filled with sorrow because the waves had become quiet."

Dante watched her mouth while she spoke to him. He cupped her cheeks in his palms, longing to kiss her, and aching to hear her say what he saw in her eyes.

"It was quiet," Gianelle told him, "and I never had the chance to whisper to it the words I would have given my life to say. I love you, Dante. I love you so very much."

Her breath mingled with his in prelude to a kiss that set her heart afire, belonging to him alone, a kiss that was as powerful as the raging sea around her. He was rock and salt, and warm like the sand. He lifted her in his arms and carried her to the shore. Falling to his knees, he laid her down in the wet sand. And then he was there, kissing her, touching her, loving her.

Their laughter filled the air and was carried on the wind to the high battlements of Graycliff, where an old, withered man sat keeping watch over the castle. He couldn't see more than five feet in front of him, but he could hear better than any tower guard. He tilted his head toward the joyful sound coming from the sea, and he smiled and set his sightless eyes toward heaven.

"Thank you," he whispered. Then, "Would it be too much to ask to have that pesky, clucking hen roasting on my trencher tonight? She keeps me awake all night . . ."

About the Author

PAULA QUINN has been married to her childhood sweet-heart for seventeen years. They have three children, a dog, and too many reptiles to count. She lives in New York City and is currently at work on her next novel.

More sultry, sexy intrigue
from Paula Quinn!

Please turn this page
for a preview of

Lord of Seduction

AVAILABLE IN MASS MARKET

December 2006.

Chapter One

2

ENGLAND, AD 1085

Lady Tanon Risande stepped into Winchester Castle's great hall and drew in an anxious breath. She looked around, letting her gaze absorb the vast expanse of tapestry-lined walls gilded in firelight. Laughter permeated the air as knights lifted their goblets in salute to one another. Ladies giggled coyly or scolded the children running around the tables like buzzing flies. A troubadour sat beside one of the great hearths, singing a song of a forlorn love while calculating the tinkle of coin as it was deposited into the wide-brimmed hat at his feet.

Tanon twirled her finger around a midnight curl dangling over her shoulder. Among the stately guests who had traveled to Winchester for the autumn tourney was Lord Roger DeCourtenay, Earl of Blackburn. What if he didn't notice her again? What if she'd endured endless hours of her handmaidens' tugging on her unruly curls and being fitted into layers of clothing for nothing? She hated all the time and preparation it took trying to look pretty for a man who preferred the more voluptuous, more scantily clad ladies of the court. But Tanon had no choice.

Roger was her betrothed. Not through any choice of her own, of course. She was a noble's daughter, and if that wasn't enough to ensure her a proper marriage to a noble of no lesser title, then being treasured by the king of England was.

Still, she was more fortunate than most Earls' daughters, who were doomed to marry men three times their age. Lord DeCourtenay was young and handsome, so when she was told that she was to become his wife, she tried not to be very disappointed.

But Roger was. During the three times they'd met before, he'd given too much of his attention to other, more curvaceous maidens to spare her more than five blinks of an eye.

She spotted her mother sitting with her uncle Dante at the far end of the hall. Lady Brynna Risande inclined her head, moving her ear closer to Dante's lips in order to hear him over the cheers coming from the table beside them. Standing a few feet away with her grandsire Richard, Tanon's father, Lord Brand the Passionate lifted two of his fingers to his lips and then held them aloft to her mother. As if he couldn't bear to be away from her for more than a few moments, he went to her. After exchanging a quiet word with his brother, Brand tossed his arm around his wife and drew her into his close embrace.

Tanon watched her parents, sighing at the love that exuded from every glance they shared, every touch, every smile. She wanted what they had. Friendship, passion, tenderness. Her mother never had to sit through hours of combing and dressing for Tanon's father to lose his breath at the sight of her.

Moving her gaze to the dais where King William

shared a drink with Hereward the Wake, Tanon smiled
and waved her fingers at the king. Poor William. He
looked weary, but that was to be expected, what with
King Cnut of Denmark threatening invasion, not to mention the unrest along the Welsh border. She had no idea
why men enjoyed battle so much.

Shaking her head, she returned her gaze to Roger.
There he was, laughing with Lady Margaret Ellerby, a
beauty whose mammoth breasts matched her enormous
ego. Tanon didn't like her, and she didn't care for any man
who did.

"A friend of yours?"

Tanon sighed without turning to the man who spoke to
her. "My betrothed." She bit her lower lip when Roger
dipped his mouth to Margaret's earlobe.

"Fool."

Tanon pivoted around and aimed a scowl at the man
beside her. "Pardon?"

A smile quirked one corner of his mouth. "Him, not
you."

"Oh." Her frown faded, along with her interest in Roger.
She was certain she'd never met this man before. She
would have remembered him if she had. Compared to the
other knights at court, his appearance was savage, beyond
beautiful. Scottish, she guessed. He'd probably arrived
with one of the many clans to compete in the tourney. He
hadn't said enough for her to place his accent, but she
didn't need to hear it to know that he was foreign. He
wore a sleeveless doeskin tunic embroidered with a border of indigo Celtic designs unfamiliar to Tanon. Golden
armbands wreathed the sleek, corded sinew in his arms.
His eyes were the most startling shade of blue, but the

confidence exuding from them was what halted Tanon's breath. That, and the way the firelight captured the different shades of gold in his long silken mane.

"Are you here to compete?" She almost kicked herself beneath her scarlet gown for asking such an obvious question. One would have to be blind not to recognize him as a warrior.

"Aye." He glanced at Roger and then slid his gaze back to her. "I guess I am. I was unaware of your betrothal, Lady Risande."

Tanon stared at him, finding it difficult not to. The decadent curves of his lips made her feel light-headed. The velvety lilt in his voice made her skin tingle. "But you have the advantage, sir," she said softly. When he lifted a curious eyebrow, she smiled, flashing her dimple. "You know who I am."

"Aye." He nodded, smiling with her. "You were described to me in great detail by one of my vassals after he met you last winter. He said your eyes rival the verdant moors of Cymru." While he spoke, he took her hand and lifted it to his mouth. "And your nose crinkles when you laugh." With an irresistible combination of tenderness and strength, he turned her hand over and pressed his lips against the inside of her wrist. His gaze brushed her face from beneath thick lashes, and his smile widened into a slow, sensual grin as he withdrew.

"Allow me to escort you to your father." His fingers caressed hers as he fitted her hand into the crook of his arm.

Unable to breathe, unable to tear her eyes away from his, Tanon took a moment to blink and slow down her thudding heart. "But Roger—"

"Grows drunker by the moment."

Tanon looked toward her betrothed's table and was mortified to find Roger completely engrossed in Margaret's bosom.

"Scoundrel," she swore under her breath, letting her companion lead her away.

"Lackwit," he agreed.

Tanon giggled, thankful that he had rescued her from having to walk by Roger and Margaret alone.

"Evan was right," the foreigner said. When Tanon looked up at him, his powerful gaze drank her in. "Your nose does crinkle."

Lifting her finger to her nose, she blushed, and then laughed. "Are you going to tell me your name, or shall I simply call you stranger for the rest of the evening?"

"If you promise to spend the rest of the evening with me, then aye, I'll tell you my name."

She liked his boldness and the self-assurance that slowed his steps to a leisurely pace. He was in no rush to end their encounter, and neither was she. He smelled good, too, like the intoxicating scent of a forest after a spring rain.

"I'm afraid I'm not permitted to bargain, my lord."

"Pity, then I shall have to concede." He turned to look behind him and nodded to a man standing alone at the entrance. A moment later ten more men entered the hall, swords drawn.

Tanon's father and uncle were among the first to spring from their seats.

"What is the meaning of this?" the king bellowed over the sound of benches being pushed away from tables as the rest of his men stood up, ready for a fight.

Still too stunned to comprehend what was going on,

Tanon instinctively took a step closer to the stranger. She watched him lift his hand to the men behind him. Immediately, swords were returned to their scabbards, and the warriors took a more relaxed position.

"Your Majesty." He turned to face the king. "Forgive me." The arrogant edge in his voice belied his apology. "I wasn't sure how my presence here would be"—he cast Tanon a rueful look when she yanked her arm away from his and ran to her father—"received." Returning his attention to the king, he bowed. As if he and his men had rehearsed this scene a dozen times, one of his men stepped forward and cleared his throat.

"His Royal Highness, Prince Gareth ap Gruffydd of Wales."

Wales? Tanon's mouth went dry with horror. He was Welsh! *Non,* he was a Welsh *prince*! No wonder she thought him savage looking. Dear God, he could have killed her! She brought a trembling hand to her throat, dipping her gaze to the daggers protruding from the cuffs of his boots, the thick belt around his slim waist. From her vantage point a few feet away, Tanon's eyes absorbed the full impact of his appearance. His muscled legs were encased in tan leather trousers. The snug fit revealed more of his considerable male attributes than Tanon cared to think about. He looked fierce, untamed, his trim body coiled tight with unleashed energy.

"Gareth?"

Tanon's gaze darted to William. Why wasn't he ordering his men to seize the Welshmen? These were enemies of the Normans. Primitive ruffians who were so fearsome that the king had had to station marcher lords along their borders to keep them out of England. And yet, here they were in his castle! They had probably strolled right through the front doors. With all the competitors arriving daily, it was difficult to tell who was who.

"I thought you were dead." The king fell back into his seat. "This is quite a shock."

"Aye, for my father as well when he finally saw me," Gareth said, his voice calm despite the hundreds of well-trained knights standing ready to kill him if he made one move toward the king. "I was imprisoned in Daffydd ap Bleddyn's holding in the north. But I have his daughter to thank for my life."

The tiny grin that crept over his lips infuriated Tanon. Now that the threat of bloodshed had seemingly passed, her fear changed to fury. How dare he deceive her with those beguiling smiles and perfectly fine manners? If his men didn't look like the types who could cut her throat and hum a Welsh ditty at the same time, she would have marched right up to him and slapped his face. She was sure this Daffydd's daughter had been just as fooled by his rugged good looks as she was.

"I'm pleased that you live, Gareth." The king offered him a faint smile before his smoky gray gaze fell on Tanon first, and then on her father.

"Brand, you remember the prince."

"*Oui.*" A warning growl before his hand closed around Tanon's.

Gareth offered Brand a casual nod, glancing only briefly at the possessive hold he had on his daughter. "Your agreement with my grandfather still remains."

Somewhere behind Brand, Tanon's mother slammed her palm down on the table. "You're mad if you think . . ."

"My lady." Gareth's voice was velvet, quiet, but the

raw force radiating from him shook Tanon to her core. "I am not here to fight . . . or to argue." He looked at the king again. "I'm simply here to collect what was promised four years ago when you put your writ on parchment and swore with my grandfather on the holy relics. It was done for peace, but I fear peace is slipping through our hands. Every day our people battle against one another and die along the marches."

"William . . . ," Brand began.

The king raised his palm to quiet him, praying that for once he would listen. But it was Gareth who spoke to Tanon's father.

"You were with the king when he met my grandfather. You agreed this was the only way. I ask you not to refuse."

"He will not refuse," William said with stern assurance mixed with a hint of regret. "Prince Rhys and I want peace. Had I known you were alive, I would have sent her sooner."

Gareth bowed again. When he straightened, he tossed back his head, sweeping his dark tawny mane off his shoulders. He looked so sensual doing it that it snatched the breath right out of Tanon. "I will relay your words to the Prince of the South. He will advise the people of your continued goodwill."

"But know this, Gareth." William narrowed his eyes on him, and the challenge in his voice was unmistakable. "If harm comes to her, it will cost you your head. Peace be damned."

Gareth smiled easily. "Her value to you is noted, Sire."

William sighed and pinched the bridge of his nose in his fingers. "*Enfer*, she is betrothed."

"So I have learned." Gareth looked over his shoulder,

and with a sickening, sinking feeling growing in the pit of her stomach, Tanon followed his gaze.

Roger was slumped over Lady Ellerby's shoulder in a drunken stupor.

Gareth's lips curled into a wry grin as his eyes met Tanon's. "It seems I have arrived just in time."

Dear Readers,

As the creators of potent military heroes, we authors would like to know if our warriors, both medieval and modern, surrendered to love in a similar fashion. Dante Risande from *Lord of Temptation* and Chase McCaffrey from *Time to Run,* both Warner Forever books published in February 2006, have bravely answered these very personal questions.

PAULA QUINN: Dante and Chase, what happened after you met Sara and Gianelle, our irresistible heroines?

DANTE: I went to Devonshire to investigate a Saxon noble suspected of treason. I left, taking with me a beautiful servant accused of murder, spilling insults and planning her escape the moment I closed my eyes. Gianelle wanted no part of me after spending years as a slave, she wanted naught but her freedom. I wanted to protect her. And to do that, I had to buy her—to possess her, body and soul. But winning her heart was another matter.

CHASE: Sara asked me to help her run away from her husband. Of course I said, no. After sixteen years in the service, the last thing I needed to do was to screw up my career. But there was somethin' about the way she looked at me that made it impossible to just walk away. That's when all the trouble started.

MARLISS MELTON: Gentlemen, how would you say that your lives have been changed by Gianelle and Sara?

DANTE: Gianelle smiles at me like an angel and then she snubs me, rebuking every attempt I make to please her. I was a devilish rake, never considering the hearts I had broken. For the first time in my life, I care about what will become of a woman after I take her to my bed. *Merde,* it scares the hell out of me.

CHASE: Emotions used to run off me like water off an oiled tarp. Now I can't get away from the way things make me feel. Shit, the first time I made love to Sara, I cried like a baby. I've tried goin' back to what I used to be, a sniper without empathy, without remorse. But it's too late now. Somewhere along the way, Sara crept inside of me. She's made me a different man. Funny thing is, I don't much mind.

There you have it, readers. Even the toughest warriors, regardless of the era in which they live, are helpless when it comes to love. In fact, it's apparent to us authors that the bigger they are, the harder they fall.

Sincerely,

Paula Quinn　　　　　*Marliss Melton*
LORD OF TEMPTATION　　TIME TO RUN
www.paulaquinn.com　　*www.marlissmelton.com*